A COLD AND BROKEN HALLELUJAH

Other titles in the Long Beach Homicide series:

A King of Infinite Space

The Pain Scale

A COLD AND BROKEN HALLELUJAH

A DANNY BECKETT NOVEL

TYLER DILTS

FOR TIM,
MY FAVORITE LONG BEACH WRITER!

THOMAS & MERCER

This is a work of fiction. Names, characters, organizations, places, events, and incidents are either products of the author's imagination or are used fictitiously.

Published by Thomas & Mercer, Seattle
www.apub.com
Amazon, the Amazon logo, and Thomas & Mercer are trademarks of Amazon.com, Inc., or its affiliates.
ISBN-13: 9781477824498
ISBN-10: 1477824499

Cover design by David Drummond
Library of Congress Control Number: 2014903902
Printed in the United States of America

For David Aimerito

PROLOGUE

The truth doesn't set you free. More often than not, it does just the opposite. It weighs on you. It imprisons you. It pulls you down into its depths. The truth is a pocketful of stones at the water's edge.

I'm a homicide detective, and I know that, with only rare exceptions, the truth is the last thing you want to hear.

The truth is that her death was neither quick nor painless and that she knew exactly what was happening to her as she lay there alone, in agony, staring into the dark.

The truth is that he saw the gun and that his last moments were filled with the most abject terror of his life.

The truth is that he raped her before he murdered her.

The truth is that it is a horror to burn.

• • •

He doesn't flail and he doesn't scream. The flaring match bounces off the sleeve of his ragged coat, and its abandoned flame surges up his arm. He grunts, mildly surprised, and tries to brush it away like it's a few stray crumbs. The action only causes his fingerless glove to ignite as well. He holds his hands, both on fire, in front of his face, and he watches them. The surprise that first fills his eyes gives way to fear, which, although it lasts only a few seconds, seems to go on much longer. Finally, the fear gives way to pain, and a low and guttural moan comes out of his grimacing mouth as he collapses to the ground. The sound grows in intensity, and he curls into a fetal ball on the hard concrete and rocks back and forth. The fire covers his whole body, and the flames grow larger, reaching up into the night sky. He writhes and moans for nearly a minute. The flames, the motion, and the sound seem to crescendo together and then begin to fade until nothing is left but a silent and charred and motionless corpse smoldering on the ground.

Case #0054732
Crime Scene Evidence Inventory
1
Shopping cart: Whole Foods Market, very good condition. Contents itemized below.

There are some evenings in Long Beach—usually in the late summer and early fall—when the air stops moving, all traces of wind disappear, and even a mile or more inland, the smells of oiled sand, of decaying sea life, of the harbor, of all the urban detritus that washes out of the mouth of the Los Angeles River, hang thick in the air. We're reminded, yet again, that a beach is not always a beach simply by virtue of its proximity to the immense blue waters of the Pacific, that we don't live in Malibu or Laguna, and that even though we're geographically centered between those two paradisiacal coasts, our real essence lies not even on the same continuum of natural beauty that they inhabit, but rather on a man-made, industrialized plane of cargo ships and containerized trains and diesel trucks. We're reminded that we long ago surrendered any claims we might once have had to the scenic beauty and purity of the natural world, succumbing to the all-encompassing demands of commerce—and that the toxic, decaying smell that sometimes hangs in the motionless air late into the night is just one of the many prices we pay in Long Beach so that other people on other beaches might enjoy the fresh and promising scent of the onshore flow.

It was nearing midnight, and I hadn't yet thought about going to bed. Sleep never came easily, especially in the waning days of summer when the heat lingered in the darkness until the first light of dawn. I was sitting on a kitchen chair in the middle of my living room, directly beneath the ceiling fan, my fingers curled around the neck of my banjo, a Deering Saratoga Star. No matter how much I worked it, I couldn't get the fingering for the C chord right. I wished I could have blamed the failure on the chronic pain I suffered as the result of having my hand nearly severed while apprehending a suspect a few years earlier, but the truth was that I just had very little musical aptitude and too little patience to change that fact.

My iPhone thrummed on the coffee table, and I knew without looking who was calling. Only people with the first name Sergeant ever called me after eleven.

I answered the way I always do. "Danny Beckett."

She told me where the body was. I took off my T-shirt and put on something with a collar. There was no need to bother with a jacket.

I sent a text message to my partner, Jennifer Tanaka. *Want me to pick you up?*

A few seconds later she answered: *Yep.*

I made sure the front door was locked and turned on the lamp I always kept burning in the living room when I wasn't home at night, and then I went out the back door. My garage is too full of my life, packed away in cardboard boxes, to be of much practical use. It's set back just enough in the alleyway to give me room to park. I wrestled the misaligned gate latch back into place and snapped the padlock shut.

In my Camry, I turned the air-conditioning all the way up as I drove. Springsteen's *Wrecking Ball* was in the CD player, but I've never been comfortable listening to music on the way to a murder scene. It doesn't feel right. The radio was tuned to KPCC's overnight BBC broadcast.

Nine months earlier, when the Southern California real-estate market had hit the lowest point of its multiyear collapse, Jen had bought her first house. Because of her relatively good financial position and a little down-payment assistance from her parents, she managed to score a beautifully restored Craftsman bungalow with its own guesthouse, in Belmont Heights. I pulled into her driveway just as she was locking the front door behind her. She climbed in, and we backed out onto Colorado and headed toward downtown.

"How was the weekend?" I asked.

"Family came over to help work on the guesthouse. It's just about ready to go." Her father had convinced her to rent it out to help defray the costs of the mortgage.

"You sure you want to be a landlord?" I asked.

"I'm sure I don't. But what am I going to do after he gave me half the down?"

"So, just get somebody in there until you can pay your folks back and then do what you want."

"That's the thing. He insists it wasn't a loan, that it was a gift. He just doesn't act like it. He acts like he's bought into Tanaka Properties Inc. I shouldn't have taken the money."

I laughed.

"What?" she said.

"I was figuring it would take longer for buyer's remorse to set in."

She didn't find that as amusing as I did.

We let our conversation trail off as we got closer to the scene. The British people on the radio were talking about an election in Africa while I thought about where we were heading.

We didn't know what to expect, but we knew it was big because of the size of the rollout. It wasn't a quiet night in Long Beach—the hot ones usually aren't—but there were already more than a dozen units at the location or en route, and even the watch commander was on his way.

As we turned off of Ocean onto Golden Shore, Jen said, "We haven't had one at the river in a while."

From its headwaters in the San Fernando Valley, the Simi Hills, and the Santa Susana Mountains, the Los Angeles River flows nearly fifty miles, mostly through concrete channels built by the Army Corps of Engineers after the flood of 1938. The river travels south across just about every kind of neighborhood Southern California has to offer. The last thing it passes on its way into the harbors of San Pedro and Long Beach is a trailer park. I've always thought there was something meaningful in that—in the motor homes and fifth wheels that witness the waters flowing into the expanses of the harbor and the Pacific beyond—but I couldn't ever put my finger on exactly what it was.

Along the river is a bike path that stretches all the way up to the city of Vernon. If you've never heard of Vernon, count yourself fortunate and don't go asking. After it flows south through the San Fernando Valley, borders Griffith and Elysian Parks, and passes downtown, the Los Angeles runs through some of the least welcoming areas of the county, places most Long Beach locals would avoid in cars, never mind on bikes. At most major cross streets, the bike path leads under bridges that allow traffic to flow freely without most drivers having any idea that they are passing over a river at all—let alone the one named for the City of Angels itself.

Jen and I parked on the shoulder of the ramp leading from West Shoreline Drive to Golden Shore. There was a pumping-station shed with a small turnout for a driveway and an access gate to the bike path. Patrol units and the Crime Scene Detail van were lined up for thirty yards in each direction.

Before we got there, the senior officer on the scene had been a patrol sergeant named Stanley Burke. He was an old-timer whom I'd known since my own days in uniform, and he'd been working recently with a rookie, as her field-training officer. We found Stan, and he gave us the rundown of the incident.

"So we've got the suspects?" Jen asked.

"Yeah," he replied.

"That should make it easy."

I looked down the bike path at the charred corpse of the murder victim. "No," I said, with more foresight than I could have possibly known at that moment. "This one's not going to be easy."

• • •

A patrol unit had been crossing the Ocean Boulevard overpass when one of the uniforms saw the flames. They called it in to dispatch, and a pair of bike officers working the Rainbow Harbor beat were the second to respond. The three suspects had not been prepared for cops on the bike path itself. By the time they realized their escape route was cut off and reversed their course, the squad car had made its way down to Golden Shore, and the officers had climbed the fence and headed south on the path.

The suspects were flanked, with nowhere to go but down the rock-paved embankment into the river. Surprisingly, only one of them went that way. The rookie from the patrol unit chased him down, tackled him in the waist-deep effluvial flow, and dragged him back up the slope. One of the other suspects had tried to make it over the chain-link fence and onto the street beyond, but he didn't have enough speed and was pulled back down to the ground by one of the bike cops. The remaining suspect knew there was no place to go and didn't even need to be told to kneel. By that time, there were two more units on the scene. It was only when the three teenagers were cuffed facedown on the pavement that the officers began to understand what had happened. Most of them would wish they hadn't.

When we arrived, the uniforms had pieced together most of the story. Several hundred yards downriver from the murder scene, according to a witness from the RV park, the teenagers had started chasing a man who was pushing a shopping cart along the bike path. Based on the cart itself and what little remained of his clothing, we assumed him to be homeless. As the suspects had run after him, the victim had tried to slow them down by spinning around and pushing his cart at them, but that only allowed them to more quickly close the distance, and then two of them doused the victim with gasoline from giant 7-Eleven soda cups. When the man finally began to flag and give in to his exhaustion, one of the teenagers struck a wooden fireplace match against the abrasive strip on the side of its box and flung it at the dripping man.

He exploded into flames.

• • •

The victim's body was facedown on the edge of the bike path, feet dangling over the rocky incline toward the river. The air felt still, but I was thirty feet away and could already smell the acrid scents of scorched human tissue and synthetic petroleum-based fabrics. There must have been a breeze too slight to perceive.

He was all alone within the taped-off perimeter. As I got closer, I could see that not only had his flesh been charred to the bone, but also that the polyester fleece vest he'd been wearing had melted into a kind of thin, hard shell covering his torso. His pants were made from some kind of artificial fiber, too; they created a patchwork of seared red-black skin and black knobs of rendered nylon that had already begun to harden into some repellent amalgam of organic and artificial waste.

He didn't have any identification that we could find. Because of the degree of damage to his hands, prints would likely be impossible to lift. Later the ME might find some kind of ID in the remnants of his clothes, the criminalists could come across something in his shopping cart, and there was a chance at a DNA match, but at that point our first priority would be determining the victim's identity. If we couldn't, it wouldn't be impossible to prosecute the three teenagers, but it would be more of a challenge.

John Doe cases, especially when the victim was homeless, were often tough to make, because without knowing the identity of the victim, it was more challenging to make him seem real, a person with an actual life, a substantial existence, something other than just a hypothetical stereotype: a genuine loss. With no name and no history, the victim was just another one of the dozens of faceless and invisible transients we see every day in a city like Long Beach. And as much as I was loath to admit it, the truth was that, although a good number of people did indeed care about anonymous vagrants, very few of those people were outside of the system. They were uniforms, social workers, soup-kitchen volunteers. The homeless and the nameless didn't have families, they didn't have loved ones, and, most importantly, they didn't have stories. If we were going to make the boys who burned this man to death pay for their crime in any meaningful way, we needed to find something.

We needed to know who the victim was.

We needed to know his story.

• • •

"Did you see the shopping cart?" I said. The cart was tipped over on its side.

"What about it?" Jen asked.

"Look at where it's from."

She leaned in and examined the little plastic flip-up child seat in the top rack. It was full of the victim's possessions, so she had to squat a bit to get a good view. "Whole Foods?"

"Yeah," I said. "Never seen one of those on the street before."

"Neither have I. Could be something."

I didn't think about it until it didn't happen, but I had half expected one of us to make some sort of joke about upscale homeless or social-climbing vagrants. But neither of us did. We maintained a degree of seriousness that was unusual for us that far into a crime-scene investigation. It's not so much that the tone lightens or that we take the work more casually, but as we work the scene and become more and more familiar with the details, a kind of familiarity and ease set in. And that's when the gallows humor becomes a part of the dynamic. We try to make each other laugh so we won't get lost in the darkness. But for some reason, that wasn't happening here. Later I would wonder if Jen sensed something in me, a distance or a reticence, that was making me hold back on the banter. I wondered if I saw that in myself.

• • •

One of the crime-scene techs, a twentysomething named Kyle, called me over to a spot a few yards away from the body. "Did you see this?" he asked, squatting down next to a cell phone on the ground.

"I didn't get a good look at it yet. Why?"

"One of them had this in his hand when the patrol units got here," he said. "Probably dropped it when they tried to run."

"What are you thinking?"

"It looks like the camera app was open. He might have been recording it."

That was good news. The case against the three suspects was already a good one. If we had video of the incident, that would make it just about as solid as it could be without a victim ID.

"What do you think about looking at it here?" I asked him. I knew the ideal method would be to take it back to the lab to check for prints and other physical evidence before they started to check for any data the phone might hold.

The suspects' DMV and school IDs confirmed that they were minors, and California law dictates that if we take juvenile suspects into custody, we have to either formally arrest them or let them go in six hours—so we were up against a ticking clock.

"Well, that's your call," Kyle said. "But I'd really like to get it back to the lab first."

I thought about it. If there was video, it might be a big help in the suspect interrogations, but with a case this solid, I worried about anything that might go wrong with the evidence. Despite his youth, Kyle had worked enough of my cases for me to know he was good at his job. I trusted his opinion.

"Okay," I said. "Think you can check it before your shift's over?"

"Sure thing, Detective."

• • •

I looked over to the perimeter. Just about as far away from the body at the center of the crime scene as she could be, a young uniform leaned on the front fender of a squad car with one towel draped around her shoulders and another in a mound on the hood of the Police Interceptor. She'd removed her uniform shirt and Kevlar and wore only a damp white undershirt. I'd been watching her, glancing in her direction every now and again, and this was the first time I'd seen her alone.

"Hey," I said as I approached.

She looked at me and when she realized that I was the lead homicide detective on the scene, she stood up straight. Almost at attention. She was fresh out of the academy, from our first class of new recruits after a five-year hiring freeze—but as I got closer, I could see that she looked older than most rookies. I made her age as late twenties.

"Relax," I said. She didn't, but she tried to look like she was at ease and leaned back against the fender again. "What's your name?"

Her academy conditioning kicked in and she looked at the ground. "Boot."

"Not anymore." I repeated my question, but she still didn't answer. "Look, you dove into the LA River and took down a killer. That was no rookie move."

"He was just a kid."

"A kid who'd just burned a man to death because he thought it would be fun to watch. You did good."

"Lauren Terrones."

"Well, Officer Terrones, why don't you tell me what happened and then you can head back to the station and change into some dry clothes."

She nodded a weak affirmation but didn't say anything. I watched her and tried to judge the best way of opening the interview.

"This your first barbecue?" As soon as I saw the expression on her face, I knew I'd made the wrong calculation. I thought if I treated her like a vet, she might be more likely to open up. But she wasn't ready for the gallows lingo yet. It was too soon for her to start depersonalizing. "Burn victims are hard," I said.

She nodded and tried to pay attention, to make sure she came off as a good student, the solid rookie sucking up a lesson from the grizzled vet. Something about her earnestness got to me.

I decided to go out on an entirely different limb. "My wife burned to death," I said. "A car accident. She survived the impact. It was the fire that got her." As soon as I spoke, I felt that I'd shared too much personal information too soon. I'd never used my wife's death like that before, and I wasn't sure where the impulse had come from. But if I let myself think about it, the interview would go so far off track I'd never get it back.

"Oh my god," she said.

"It was a few years ago." I tried to spin it back into a reasonable thing to say in the situation. "I've never been able to look at a fire victim the same way since. Sometimes I overcompensate." She hadn't expected the candor. "Like that 'barbecue' crack."

That did it. She loosened up, her defenses came down, and when she looked at me her eyes were filled with an empathy that had pushed out the agitation and intensity and left no room, at least for the moment, for them to take hold again. I could probably count on a few minutes of clarity.

"Tell me what happened," I said.

She ran it down for me, and I had only a few follow-up questions. Her account lined up with what everyone else had said and with everything else we knew. By the time we were through, she was still relatively calm, but the distraction was beginning to wear thin.

Stan had been watching us from a few yards away, just out of her field of view, and when he saw that our conversation had nearly run its course, he came over.

"Thanks, Lauren," I said.

"You're welcome," she said.

"Here comes your FTO."

"Get in the fucking car, Boot," Stan said with even more gravel in his voice than usual. When the rookie was a few steps ahead of him, Stan looked back over his shoulder and gave me a nod. I gave him one back.

• • •

I'd only spent two hours at the scene. Even though I felt like I had a good sense of things, I wanted to get to the suspects and make sure we had them booked within our limited time frame. Ordinarily, I'd never leave a scene in progress, but I trusted Jen to make sure everything got done right.

Kyle told me they were ready to load up the shopping cart.

"Let me take one more look at it." If we got an ID on the victim, it would probably be from something in the cart.

Even though it had fallen onto its side, almost nothing had spilled out—only an old Powerade Zero bottle half-filled with water and a relatively recent *Time* magazine shouting "A WORLD WITHOUT BEES" in white-and-yellow caps on a black background. The magazine had apparently been tucked into the top of the cart; one corner of the cover, with its familiar red border, had torn off and remained lodged there. Everything else was secured with a fleece blanket that had been folded to the size of the cart's open top and held in place with three crisscrossing bungee cords. There was a similar setup in the child seat: a dark-blue bath towel and a single cord. I'd never seen so neat an arrangement in a homeless person's cart before. In an odd way I was almost envious of the organizational discipline required to keep things so orderly. Even the cart itself was in far better shape than most I'd seen on the street. Whoever our murder victim was, he was obviously conscientious when it came to keeping track of and maintaining his possessions. I wanted to believe he took a kind of pride in this, that it meant something to him to maintain his belongings so carefully, that it indicated something about his character, something hopeful about him and how he faced his hopeless situation. I didn't realize it then, but what I really wanted to believe, deep down, in the part of myself that I didn't like to look at or even acknowledge, was that this fastidiously organized shopping cart somehow made the dead man more worthy than the many transients I passed on the street every day and didn't even see. I wanted to believe that the way he'd maintained this stolen basket made him real enough, human enough, to warrant our attention, and that closing this case and acknowledging this single victim's humanity would somehow be enough to assuage us—the cops, the bystanders, the system—of all of the guilt we should have been feeling at his plight and that of so many more like him.

I wanted to give him a name.

2

FLEECE BLANKET: MEDIUM BLUE, FRAYED AT ONE CORNER, THREE DARK STAINS NEAR SAME CORNER, RECENTLY LAUNDERED.

"Morning," I said to Lieutenant Ruiz, the Homicide Detail commander, as he came into the observation room. I was getting ready to begin the interrogations. The suspects had been separated and placed in individual interview rooms. "You're in early." He was—it wasn't even three a.m. yet. I'd meant the statement as a joke, but either he didn't get the intended humor or he decided to ignore it.

"Yeah," he said. "Figured I'd try to get a jump on the media attention. Things squared away at the scene?"

"Jen's on top of it. Still a bit of evidence to be collected. Got patrol helping with the canvass. Not expecting much on that front until everybody wakes up. We've already got statements from the uniforms who responded and a guy from the trailer park, and it looks like we might have smartphone video, too. This one's tight."

"Anything on the victim?"

"Nothing you probably don't already know. Apparently homeless, no ID. He had a shopping cart. We're hoping we find something in there to help, or that maybe the canvass will turn up someone who knew him. How about the suspects?"

"We've confirmed their IDs."

He handed me three sheets of paper with the suspects' IDs and any background that had been discovered on them so far. There wasn't much there.

"Why'd they do it?" he said. We both knew that at that point his question could only be rhetorical.

"I don't know."

"Maybe just trying to make their bones."

"Could be," I said. "They got everybody's attention."

"We'll keep working on background." He looked at his watch. "How much time do we have?"

I looked at mine, too. "A little less than three hours."

"Why don't you get in there," he said. "Anything big comes up, I'll let you know."

I watched all three suspects on the live video feeds in the observation room. Omar Guerra, at seventeen the oldest and the suspected ringleader, seemed calm and collected. His sheet was the only one with priors: two arrests for minor gang-related offenses, but nothing that had stuck. He was reclining in the chair, his head against the wall behind him, eyes closed. I wondered if he might have dozed off. The other two, though, weren't holding up as well.

Francisco Carillo was at the other end of the spectrum from Omar. He couldn't sit still. He rubbed his hands together, bounced his feet, bobbed his head up and down, side to side. At one point he stood up and paced back and forth in the small room, then looked right at the camera with the laser-eyed focus of a surprised cat, and then sat back down as if he thought getting up might somehow put him in even more trouble.

Between those two extremes was suspect number three, Pedro Solano. He was nervous and fidgety, too, but without Francisco's pent-up, caged-animal energy. Pedro's head was down, so I couldn't get as good a read as I would have liked on his face or his expression, but at one point he raised his hand to his cheek as if he might have been wiping away a tear. That made my decision for me. Pedro would be number one.

In the bathroom I washed my face, combed my hair, rinsed my mouth out with Cool Mint Listerine, and put on a tie. On the way back to the interview room, I detoured to the vending machines and bought two Cokes, a Snickers, some M&Ms, and a bag of Nacho Cheese Doritos. I turned the video recorder on and opened the door.

"Pedro?" I said. Before I was even all the way into the room, I'd already gotten a nod of agreement. The room was small, no more than eight by eight, and had a table pushed back into the corner with a chair on each of the accessible sides. Pedro was sitting with his back against the far wall, his left arm resting on the table. I pulled the other chair out and around to face him and sat down directly between him and the door.

"How are you?" I asked.

He didn't answer, but I didn't expect him to.

"I know it's been a long night. You thirsty?" I slid one of the Cokes toward him. "I got some snacks, too. Here you go." I pushed the candy toward him, too.

He looked at it, then at me, then back down at his hands in his lap, but he didn't reach for anything.

"It's okay," I said. "Go ahead."

He resisted the impulse for a few more seconds, then reached for the Coke and took a long drink from the can. Then he tore open the Snickers wrapper and dug in as if he hadn't eaten in hours. Which, of course, he hadn't.

"You are hungry. Is that going to be enough? You want me to go grab you a sandwich or something?"

He looked at me, finished chewing, swallowed, and then said, in very small voice, "No, that's okay."

"You need anything else?" I asked.

He shook his head.

"Okay," I said. I put a handkerchief down on the table, knowing he'd think I meant for him to use it to wipe his hands and mouth. Really, though, I wanted him to have it when he started crying.

"You go to Poly High, right?"

"Yeah."

"How do you like it there?"

"It's school," he said, as if the idea of liking school was as absurd as the idea of a fish liking fresh air.

"But you go there with Francisco and Omar, right?"

"Francisco, yeah. Not Omar anymore."

"No?" I said. "Where does Omar go?" I knew the answer. He'd had his student ID in his pocket when he was booked.

"He goes to Saint Anthony's now."

"Really, since when?"

"The middle of last year."

"Why'd he transfer?"

Pedro was quiet. He didn't want to rat out his friend.

"I'll see it in his file in a couple of hours anyway."

He still didn't want to talk. He was too loyal.

"That's okay. We'll come back to that one later. You guys are tight, right? You and Omar and Francisco."

Nothing. He took a drink of the Coke, and I waited for the silence to start to work its way through his armor. It was a lot thinner than he believed.

"I know you guys are tight. I understand that. You're alone, you're fucked. All you have is your crew."

I could see his chin move. An embryonic nod.

"So it's all about your crew. You gotta back your brother's play. No matter what."

He actually moved his head this time.

"Yeah," I said. "Of course you do."

Another agreement. Time to press a little harder.

"But we know this was Omar's play. No doubt about that."

His eyes went down to the hands in his lap again.

"The thing is, for me, for us, it's not the same—what you did and what Omar did. It's not."

I let that sink in for a few seconds.

"Omar knows you're gonna stand up. Francisco does, too. He just told me you were the one with the stones."

Pedro looked at me. I could see a little sprout of pride in his eyes.

"Yeah, of course," I said. "What else is he gonna say?"

"I don't know."

"But he is saying something else, though."

"What?"

"I probably shouldn't talk about it."

"Why?"

"I don't think you're gonna like it."

"What did he say?"

"You sure you want to know?"

"Yeah."

"He's saying that he didn't have anything to do with this thing tonight. That it was all you and Omar."

"What?"

"Yeah. He's saying that he even tried to stop you guys."

"No, he didn't."

I couldn't tell if he meant that Francisco didn't say that to me or that he didn't try to stop them, but it didn't really matter. Pedro was buying it.

"The thing is, Pedro, I know he's lying. I've seen your school records." I hadn't, of course. It would take days or weeks and a court order to get them. But he didn't know that. "I know what people say about you. I know you didn't put this thing together. I know. But nobody else here knows you. They're gonna believe Francisco. They're gonna believe him unless you tell me what really went down."

For a few seconds, I thought I had him. He looked at me with a purpose in his expression, and his mouth began to move, but he stopped himself before any sound could escape. In his lap he interlaced his fingers and wrung them together, and he just stared down at his clenching hands.

I knew I'd lost him.

Still, I tried for another half an hour to coax and cajole him into opening up. But even though I'd gotten him right up to the line, I couldn't convince him to step over it.

The handkerchief was still on the table. I reached over, picked it up, and folded it twice. Then I gave it to him.

As he rubbed at his eyes and nose with it, I was surprised by the delicacy in his movements. I hadn't noticed how small his hands were.

• • •

"Pedro told me how it went down. You and Omar talking him into it, how he didn't even want to be there."

Francisco was a nervous ball of energy. He couldn't sit still. Containing himself in the chair across from me seemed to take a Herculean effort on his part. His Nikes were bouncing up and down on the floor in a hectic arrhythmia, and the back of his chair was touching the edge of the table, making it jitter as if a mild earthquake were rattling the building.

"Francisco?"

His eyes, pupils dilated by the stress response, finally met mine.

"Just take a few deep breaths, okay?"

It took a few seconds for the words to sink in, but when they did, he took a deep, quavering breath and let it out.

"Good," I said. "Good. Again."

I took a deep breath myself and exaggerated the physical motions, expanding my chest, lifting my head, and easing my shoulders back. He followed along with me.

"That's good, just keep breathing."

I silently counted to ten as we inhaled and exhaled. By the time we finished he was still visibly agitated, but he was calmer than he had been.

"Okay," I said. "That's good. Did you hear what I said a minute ago about Pedro?"

"Yes."

"Is that what happened? You and Omar forced him into this thing?"

"No."

"Tell me. Tell me what really happened."

"It was all Omar."

"Tell me about it."

"Omar, he . . ."

"He what?"

Francisco didn't continue. He started trembling again and we took ten more breaths. It helped to calm him, but I'd found his line in the sand, too.

That was all I was able to get out of them. It came as no surprise that both Pedro and Francisco were more afraid of Omar than of anything I could do to them.

• • •

Omar was still reclining in the chair with his head against the wall and his eyes closed, pretending to sleep, when I came in and closed the door behind me. I put a cup of water on the table in the corner and pulled the other chair around to face him. He made a show of not acknowledging my presence.

"How's it going, Omar?" I said as I sat down and slid my chair in closer to him. He wore Timberlands and khakis under a white T-shirt and black hoodie. Slowly, with every ounce of cool he could muster, he pulled his head away from the wall, opened his eyes, sat up straight, and said one word: "Lawyer."

That surprised me, but I didn't let it show. I nodded, stood up, took the water off the table, and closed the door softly behind me as I left.

• • •

The lieutenant met me in the hall with a guy in a pricey suit. "Detective Beckett, this gentleman is here to see Mr. Guerra."

"Wow, that was fast," I said.

"My name is Hector Siguenza. I'd like to see my client."

"Sure thing." I led him back down the hallway and opened the door of the interview room. "Go on in."

Omar scowled at the lawyer and said, "Where's my uncle?"

"Fuck you," Siguenza said to him. "That's where he is. Fuck you."

The teenager's jaw hung slack; he looked like he was at a loss for words. I'd have to find out who his uncle was.

The man in the suit looked at me. "I need to talk to my client."

"Of course," I said and left them alone in the interview room.

Ruiz was waiting in the hall.

"We know who his uncle is?" I asked.

"Yep. Benicio Guerra."

Guerra was a big-time criminal defense attorney who'd started on the street and transformed himself through a decade in prison into an apparently upstanding citizen. No one really believed he'd gone legit, but no one had been able to pin anything on him.

"No shit? Benny War? So that's how he got a guy in a thousand-dollar suit here before the sun came up."

• • •

On the way back to the squad room, I checked my watch. We still had two hours until the deadline to file charges. Before I could sit back down at my desk, my cell phone rang. I checked the display: it was Kyle, the crime-scene tech. "What's up?"

"You gotta see this."

"See what?"

"The video from the smartphone."

"What's on it?"

"Everything, man. All of it."

I made it downstairs faster than I ever had before.

3

SHOES, TWO PAIRS: NEW BALANCE 1123 RUNNING SHOES, WELL USED AND STAINED, SIGNIFICANT WEAR ON OUTSIDE EDGES OF HEELS, MEN'S SIZE 12; MERONA LOAFERS, BROWN, GOOD CONDITION, MEN'S SIZE 10.

The video begins with Omar Guerra in the fluorescent nighttime glare of a parking garage, taking a two-gallon red plastic fuel can out of the trunk of a relatively new Honda Civic.

"Gimme the cups," he says as he unscrews the can and extends the nozzle. From off camera, a hand extends a Super Big Gulp into the frame. Omar removes its plastic cover and carefully fills the cup. They repeat the process and the camera spins around to show Francisco, with one arm in the customary selfie position and the other holding a gasoline-filled cup. Omar raises his own cup in a gesture that almost looks like a toast.

There's an expression on his face I can't quite read. It could be anything from a gleeful grin to an uneasy grimace. I wonder what he's thinking in that moment.

Omar hands his cup to Francisco and carefully screws the cap back on the gas can, puts it away, closes the trunk, and makes a point of setting the car alarm.

The picture cuts out, and then we see Omar's back as he walks out of the parking structure.

"That's the Pike," I said, immediately recognizing the oceanfront shopping and dining complex.

"Yeah," Kyle replied. "Right between Bubba Gump's and the Aquarium of the Pacific."

"Surprised they parked so far away from the scene."

"What is it?" he asked. "Maybe a quarter of a mile?"

"Probably about that. I'll check it later."

On the video, they keep walking along the path toward the harbor.

I expect them to take a right and cut toward the river sometime soon.

Omar's phone chimes, and he reads a text message to Francisco, who is still holding the camera. "Pedro's over by the trailer park. He found the guy."

Another cut in the video, and now they're just passing the California State University Chancellor's Office and getting close to the Golden Shore RV Resort.

Kyle and I knew what was coming, but it was still a shock.

Omar and Francisco are walking along the bike trail, and the camera pans forward to find another boy waiting for them close to a short wall with a motor home on the other side. He waves when they see him.

"Pedro!" Omar says, nearly shouting. As they get nearer to him, Pedro gestures toward the mouth of the river, and the three of them begin to move faster, as if they fear their target might get away. "Where's Jesús?" Omar says.

I paused the video and made a note: *Jesus? Fourth suspect?*

After I hit "Play," Pedro shakes his head and raises his hands.

By the time the victim's distant figure appears in the frame, the boys are practically running. The picture begins to shake erratically from the motion. They close in on him, and he looks over his shoulder. It seems to take a few moments for him to realize they are coming after him. When he does, he turns and begins to shuffle more quickly up the bike path. The boys close in on him swiftly, and when they're only a few yards away, he turns around and pushes his cart directly into their path. It does nothing to slow them down.

They catch up to him, and Omar shoves him to the ground. As he struggles back to his feet, panting and stooped with fear, he says only, "Please" in a voice so soft it's barely audible.

The three boys are in a semicircle around him, shifting their weight on the balls of their feet, as if the old man were capable of some kind of superhuman burst of speed or dexterity and they need to guard against his inevitable escape.

Omar makes a noise that might be a laugh. There's a brief pause in which the other two boys look at their leader, as if they can't quite believe this is really going to happen, and then Omar makes his noise again and throws his cup of gasoline on the unsteady man. Francisco follows suit, and then Omar drops his empty cup and strikes a match, and the man bursts into flames.

Omar's visceral excitement is palpable and seems inexhaustible. It only edges into panic when the lights and siren of the squad car on the bridge pull him back from his reverie and remind him of where he is.

After we finished watching the video, I said, "Is there a shot of the victim's face anywhere in there that might be good enough to help us?"

"I'll go through frame by frame, but I don't think so. Too dark."

Even without the ID, it was enough. With nearly an hour left before our deadline, we charged all three of them with first-degree murder.

• • •

Things were settling down by the time the morning light glowed gray in the eastern sky outside the Homicide Detail's lone window at the far end of the squad room. I spent another hour preparing the initial inquiry for the California DOJ's Missing and Unidentified Persons Unit. Because law enforcement never met an acronym it didn't like, everyone referred to it as MUPS.

It was just past seven when Patrick Glenn, one of the other homicide detectives, came in and sat down.

"Long night?" he asked.

"Nah," I said as I headed toward my desk. "I'm just getting warmed up."

"You caught the case last night, right?"

"Yeah."

"How you holding up?"

I wasn't sure what he meant. It wouldn't occur to me until much later that I wouldn't be the only one connecting our homeless victim's death by fire to that of my wife. "Fine," I said. "Why wouldn't I be?"

"No reason." He had a good enough poker face that I didn't think any more about it. Rather than give me time to make the connection, he pretended to be engrossed by something on his computer screen. "You get that link I sent you?"

"No. What link?"

"It's not work related. I sent it to your Gmail."

"Been at this all night. Haven't had a chance to check. What is it?"

"Watch it. You'll like it."

"I will. Could you help me out with something?"

Patrick grinned. "Sure. Just give me their names."

He had the least seniority of anyone on the detail. Before Homicide, he'd been in Computer Crimes. Every time I caught a new case with any loose threads, I went to Patrick to ask him to check out the suspects' digital footprints. It wasn't laziness on my part, he was just much better at it than I was and regularly came up with things I'd miss. I was always good with the quid pro quo, though. "Can I bring you back something for breakfast?"

• • •

The Potholder Too, a greasy-spoon breakfast joint across the street from the police department headquarters, had opened the year before, replacing the mediocre Mexican restaurant that had operated there for as long as I could remember. I got my usual—the Rancher, an omelet filled with corned-beef hash and bacon—and had begun to think about the case when Lauren, the rookie from the crime scene, came in with Stan. I didn't really feel like company, and I could have kept my head down in my notes and they would have found another table, but instead I smiled and waved them over. I didn't want her to think that detectives are all assholes. We pretty much are, but she didn't need to learn it from me. Stan was still in his uniform, but she had changed into jeans and a sweatshirt. In her street clothes she looked different than she had at the scene. I might not have recognized her if she hadn't been with her FTO. But it had been a long night for all of us. She was probably just tired, and even though I'd never admit it, I probably was, too.

"How you guys doing?" I asked as they sat down.

"Peachy," Stan said for both of them.

I looked at Lauren, inviting a comment, but she only managed a weary half smile.

"What's the case looking like?" Stan asked.

"Tight. Don't see any problems." I was feeling good about it. We hadn't even finished breakfast and things were already lining up. Except for two big questions. "Need to identify the victim and try to figure out a motive. Ruiz authorized some patrol hours. You two interested in some overtime?"

"Yes," Lauren answered quickly. I couldn't tell where the enthusiasm came from.

Stan gave her a stern look. "You sure you're up for that? Ten minutes before we sat down you said you were going to sleep all day."

"I'm up for it." She looked at me as if for validation of some kind.

"You can go home for a couple of hours and get some rest. We won't be ratcheting things up until this afternoon." I looked at Stan. "You in?"

"Have I ever turned down overtime?"

The waitress came back to the table. Stan ordered a Baja omelet while Lauren studied the menu. "The Sailor?" She asked the waitress, "There's no meat in that, right?"

"That's right."

She still didn't seem happy with that option. "I think I'll just have some coffee."

"Eat something," Stan told her.

"Toast," she said. "Sourdough."

Stan eyeballed her and was about to say something, but I caught his attention and gave my head a slight shake. There's nothing wrong with a bland diet after a tough crime scene. At least not when you've only got a few weeks on the job.

We finished our breakfast, and they left me with my files.

It wasn't very complicated. We had a solid case with the video recording of the crime. We had the reports of the cops on the scene and the witness at the trailer park. We knew they did it, and we knew how they did it. We'd work on getting more information about the suspects—motive, background, that sort of thing. We'd try to turn the other two against Omar and attempt to find the Jesús mentioned in the video and determine if he'd been involved in the crime. We'd do everything we could to strengthen the case, but really, everything else would be just like wrapping paper and bows. We already had the gift.

Except for one thing. The identity of the victim. That was the one big question. Maybe we'd get lucky and ID him through missing-persons reports and medical records, maybe the autopsy would give us something, maybe a DNA match would come through, maybe a witness could identify something in his possessions that would give us an answer.

• • •

Back in the squad, after Jen had wrapped up the scene and headed home to get a few hours of sleep, I found Ruiz in his office checking on the morning news shows. He flipped back and forth, and we saw that both KTLA and KTTV led with the murder-by-fire of a homeless man in Long Beach. Neither station gave the story more than ninety seconds. That was good for us. The media always make an investigation more complicated. With any luck, we'd only get one more publicity bump if the video got out, and that would be it. If there was an upside to the lack of identification of our victim, it was that as long as he remained unknown, the media wouldn't regard the story with any interest. Without a past, they wouldn't consider him a worthwhile subject. If he'd been a cute middle-class white girl, we'd have had to beat them off with sticks.

"That wasn't too bad," I said after KTLA cut to a story about the recent resurrection of the Twinkie.

"You get any calls from reporters looking for statements?" Ruiz asked.

"Nope, and I hope I don't."

"Well, if we can keep the video quiet, you might get your wish."

I knew that was true. No matter how gruesome the crime itself, the public never really cares when the murder victim is homeless. But if the footage of the murder got out, everyone would want to watch.

• • •

By nine o'clock in the morning, the thermometer was already close to the triple digits, and the sun reflecting off the concrete of the LA River channel was making me regret my decision to check out the bike path upstream from the crime scene in the daylight. I knew I wouldn't get as far as I had hoped to, but I decided to see how much distance I could cover before the impending sunstroke made me turn back.

It wasn't very far. A few hundred yards. I stopped beneath the Ocean Boulevard overpass to cool off for a minute in the shade. Someone else had the same idea. There was a small man in tattered, stained jeans and some kind of Converse knockoffs leaning against one of the concrete support columns. He was caked with the ground-in dirt and grime of several weeks on the street, and he had removed his thinning T-shirt and draped it over an olive-drab surplus duffel bag that looked old enough to have seen action in World War II. I couldn't tell if he had an extreme farmer's tan or if the portions of his body usually covered by his shirt were simply considerably cleaner than his arms and face. Either way, there was stark contrast.

"How's it going?" I asked him.

He didn't answer. He just gave a kind of noncommittal nod and looked back down at the ground between his feet. The uniforms had done a canvass before the sun had come up and hadn't found anyone along the path for at least half a mile. That wasn't a surprise. Nobody who's lived in a bad part of town for very long ever heads toward a crime scene. No, the smart traffic always flows in the other direction. I wondered how long he had been there.

"You know what happened down there last night?" I gestured toward the harbor.

He still didn't speak, but at least he was looking at me. There was something in his eyes that I couldn't figure out—a hesitance, a trepidation, maybe even a fear, that gave me a sense of empathy for him.

"It's okay," I said. "I'm a cop." I wasn't sure how he'd take that. There was a good chance that he'd be as leery of a police officer as he would of the killers themselves. In fact, I thought, it was more of a likelihood. Most people in his position would have a lot more to lose at the hands of a cop than they would from a couple of teen wannabe gangbangers.

"A man was killed. We think he was homeless."

His expression remained the same, but I seemed to have his attention. "We don't know who he was."

Nothing.

"Any chance you might be able to help us?" I took a ten-dollar bill out of my wallet, crouched in front of him, and held it out.

He looked at the bill, then up at me, and then back at the bill, as if he was trying to determine if it might be some kind of trick.

After a few seconds, I had apparently convinced him of my sincerity and he reached for the money.

"Do you know who he was? He was tall, about six feet. Had a Whole Foods shopping cart."

That seemed to trigger something in him. "Bishop," he said.

"Bishop? That was his name?"

He gave me a slight nod.

"Was that his first name or his last?"

He looked at me very seriously and said in a voice barely louder than a whisper, "Bishop danced . . ."

Without missing a beat, I answered him, completing the lyric about the thumbscrew woman.

His eyes widened in recognition, and I knew that, at least for the moment, I'd cut through whatever fog was enveloping him and made a connection.

4

PAPERBACK COPY OF THE GRAPES OF WRATH, BY JOHN STEINBECK: VIKING CRITICAL EDITION, 1992, OLD, WELL WORN, MARGINAL NOTATIONS THROUGHOUT.

The autopsy was harder than I expected. Truthfully, I hadn't expected it to be difficult at all. After a detective's been working homicide for a while, if he's still having trouble with autopsies and crime scenes, he needs to get out. It's not going to get any easier. You reach a point early on when you realize whether or not you're capable of dealing with the realities of death on a daily basis. Most cops know before they ever ask for the assignment. Every once in a while, though, someone slips through. A few years ago, we had a guy transfer in from Sex Crimes the same way Jen had. His name was Grogan. We rotated him through the squad so he'd have the chance to spend some time with each of the vets. Usually working rapes and molestations and the rest prepares someone to deal with very nasty stuff, and we all thought he was cut out for the job. One day when we were working a particularly brutal child murder and we got our first look at the little girl on the ME's stainless-steel table, Grogan looked down at her and turned an ashen color. Her head had been cut off and there was a two-inch gap separating the severed ends of her neck. The odd thing was that her long blonde hair still reached down past her shoulders and was visible in the space between the raw edges of her neck. He looked at it for several seconds, turned to me, and said, "Excuse me a sec, I'll be right back." I never saw him again. Ruiz told me he maxed out his leave time and then requested a transfer back to patrol.

I'd never had strong reactions to autopsies. Homicide had always been my goal, and I worked hard to get it. I never struggled with the grisly realities of the work the way many cops did. Something in my psyche had prepared me for the realities of the job. I'd always known I was cut out for it.

So I was surprised by the feeling of tightness in the pit of my stomach when the ME, Paula Henderson—her gray hair trimmed short and her eyeglasses, as always, hanging on a chain around her neck—led me in to begin.

As soon as I saw the face of the victim, burned into a blackened rictus, the hair gone, the flesh seared away into taut, leathery ropes of tissue, the deep reds, purples, and browns of the remnants of flesh, it took me back to the first time I'd seen the accident-scene photos of the auto accident that had killed my wife. It had been five years since Megan's Toyota had been sandwiched between two eighteen-wheelers. We had been going through a rough patch, and she was on her way to stay with her mother for a while. Unbeknownst to me at the time, she was pregnant with our first child. She survived the impact, but her car caught fire and she perished in the flames. I never should have seen the photos of the aftermath of the collision, but I had connections, and I worked them hard to get copies of all of the files, too. I even have autopsy pictures. A lot of people tried hard to keep me from looking at all of those investigative materials. No one could have tried hard enough, though. I had to see. I had to know. All of the gruesome details have long been fixed in my memory.

When I looked at the victim's body on the table, it took a concerted effort to put Megan out of my head and focus on the task at hand.

Ten minutes in, Paula looked me in the eye with a compassionate, motherly expression and asked, "Are you okay?"

I pretended too hard to be offended and said, "Of course I am. Just keep going."

There were no big surprises. We did get a bit of useful information. He was Caucasian, late fifties to midsixties, between five foot ten and five foot eleven, 150 to 160 pounds. Graying black hair and brown eyes. Size twelve shoes on size eleven feet with three pairs of socks in between. Moderate level of liver disease. A scar on his lower-left back from a wound that had been stitched up.

"Could that be surgical?" I asked.

"It could, but there are no other indications. Looks like a knife, but I doubt a doctor was holding it."

I called in the physical description and possible name to Stan and told him to spread it around the other uniforms helping with the canvass. It felt like things were starting to come together.

• • •

"What the hell does that even mean?" Jen asked me that afternoon over lunch at Enrique's. The location wasn't convenient for either of us, but she knew it was my favorite food in Long Beach.

I'd told her about the shirtless man under the bridge. "It's an old Springsteen song. 'Bishop Danced.'"

"I've never heard of it."

"It's kind of obscure. From the *Greetings from Asbury Park* days, but it was never available on anything until *Tracks*. It's not one that—"

"Don't go all fanboy on me. I'll take your word for it. You really think his name was Bishop?"

"I'm not sure. Going to keep the uniforms on the canvass, and I want to get the description to the homeless shelters and see if the name rings any bells for anyone else."

"Sounds good. You holding up okay?"

"Sure."

There was doubt in her eyes.

"Why is everybody asking me that?"

"Because it's a burn victim."

"You guys really think I'm that unstable?"

"Nobody thinks you're unstable. We just think it might be hard."

I considered what she was saying. Not the fact that it would be perfectly natural for a man who'd lost his wife in a fire to be rattled by investigating a homicide by fire, but the sudden concern my colleagues were showing for my ability to handle the difficulty. I felt a momentary twinge of resentment, but it passed as quickly as it had come, and I reminded myself who I was sitting with.

I said, "The autopsy was kind of tough. More than I expected it to be."

"Don't worry about it. Just don't let it stew like you always do. It's okay to talk about it."

"I'm not bottling anything up. I have talked about it."

"To who?"

"Lauren. Stan's partner." I didn't realize how absurd that would sound until I said it out loud. Of course I hadn't talked about Megan's death. I'd only used it in a weak attempt to build rapport in an interview.

"You told that rookie about Megan?" Jen asked.

"Yeah."

"Why?"

"She was tense. I was trying to get her to relax."

"By talking about your dead wife?"

"I needed to personalize. Get her to think of me as something other than her superior. So she'd be comfortable talking."

"You think that's it?"

"Yeah."

"If it was anybody else, I'd say they were hitting on her."

"But not me?"

She rolled her eyes. "Seriously? Have you ever hit on anybody? Ever?"

I thought about it. "I asked Megan out."

"In college."

"You're oblivious."

"To what?"

"How's the carne asada?"

• • •

Back in the office after lunch, I checked my messages and found one from the MUPS unit. They found six hits on the name Bishop, but none of them matched the physical details of our victim. I added the new information from the autopsy to the MUPS report and told them the DNA sample was on the way. There wasn't too much—just the scar as a distinguishing mark and more accurate numbers for the height and weight and other descriptors. I'd have to wait awhile to see what, if anything, they came up with.

When I hung up the phone, Jen said, "I found Jesús."

"Yeah?"

"Didn't have to look far. He's Pedro's brother. I cross-checked all three of their cell-phone contact lists. There's a couple more Jesúses, but only one who's in all of them. What do you want to do?"

"I want to talk to him." I checked my watch. "He go to Poly with the others? Maybe we can catch him there."

"No dice. I already called the school office. He didn't show up today."

"Let's wait awhile before we try his house. I want to see somebody else first."

• • •

Outside, the heat was radiating off the street and sidewalk in visible waves. The weather app on my phone said the current temperature in Long Beach was ninety-one, but it felt fifteen degrees hotter.

I'd done some research on Benicio Guerra, and I filled Jen in as we walked. By the time I finished, I'd already worked up a sweat. "You still think it was a good idea to walk?" I asked.

"It's barely a block away. We'd spend more time navigating our way out of one parking garage and into the other than we'll spend walking out here. Chill out."

"Funny."

We'd exited the department through the back parking lot and cut behind the courthouse to turn left on Magnolia. As we crossed the street and headed west on Ocean, we passed the Federal Building. Several months earlier, an ICE agent who was apparently pissed off about not getting a transfer he requested went batshit there and pumped six rounds into his boss. One of his colleagues thought that was inappropriate behavior and dropped him. He died on the scene, but the supervisor survived. The incident was still fresh enough that, unless they were alone, no one in the LBPD ever walked by the building without either making an ICE crack or hearing one.

"Should have worn your vest," Jen said as we passed the lobby doors.

"I'll bet the IRS is happy that nobody who comes here rags on them anymore."

"You know, Patrick made the same joke five or six months ago."

"Really? Shit."

"Don't take it so hard."

"Without my razor-sharp wit, I'm nothing."

"That's what you base your self-worth on?"

"Yes. That and the number of 'likes' my status updates get on Facebook."

• • •

Guerra and Associates took up a whole floor of the World Trade Center building on Ocean. From the look of the lobby, they were doing pretty well. Lots of glass and wood and brushed metal. The receptionist offered us a latte. We declined.

Benny didn't keep us waiting long. A young suit, who looked at least as much like muscle as he did like an attorney, came in and introduced himself. "Hello, Detectives, I'm Gregory, Mr. Guerra's associate."

"Danny Beckett," I said, extending my hand. He gave it a solid shake, but I knew there was more strength in his arm than he used. I couldn't tell if I knew that because of my amazing perceptive abilities or because he wanted me to know it. "This is my partner," I said, "Jennifer Tanaka."

"Hello," he said to her, smiling. He initiated a handshake, but when he saw she wasn't reciprocating, he brought his left up as well and clasped them both in front of his waist. "Can I get you something to drink? A latte?

"No," I said. "Thank you." I made a show of looking at Jen and raising my eyebrows.

"I'm fine," she said. "Very kind of you to offer."

"Let's head back, shall we?"

Jen looked him in the eye and said, "Yes."

The walk was long, as I'm sure it was intended to be. Lawyers with their names on the wall behind the reception desk always want to make sure you have plenty of time to think about how important they are on the long walk back to the corner office.

I was trying to figure out what to make of Benicio Guerra playing the same game as all the other high-end attorneys in Southern California, because he certainly wasn't like anyone else.

He'd done eight years for a triple murder when he was a soldier in one of the Long Beach Longo sets. No one involved in the investigation thought he had actually pulled the trigger, but he stepped up and took the hit for someone higher up in the pecking order. He served his time, and while he was in prison he was believed to have killed at least two of his fellow inmates. I wanted to appreciate the irony of Guerra going away for murders he didn't actually commit only to become a murderer inside, but I just couldn't. That was too cynical even for me.

We came into his office, and he stood, made a show of walking out from behind his expansive desk, and shook our hands.

I'd never met him before, but his history was well known. He'd always been smart, and while he was inside, he took full advantage of his time to study. He'd stacked his time before prisons had started reducing access to their law libraries in the late nineties, and he walked out of prison and into Long Beach City College. After his eight years, Benny found higher education a breeze and transferred to UCLA with a 4.0 GPA and a redemption story that carried all the way through law school. He started as an associate with

Sternow and Byrne, a huge Century City firm that allowed him to learn from some of the highest-paid criminal defense attorneys in Southern California. After four years, he started his own practice. And wound up here.

Since his release, he had stayed clean as a hound's tooth. Not even a parking ticket. Benny had figured out how to make crime really pay.

"Hello, detectives. Welcome." He gestured toward a pale-beige leather sofa, and we sat. "Can I get you something to drink? An espresso, perhaps?" I wondered if they had just invested in a fancy new coffee machine. When we declined the beverage offer, he took a matching chair opposite us. Our backs were to the window, so he got to enjoy the view of the ocean and the harbor. We didn't mind. Cops always sit with their backs to the wall whenever they can. Besides, Jen and I had both seen everything on the other side of the glass.

"How can I help you?" he said.

"Do you know why we're here?" I asked.

He had a narrow, inch-long tendril of scar tissue that ran down his cheek under his left eye from the removal of the three jailhouse teardrop tattoos that his records indicated he'd had removed while on parole. When the light caught it just right, it appeared as if he really was crying, an effect I'm sure the blue-black ink that had been there before had never achieved.

"I'm assuming it's because of my nephew, but it would be nice if I was wrong."

Jen said, "You're not wrong."

"Tell me how I can help."

He was studying us. Putting the question to us in the broadest possible terms, trying to read us at the same time we were reading him.

If his statement was a slow and high lob over the net, I wanted to spike it back in his face. The best I could do, though, was, "You can tell us why your nephew thought burning a homeless man to death would impress you."

He didn't even flinch. "Is that why he did it?"

"What do you think?" I said.

"I don't have the slightest idea. I'm not close to him. Haven't been for years. Not since he was in elementary school."

"Because of the falling-out you had with your brother?" Jen asked.

"Exactly." He leaned forward and gave us a sad smile. "You know about my past. That's why you're here. I don't blame you. In fact, I'm sure I'd be doing exactly what you are, were I in your position. The reason I haven't talked to my nephew in such a long time is because my brother chose to continue down a path I could no longer condone. You're right to doubt me, but the fact is that I left that life behind me a long time ago. I still make a living from crime. Just look around, I'm sure that's obvious. But working on the other side of the fence is a fool's game. Why would I risk all of this?"

His frankness was surprising. And worse, it left us no angle to work on him. So I let go of the angles and just asked a simple and straightforward question. "Then who was he trying to impress?"

"I can only guess," Benny said. "But I assume it was his father."

"His father's in prison," Jen said.

"Yes. Corcoran."

"And you think he's still that big an influence on his son?"

"His old man's standing up. A word from him could still open doors."

We knew the doors he was talking about.

"I know you've been off the streets for a long time," I said, "but is torching a helpless old man really going to impress anyone?"

"Of course not."

"Then why did he do it?"

"Because he's a fucking idiot."

• • •

We were outside of Benny's building on Ocean Boulevard and on our way back to the station before I asked Jen, "What do you make of Benny?"

"Got a good song and dance."

"I know. So good I wonder if it might even be true."

She said, "I think it's too good. Let's see if he's got any connection to Omar's lawyer."

"What if he does?"

"Then we'll know he's full of shit and we can look harder at him. Maybe we can shake something loose."

"Maybe." I didn't say anything else.

"What?" she asked.

"I don't know. I just want to ID the vic."

"You don't think the name 'Bishop' will lead us anyplace?"

"There were a couple of hits on the name with MUPS, but none matched the description. I'm thinking it must be a street name or something."

"Maybe we'll get a DNA hit."

"That would be nice," I said. "But we've still got a few threads we can pull on."

"There's something different about this victim for you, isn't there?"

"Yes."

"Is it because he burned? You thinking of Megan?"

"Maybe."

"But that's not all of it, is it?"

"No."

She waited for me to go on. Jen was always better at interviews than I was.

I watched the traffic, waiting for the crosswalk signal to change, and thought about why Bishop's identity seemed to mean so much to me. All I could come up with was this: "He had three pairs of shoes and none of them fit."

5

Key ring: plastic fob w/ blue abstract design. One VW automobile key. Six other keys, miscellaneous.

Pedro and Jesús Solano lived in a neighborhood called Zaferia, which was just east and north of Cambodia Town. I'd never heard the name until a year or two earlier, when the city started hanging up banners on the light poles along East Anaheim Street that said "Stop Shop Dine, Historic Zaferia District, Est. 1913." The drill was familiar—hang up banners everyplace the city council hoped had a shot at gentrification. It didn't seem to be working around Ohio and Tenth, though, and especially not for the Solano family. They lived in a run-down bungalow that was hidden behind a larger though equally aged home that fronted the street. If I hadn't checked the place out first on Google Maps, it would have been hard to find it.

Jen and I parked on the street half a block away, in the closest empty spot we could find. Next door was a four-story apartment building. As we walked up the long and narrow driveway past the front house on the lot, someone on one of the balconies said "Five-oh" in a matter-of-fact voice that wasn't quite loud enough to qualify as a shout. I couldn't tell if it was a warning or a greeting.

Thirty yards in from the street, there was a small porch up three steps from the driveway. To the left, with doors perpendicular to the front of the house, was a shed that wasn't quite big enough to qualify as a one-car garage. There was a large ash tree in the small space between the two structures, and its roots were pushing one side of the shed so far out of square that there was a six-inch gap above the left-side door, and a similar one beneath the right. The two sides of the padlock hasp didn't line up, and a bike chain slipped through the handles was all that secured the doors. It didn't look like the wood frame could withstand much more displacement from the ash.

Jen leaned against the short stairway's railing, looked up, and scanned the balconies as I climbed the steps up onto the porch and knocked on the rusty metal security door. The dull, hollow clanging echoed through the small house. Even though visibility through the screen was poor, I could see that there was a couch along one wall of the living room. A small woman in a zip-up hoodie and sweatpants, who I hadn't realized was there, struggled to her feet and lurched toward the door. I couldn't get a good read on her, but she appeared to be under the influence of alcohol or something else.

"Mrs. Solano?"

"What do you want?"

I held up my badge. "Are you here by yourself?"

"Yes. What do you want?"

"Where are your kids?"

"Jesús is at school still. Maria's at the daycare. What do you want?"

I thought about asking her more about Jesús, but it was clear she was wary of police, and I didn't want to tip her off to the real reason we were there. And she gave me a good opening. "What about Pedro?"

"Pedro?" She raised her voice. The slurring became more pronounced as she grew angrier. "He's in your jail! You don't know that? You already have him."

I faked surprise. "We do? Since when?"

"Last night." The anger dissipated as quickly as it had risen. Then, sounding vaguely hopeful, she added, "You do have him, don't you?"

I turned to Jen. "Mrs. Solano says Pedro's already in lockup."

Jen played along. "Seriously? What are we doing here, then?"

"I don't know." I turned back to the screen door. "I'm sorry we bothered you, Mrs. Solano. Our mistake." I spun around and started down the stairs.

Behind us, Mrs. Solano was shouting, "You have Pedro, don't you? You have Pedro?" By the time we got to the sidewalk, we couldn't hear her anymore.

• • •

As Jen drove west on Anaheim, she said to me, "Think maybe you were a little hard on her?"

"Yeah, but it was the right way to play it. We got lucky that we didn't tip our hand and she didn't figure out we were looking for Jesús. I don't know if he's laying low or what, but if there's any doubt about where he stands, where he thinks Pedro stands, that's going to work in our favor."

"How do you figure?"

"If his mother's got some doubts about what's going on with Pedro, and Jesús has to figure it out, then he's going to have to be talking to people, asking questions."

"And everyone he talks to is another potential lead."

We slowed for the red light at Gundry, and I looked out the passenger's window at the Mark Twain branch of the Long Beach Library. It was only a few years old, opened just before the recession hit, one of the newest in the system. Its contemporary architecture stood out against the older and more run-down buildings in the area, like Tech's Tires and La Bodega #4 across the street. The gleaming new building, though, told only half the story. Inside, they offered tutoring services for neighborhood kids and the area's best Internet access. The branch also housed the largest collection of Khmer-language literature in the United States. The first time I'd seen the new library, I'd been troubled by its presence, thinking the cutting-edge design not only seemed out of place in a poor neighborhood but that it also sent the wrong messages about where the city was placing its priorities. Now, though, looking out the window as Jen accelerated, I realized this ostentatious building named after one of literature's most famous dead white males in a neighborhood filled with poor Asian and Latino immigrants was actually a symbol of the best of Long Beach's Frankensteined urban stew. The cultural and socioeconomic jumble of pressure and influence and privilege and poverty don't often come together in any productive way, but on those rare occasions when they do, I try to let the cracks in my preconceived notions widen and let in a little bit of light.

• • •

When we got back to the station, I called Robert Kincaid, the ADA who'd be prosecuting the case. He'd already seen all the case files we had so far. After I told him about our visit with Benny War, I asked him about Hector Siguenza.

"He's part of Benny's cabal," Rob said. "Him and four or five other guys. All lawyers. They've got a standing tee-time at the Virginia Country Club every week."

"You figure Benny's calling in a favor?"

"Yeah. No way Benny would touch it himself, but he wants to stay close. Makes sense that he'd pull in one of his cronies."

"Think he might be pulling Siguenza's strings?"

"Benny's usually too smart to get directly involved, but I'm sure there's some influence there. Why?"

"Just trying to get a sense of things," I said.

"Keep me in the loop."

"I will."

Maybe I was wrong about Benny, but I couldn't shake the feeling that he'd been trying way too hard to seem like he didn't give a shit.

• • •

That evening I felt like I needed to get my head out of the case for a little while, so I stopped at Ralphs for some beer and drove to Belmont Heights.

"You been practicing?" Harlan Gibbs asked as he led me into his living room. I took the first bottle of Sam Adams out of the six-pack, popped the cap off, and handed it to him.

He was a retired Los Angeles sheriff's deputy whom I met on a murder investigation a few years earlier. The victim had been an English teacher who rented a small house from Harlan. The first time I saw him, he was pointing a Smith & Wesson .357 Magnum at me. He'd mistaken Jen and me for intruders. We'd been friends ever since.

"Yeah."

"How often?"

"Every day."

"Bullshit."

"Seriously."

He stood up, went into the next room, and came back with a banjo. It was one I didn't recognize. He checked the tuning, made a small adjustment to the third string, and handed it to me.

"This looks nice." And it did. It was a Gibson. I couldn't identify the model, but it looked top-of-the-line with an ebony fingerboard, a figured maple resonator, gold hardware, and pearl inlays. Probably worth ten grand or so. It looked new, but I knew that with Gibsons, new wasn't always as good as old. "You just buy this?"

"Got a deal."

Almost a year earlier, when my physical therapist told me I needed to start playing the guitar to treat my chronic pain, Harlan had made a gift to me of a beautiful Deering Saratoga Star and told me it would be even better for rebuilding the strength and dexterity I'd lost with my injury. It was every bit as valuable as the instrument I was holding in my hands, and I thought he'd resigned himself to giving in to the stomach cancer he'd been stricken by. I never figured out if I was right, but Harlan kept fighting, and he was closing on nine cancer-free months. The new banjo seemed to me a good sign, an investment of sorts in the future.

"Flashy," I said. "You run into some pimp with buyer's remorse?"

"Bought it for the sound."

I adjusted the banjo in my lap and picked a forward roll across the strings. Sounded very nice. I tossed a knowing nod in Harlan's direction.

"Please," he said. "Like you could recognize a decent sound."

He was right, of course, but I wasn't about to give him the satisfaction of indicating I knew it.

"Okay, Béla," Harlan said, "show me a basic chord progression. G, C, D7."

It wasn't pretty, but I managed a slow and clumsy alternating roll through all three chords, relieved that I managed the C without the dead plunk from my poor fingering on the fourth string.

"That was lovely," Harlan said and took a long pull from his beer. "Thought you said you were practicing."

"I have been. Half an hour every night before bed."

"Well, it's not working. You need some lessons."

I'd tried to weasel some lessons out of him when he'd given me the Deering, and he made an effort, but he wasn't a teacher. Didn't have it in him. And because I'd hoped the lessons would be as good for him as they were for me, I hadn't pushed him to continue.

"I'm taking lessons."

"With who?"

"Tony Trischka."

"Yeah, right."

"Seriously. Tony Trischka's Online Banjo School."

"Online? You're learning banjo on the computer? Jesus."

"It's the best I could do. Maybe if I knew any real banjo players, they could help me find some decent lessons."

The jab landed and earned me half a snort. "All right," he said. "I'll ask around."

We drank in comfortable silence for a bit, and then he said, "Saw the homeless guy on the news. You caught that, right?"

I nodded. Then we talked about banjos and music and old movies for two hours, and I went home.

• • •

The heat had been building in my ground-floor duplex apartment all day, and even though the sun had gone down hours earlier, it still felt like a blast furnace when I stepped inside. I had intentionally kept the ceiling fan on when I left, but it hadn't made any noticeable difference in the temperature. All it did was move the hot air around like a convection oven. On the way back to the bedroom, I opened every window I passed, even though I suspected the air outside was too still to provide enough cross ventilation to cool the place down.

I went into the kitchen to get myself something to drink. Years ago, the previous tenant, a graphic designer, had painted the room in a bright, Caribbean-flavored color scheme—all primary colors, yellow and red and blue—and I still liked it. It's not the kind of thing I'd ever come up with myself. If I had to choose the colors to paint a room, I'm sure my choices would range from ecru all the way to Navajo white.

The message light on my landline was flashing. It was my landlord, saying that in the next week or so, someone would be stopping by to work on the plumbing and to install new low-flow fixtures. I didn't like the sounds of that. One of my favorite things about the duplex was the fact that it still had all the original hardware. I thought of every hotel shower I'd taken in the last few years and made a mental note to ask him if he'd skip my place.

Even though there hadn't been a Grey Goose bottle in there for two months, habit still made me reach for the freezer door first. I didn't even have it all the way open before I pushed it closed and opened the refrigerator for a Diet 7Up.

After a year of juggling Vicodin and vodka to deal with my pain, I finally succumbed to the horrible notion that had been nagging at the back of my head like a fly in a dark room, and I combined the two.

The result was terrifying.

The combination of the alcohol and painkillers was so effective in treating the burning ache that twisted from my wrist up through my arm and into my neck and shoulder, the corrosive hurt that tormented me, that it felt like an amazing deliverance. The first time I did it, I told myself it would only be once. Only once. The second time I did it, I told myself it would only be twice. Each time, I'd add a little more vodka and the relief would be a little bit deeper, the sleep a little bit more sound.

But every silver lining has a cloud.

I give myself credit for cutting myself off after night number six. Even then I knew that if I didn't stop soon, it would be harder.

Some nights, when the pain and the insomnia are particularly rough, I think about the relative ease with which I stopped, and I think that maybe just one more time wouldn't hurt. And I know that's probably true. I also know bargaining when I see it.

• • •

The first full night at home after taking on a major case is always an ordeal. Insomnia has been a problem for me for years, for far longer than the chronic pain, and especially so when my mind is racing with the details of a new murder investigation. The inability to disengage, though, is a double-edged sword. I discovered that fact a year earlier on a triple murder case, the first upon my return to active duty after the long medical leave for my injury. The excitement of a new case was a balm for my pain—it occupied my mind and being in a way that nothing else could, and that forced my attention away from the chronic affliction of my injury. When I became immersed in work, I forgot to hurt, and even now it's the only real relief I can count on.

But in the brightness of one of my many insomniac midnight-to-dawn struggles, the magic fades and the pain mixes with the befuddlement of the sleeplessness and makes those few brutal hours stretch out in front of me like an unending march toward a forever-receding horizon.

It's kind of like watching a Terrence Malick movie.

The way I deal with it is by working the case. It's actually a good chance to get squared away and organize the mass of information compiled in the first hours of an investigation. This case, though, was different. Sure, it was high profile, but we had suspects in custody, and it was as close to an airtight case as I'd seen in all my years of working Homicide. Once, several years earlier, I'd worked a killing that was recorded on the surveillance camera of a Circle K mini-mart, but the images had been relatively low-resolution and the tape wasn't the definitive evidence in the trial. With this case, though, the recording would be crucial. Not only were there shots in which the suspects were unmistakably identifiable, there were also multiple incidents of them using each other's names, and footage of the preparation and lead-up to the murder as well as the act itself. There was also a considerable amount of forensic evidence tying them to the crime and the crime scene, and multiple LBPD officers could testify to their presence in the immediate aftermath of the incident. They were going down for this.

Aside from motive, there was only one question that seemed urgent: who was the victim?

I couldn't answer that question with the information I had at hand, but, as with most cases, I knew that the better I knew the evidence, the more likely I'd be to make connections down the road. So I went back to the murder book.

The list of contents from the shopping cart was the one item that kept drawing my attention. It was the only thing we had that allowed for any speculation or interpretation. I didn't know it then, but I would spend so much time with that list that I would virtually commit it to memory. That night, though, it was still fresh and new, and it seemed to me that if I studied it and looked deeply enough into it, that it just might hold the key to unlocking the universe of our victim. I looked at it as if it were a puzzle, and if only I could figure out how to properly assemble the pieces, I'd be able to unlock some meaningful truth about our victim. Bishop? I couldn't help but wonder if that name was actually useful information or just the rambling of a man who wasn't able to make any more sense of my questions than I was myself.

I read through the inventory again. It seemed only a random collection of items, the debris and the dregs of a life that was slowly waning away into insignificance. But I couldn't let myself believe that. If I did, I'd be no better than the community and culture that had ignored and neglected him long enough for him to meet the fate he had met.

No.

I wouldn't let that happen. I needed more. I needed to know who he was and where he came from.

In my experience, it's actually a very rare thing for homicide detectives to feel as if they affected any real closure or resolved anything of great significance for those left behind by the victims of murder. The truth of the matter is that when someone dies of anything other than extreme old age and natural causes, and often even then, the death leaves a great void in the lives of the survivors, an emptiness like an abandoned mine that can never be filled. A deep chasm. If you're lucky, you might be able to cover it with plywood and rebar, to surround it with chain link and "Danger" signs, but at best, these are only ever temporary remedies, patches that might briefly hold up to the storms that will come and come again until the ground around the chasm grows so weakened and diminished that to approach the emptiness becomes ever more dangerous. And that's if you're lucky. If you're not, then the loss leaves a void as dark and desolate as a black hole, with a gravity so great that no light can escape.

I'm not sure why it struck me as so vital and important to the success of the case that our victim had someone to mourn deeply for him. What was wrong with me? Any other detective I knew would be glad to be in this situation—no next of kin to notify, no bereaved wife to console, no children whose lives would be forever changed because of a stranger in a coat and tie knocking on the front door. With a victim like this, there was no one left to hurt. The damage had been done. Why couldn't I just be satisfied with that?

6

LEVI'S JEANS, MEN'S, TWO PAIRS: ONE SIZE 34/32, FADED, HOLE IN RIGHT KNEE; ONE SIZE 36/30, DARK BLUE, GOOD CONDITION.

When I got to my desk in the squad room, I had a message waiting from Kyle.

"Good news," he said, answering my return call. "We got prints off of the chess set. Two sets of prints. No hits on one, but we got an ID on the other."

"Could the good set be our vic?"

"Doubt it. The guy was army. Only twenty-nine."

"Please tell me we can find him."

"We do have a current address. Less than two months old, so it's probably still good."

Jen came in while I was still on the phone. I told Kyle thanks and to let me know if anything else came up.

"Good news," I said to Jen.

"Yeah?"

"There was a chess set in the shopping cart. Two sets of prints, one with a solid ID and an address."

"And the other?"

"Hopefully," I said, "our victim."

• • •

The Century Villages at Cabrillo was a transitional and low-income housing development just north of Pacific Coast Highway and nestled up against the Terminal Island Freeway, State Route 103. We were on our way there to interview the man whose fingerprints were on the chess set. Jen was behind the wheel.

"You know they filmed *Terminator 2* on the 103, right?" I asked.

"Yeah. You tell me that every time we get anywhere close to it."

"*Mr. & Mrs. Smith*, too," I said. "I never mention that one because I know how you feel about Angelina Jolie."

"Well, thank you for that."

"You think it might be the shortest freeway in the state?"

"Why are you trying to annoy me?"

"I'm not. I'm trying to be witty and charming."

"Oh. I couldn't tell."

"I have a good feeling about this. We're going to get an ID for our vic."

She bit her lip and kept quiet.

"What?"

We were nearly at the entry gate for the Villages. "That worries me. You faking optimism is never a good sign."

Jen badged the guard at the gate, and he asked if we knew where we were headed. We lied and drove on through. Neither of us had been there before, and we were both surprised. From the look of things, it was difficult to differentiate the place from any of the other gated communities that had sprouted like weeds in cracked concrete all across Southern California until the big housing collapse. The Villages were different, though. They'd been one of Long Beach's most successful charitable enterprises of the last decade. The organization behind the development had raised tens of millions of dollars and invested it all in the complex that provided transitional housing for the homeless and destitute. There was a lot of support from Veterans Affairs and other government agencies as well, and things really got rolling when the soldiers returning from Iraq and Afghanistan started needing help and began to take advantage of the opportunity.

"I didn't expect it to look so nice," Jen said.

"I know," I said. "I thought it would be more projecty. I almost don't want to make fun of the name anymore." Looking around at how very normal the place looked, it occurred to me that the clichéd name of the development had been chosen precisely because it was indistinguishable from a million other communities. The people this place served would welcome that kind of uninspired normalcy. The realization left me with more respect for whoever was in charge here than I expected to have.

The set of fingerprints we'd matched belonged to a man named Henry Nichols. He'd done two tours of duty in Iraq and one in Afghanistan. Twice in the last fifteen months he'd been questioned by the LBPD on vagrancy-related misdemeanors, but he'd been released each time. I'd talked to one of the uniforms who'd picked him up. Nichols had apparently suffered a head wound before his medical discharge that had left him with some lingering effects.

We found the street we were looking for, and Jen parked in a small visitors' lot close to his building. It was a nice-looking place, all two-story earth-toned stucco with tile roofs. The style had a southwest Orange County vibe.

"That's his car," she said, pointing to a white late-nineties Jetta. "According to the DMV, he's had it less than a month."

"That means he got it about three weeks after he filed the change of address to this place."

"Think he came into some money?" she said.

"He came into something. This looks like a decent place to get back on your feet."

Inside, the building had a shared living room, kitchen, and restrooms, while each tenant had an individual bedroom. Kind of like an old-school boarding-house arrangement. We found Nichols's door and knocked. Nothing happened, so we knocked again, harder. Jen leaned in close to the door and said, "Mr. Nichols? Long Beach Police Department. We need to speak with you."

A few seconds later, we heard a muffled voice from inside the room. "Hang on. I'll be right there."

The door opened. Nichols was wearing sweat shorts and a gray T-shirt, and his hair was disheveled. "I'm sorry," he said. "I was sleeping. Been working nights." He ran his hands over his head in a fruitless attempt to make his hair more presentable. "How can I help you?" There was concern and a vague distrust in his expression, but he didn't respond with the kind of wariness or fear I'd thought likely.

"A man was killed last night," Jen said. "We're trying to identify him. We think it's likely that he was homeless."

"Can we come in?" I asked.

"Yeah," he said. "There's not much space." He was right. The room was maybe ten by ten, with a twin bed, a small dresser, a writing table, and a cheap-looking wardrobe tucked into the corner in lieu of a real closet.

"I only have the one chair," he said. He pulled it out and turned it toward the bed. Jen sat down and motioned for him to take the spot across from her on the bed. I backed into the corner and leaned against the wall and tried not to seem intimidating.

"Thank you," Jen said. "The man who was killed, we don't know who he was."

"And you think I can help?"

Nichols was backlit by the sun coming in through the window. From my position, I noticed something odd about the shape of his head. When he would move and the light hit his dark hair from a different angle, it appeared as if there was a significant dent in the right side of his skull.

"We hope so." Jen smiled warmly at him, and he seemed to relax. "You're a veteran?"

"Yeah," he said. "Army, six years." His voice was flat, and I couldn't get a solid read of how he felt about it.

"And you got a medical discharge?"

He nodded. "IED. Traumatic brain injury. Still kind of messed up with it."

"You were on the street for a while."

It was clear that he was embarrassed by the fact.

"I was. Took a long time for my VA benefits to come through. Had to stay in my car for a while."

"That must have been tough," Jen said.

"Wasn't great," he said. "I saw a lot worse, though. Had a minivan, you know, so it wasn't as bad as it might have been."

"How do you like it here?"

"It's good. There's a clinic and people to help you with the VA stuff. They helped me get a job, too."

"I'm glad to hear that," Jen said. "Where are you working?"

"At the Home Depot in Signal Hill. Doing overnights right now. Unloading and restocking, cleaning."

"How do you like it?" Jen asked. The warmth in her voice was genuine, and he was responding to it. He was starting to get comfortable.

"It's okay. I never thought I'd have to work retail after I got out, you know? But it's a good opportunity. I think I can make it work."

"Sure you can," I said.

"I want to go full time, you know? I can't right now because I'm on partial disability. But I want to get off of that and go full time."

"Of course you do. Who wouldn't?"

"Oh, there's guys who don't want to. Or can't. Some of us are luckier than others, you know?"

"That's the truth," I said.

His eyes lost their focus and he blinked twice. "Could you tell me why you're here again?"

"Sure. We're hoping you can help us."

"Oh, yeah. Somebody died, right?"

"Yes. Did you know a man named Bishop?"

A look of concerned sorrow flashed across his face but disappeared almost as quickly. He was used to losing people. "Bishop died? Oh, man. What happened?"

"He was murdered."

"Really?" He shook his head and clenched his hands into fists. "Fuck," he said as he pressed the bottoms of his fists into his thighs. "Shit. Do you know who did it?"

"Yes. They're in custody."

"Who? Who did it?"

"We can't say yet, but we believe it was gang related."

"Fuck, man. Shit."

"I'm sorry. Did you know him well?"

"Yeah." He thought about it. "Well, yes and no."

"Tell us about him."

"We used to play chess sometimes. He was nice to me. Used to let me win when I was having a really bad day."

"How did you meet him?"

"We both used to like it down at the harbor. All that industrial stuff. There's a lot of places you can stay and not get hassled. Be by yourself, you know? We both liked that. Didn't like being around other people too much."

"How'd you meet him?"

"I was down at Palm Beach Park one day back at the beginning of summer. I had the minivan, but sometimes I just liked to be by the water, you know? He was there, too. We were both there awhile, probably an hour or two. I was sitting in the shade under one of the trees, kind of forgot anybody else was around, and he comes over and says, 'I don't want to bug you, but you play chess?' I told him I wasn't very good at it. He said, 'Long as you know how the pieces move, that's good enough.' So we played. When it was over—he didn't let me win that first time—he said, 'Thank you for the game. 'Preciate it.' And that was it. Figured I wouldn't see him again."

"But you did?"

"Yeah. I liked that park. It's pretty quiet during the week. So I'd hang out there sometimes."

"How long until you saw him again?"

"Four or five days maybe? I don't know. Sometimes it's hard to keep track, you know?"

"What happened then?"

"He just came up to me and asked, 'Feel like another game?' So we played. Then I'd see him every couple of days or so, and we'd play."

"What can you tell us about him?" Jen asked.

"He was kind of quiet. Never talked about the past. Not his past, anyway. Always wanted to talk to me about my time in the desert. Asking if I was okay, shit like that. The funny thing was I never thought I wanted to talk about it. But he pulled it out of me somehow, and most times it even made me feel a little better, you know?"

"Did he tell you anything about himself?" Jen's voice got softer with each question.

"No, not really. He'd talk about his day sometimes, but never anything from his past. I asked a few times."

"What did he say?"

"He'd always either change the subject or just ignore the question."

As they talked, I let my focus drift down toward the carpet so he wouldn't feel compelled to meet my gaze and could focus only on Jen.

"Do you know his first name?"

"No, just Bishop. I don't think that was his real name, though. That first day we played chess, I introduced myself. He said, 'Everybody just calls me Bishop.' Like it was a nickname or something."

"Any idea why they'd call him that?"

"No, not really. I just figured it was because of the chess set or something."

"Do you know why anyone might have wanted to hurt him?"

"I can't think of a reason. He was really low-key. Kept to himself, mostly. He was streetwise, too. Used to give tips on places to park overnight where I wouldn't get hassled. He was right, too. Those were good tips."

He looked down at his hands. They were folded in his lap. There was a subtle tension in his posture. I wasn't sure if it was from emotion he was feeling or if he was just uncomfortable talking to us. The army had done a good job of teaching him to keep a lid on his emotions. They'd probably also done a good job of teaching him how to deal with news of a death. He seemed fond of Bishop, but I couldn't tell what else he was thinking.

"Do you know anyone else who might be able to tell us about him?" Jen asked. "Did he have any other friends you know of?"

"Not really. I only ever saw him away from the park a couple of times. Usually just around the street or something. Once I saw him at Saint Luke's Homeless Shower Program. We both just showed up at the same time."

Jen said, "Only once?"

"Yeah. Neither one of us really liked the Jesus stuff, you know? So we both tried not to go unless we really needed to and couldn't get cleaned up anyplace else."

"When was the last time you saw him?"

"I moved in here the first of August, so maybe a week before that?"

"Did he seem any different?"

"No. He never seemed different. I think that might be what I liked most about him, you know? He was always the same. Consistent."

"Did you know you were coming here?"

"Not for sure."

"Did you tell Bishop about it?"

"Yeah, told him I was hoping. He said, 'That's good. Real good. You don't want to be out here too long.' Like he knew from experience."

"Any idea how long he *was* out there?"

"Long time. A lot longer than me. I told him if I got in here, I'd still play chess with him. That just made him laugh."

"Why do you think that was funny to him?"

"Because he knew I wouldn't. I mean, I meant it when I said it, but once I got here, I never really looked back. Now I wish I had."

"I know," Jen said. "I know."

7

ONE CAN DEL MONTE FRESH CUT SWEET CORN, CREAM STYLE.

"Well," I said when we were back in the car, heading east on PCH passing Long Beach City College's Pacific Coast campus, "that wasn't as fruitful as I hoped."

"What did you expect? That Nichols was hanging onto Bishop's wallet with a driver's license and Social Security card? Something like that?"

"I guess I was just hoping."

"We got plenty. Give MUPS a chance. You said it yourself, we've got three murderers in jail with a rock-solid case against them. We'll figure out who Bishop really was."

I knew she was right. The impatience I was feeling was not something I normally experience with a case, and the frustration was expressing itself as a twisting pain running from my elbow up into my shoulder. I took a few deep breaths. At the next stoplight, she studied me.

"Six?" she asked.

I took a brief inventory of my pain at the moment and said, "Yeah. That's just about right on the nose."

In the time I'd been dealing with chronic pain, Jen had heard me vent my frustration with the diagnostic tool everyone in the medical field calls the pain scale. Every time you see a doctor or nurse, they ask you to assign a number between one and ten to your level of pain. The higher the number, the more you're hurting. Somewhere along the way, Jen had realized that she could read my symptoms from my physicality—the tightness in my neck, the way I held my arm, the rolling of my shoulder, and any of a dozen other characteristics—and place me on the scale with an astonishing degree of accuracy. She claimed it was because of her years of training in aikido and jujitsu, that those particular martial arts had so sharpened her ability to perceive stress and tension in someone's body that it was really just a more subtle version of what she did on the mat every day. I knew that was most of it, but I was also certain that she knew me better than anyone else, and I liked to think that it was our friendship as much as anything she brought with her from the dojo that allowed her to see me the way she did. Maybe, though, I just needed to believe that. To believe that I wasn't alone.

• • •

"Jesús didn't go to school yesterday. Think he's there today?" Jen asked.

"Let's find out." I found the number for the Solanos' landline in my notebook and dialed it. A young man answered.

"Doug?" I said.

"No," he said. "There's no one named that here."

I read him back a phone number that was one digit off from his.

"No, that's the wrong number."

I apologized and cut the line.

"He's home."

In the late-morning traffic, we made it to their house in less than ten minutes.

From the porch I could see Mrs. Solano's semiconscious form collapsed on the couch in the same position she had been in yesterday. I tapped on the door and tried to get her attention.

"Mrs. Solano?" I said.

She didn't seem to hear me.

I hadn't noticed the sound until it stopped, but the water had been running in the kitchen. Through the rusty security door, I could see a young man come into the living room, drying his hands on a kitchen towel. He froze and eyeballed me through the screen. I didn't know what he was thinking, but if I'd been a betting man, I would have put down a good chunk of money that he was calculating his odds of making it out the back door and over the fence into the neighbor's yard before I could catch him.

"If you're thinking about running, stop now," I said.

He slung the towel up over his shoulder and let it hang there as he approached the door.

"What do you want?" he said.

I held up my badge and said, "We need to talk to you."

He looked at his semiconscious mother on the couch, unlocked the bolt, and stepped out onto the porch with me. The space was tight enough that it was easy to make him feel crowded.

Jesús was small and thin, maybe five-six, one-forty, and looked like he was dressed for school in dark-blue pants and a white polo shirt.

"Can we come inside?"

He looked over his shoulder. "My mom's not feeling too good right now."

"It's not a good idea for us to do this out here. If you'd rather, we can go to the station and talk there."

"I have to be here for when my little sister is done with daycare."

I didn't say anything, and he thought about it, pulled the security door open, and let us follow him back into the living room. The house was small—the living room, two bedrooms, a kitchen, and a bath. Standing near the door to the hallway, I could see almost all of it with a glance over my shoulder. It must have been close to a hundred degrees inside. The windows were all open in a futile grasp at comfort. Above our heads, a ceiling fan was spinning and churning the hot air, but the only effect it had was to make me think again of convection ovens.

"Mom!" Jesús said. "Get up, you got to go in the bedroom."

She opened her eyes and tried to sit up but didn't make it.

"Cops again?" she said, looking at Jen and me. She was wearing the same clothes she'd had on the day before, and it sounded like she had a mouth full of toothpaste.

"It's okay, Mom. Just get up." He took her arm and pulled her to her feet. She was shorter than him and probably about thirty pounds heavier.

"What did you do?" she asked as he dragged her past us. I caught a whiff of her breath as she went by. I was wrong about the toothpaste.

Jesús put her in the bedroom at the front of the house and came back into the living room. I could already feel the sweat gathering along my forehead and at the back of my neck.

"What'd you want to talk about?"

"You know where your brother is?"

He looked at my face and then at Jen's. I suspected that he knew the answer to my question. "No," he said. "Where is he?"

"Sit down," I said. He sat on one end of the couch and Jen sat on the other. I stayed on my feet.

"Did your mom tell you we were here yesterday?"

"She said something about cops. She's been drunk for two days. It's hard to know what she's talking about."

"I'm going to ask you again. Do you know where your brother is?"

"He in jail?"

"You know the answer."

"I didn't for sure until now." I couldn't tell yet if he was lying. We hadn't talked enough for me to get a feeling for how he sounded telling the truth, so I had no baseline to compare with his statement.

"What can you tell us about why he's there?"

"Nothing."

"You answered that pretty quickly. I think you must know something."

"I don't."

"Where were you two nights ago? On Monday."

"Here."

"Where were you supposed to be?"

"Supposed to be? I don't know what you mean. I'm always here. Somebody's got to take care of my sister."

"What about your mom?"

He tilted his head and looked at me as if I'd just suggested he take the yacht out for a sail or challenged him to a game of polo. I didn't push that one any further.

Jen said, "That's good the way you take care of your sister."

He allowed himself the barest hint of a smile at that. He knew that it was good, and he was proud of the fact. It made me want to go easy on him, but I didn't.

"I think you're a good kid, Jesús. I do."

His face iced over. He knew something was coming.

"But that's not what Pedro says."

Nothing.

"Pedro says you were supposed to be with him on Monday night."

"I don't care what Pedro says."

"That's not what I've heard. Everybody says different."

"Who's everybody?"

"Francisco, for a start."

His jaw tightened, and for maybe a second before he caught himself, his eyes narrowed. He didn't like Francisco. "Is Francisco lying about you?"

"I barely know him. He's my brother's friend."

"But you wanted to be his friend, too."

He didn't say anything.

"Why? Because he's connected? He could help you make your bones?"

Still nothing.

"You're a good kid, Jesús," I said. "I know that. But you've got to talk to us, or everybody's going to believe Francisco. The shit he's saying about you. You'll wind up in there with them."

I kept expecting him to look away, to break my gaze, but he didn't. He was studying me the same way I'd been studying him. After what seemed like a long time but surely wasn't, he shook his head, and I knew that we were done. At least for the time being.

"Okay, you want to play it that way, that's your call. But you're going to change your mind, and I really hope it won't be too late." I handed him my card, and to my surprise, he took it without hesitation and held it carefully between his fingers as if he were afraid of damaging it. Then I got out my iPhone and dialed the number Jen had found earlier on Pedro's cell. A banda tune sounded from his pocket.

"You got my number?"

"Yeah. And now you've got mine."

We showed ourselves out and left Jesús sitting on the couch and looking at the business card in his hand.

In the car, Jen said, "You think he'll come around?"

"Don't know," I answered. "But I didn't hate him nearly as much as I wanted to."

• • •

"You two having fun out in all the sun and fresh air?" Patrick asked us when we came back into the squad room.

"It's about a thousand degrees out there, so no, not really," Jen said.

"You went to see Jesús Solano, right?"

I nodded.

"What did you think?"

"Seemed like a good kid," Jen said.

"He knows something," I added. "But he thinks he's got to stand up."

"I checked him and the other three out on social media, looking for connections. None of them are big on Twitter, but there's some interesting stuff on Facebook."

"Yeah?" I wheeled my chair toward his desk.

"Omar and Francisco are neck-tattoo deep in gang associations. They might as well have an East Side Longo fan page. Pedro's got a few, too, nowhere close to as many as them, though. But Jesús? Nothing. I need to go deeper, but it looks like the only connection he has to anything even vaguely questionable is his brother. Kid looks clean. You know what most of the pictures he's posted are?"

"What?" I asked.

"His little sister."

Patrick spun his laptop around so we could see the screen. Jesús had an album titled "Maria's Birthday." There were a dozen or more photos of a happy little girl with five or six of her friends, celebrating in the backyard of the bungalow on Ohio. There was a little cake and a little piñata and lots of laughing. It looked like Jesús was the closest thing to an adult in attendance.

"You have to hack into his account?"

"He's sixteen. Everything's set to 'public.' Hardly anybody under twenty sets anything to 'private' these days."

I thought about that. My Facebook page was locked down tighter than a submarine. What did I have to hide that was so much more secret and privileged than Jesús's life? What was I trying to protect?

Patrick straightened up his desk as if he were getting ready to leave. "I haven't eaten. You guys want to go grab a sandwich at Modica's?"

Jen said, "I'm up for it." She looked at me. "Danny?"

"You guys go ahead. I'll meet you there in a few minutes."

Patrick was about to close his browser window, but I stopped him.

"Can I look at that a bit more?"

"Sure," he said. "Just be sure to shut it down when you're done."

I pushed Patrick's chair to the side and rolled myself in closer for a better look.

Seeing those pictures made me want to like Jesús. They made me want to believe that he really was the good kid who refused to let his brother pull him down into the darkness. I wondered, too, what might have motivated Pedro. Why would he commit such a horrendous crime?

After closing the Firefox window on Patrick's desktop, I wheeled myself back over to my own computer and clicked on the icon for the murder video from the Samsung. I watched the whole thing again, from start to finish. I'd seen it so many times at that point that I knew every moment before it came, but I focused just as intently as I had the first time I'd watched. I didn't expect to discover anything new, but I wanted to confirm some of my observations about the three suspects.

Omar, I could believe, was a monster. Watching him in the video of the crime made that possibility clear. He enjoyed the killing. The pleasure he took in the violence was obvious in his gleeful excitement.

Francisco didn't share in the monstrosity, but his cold and calculating response made me think of a veteran soldier with a job to do who was getting it done.

Pedro was the least enthusiastic of the trio. He held the Galaxy and, as the cameraman, was the least visible. But I could hear his voice. "Oh, man," he said. "Oh, man." If there wasn't regret in his voice, there was at least a realization of the magnitude of their actions. In those four syllables was the recognition of an unalterable change in the course of his life. Even before the sirens and the flashing lights and the uniforms, Pedro knew that nothing would ever be the same again.

• • •

We were back in the squad room after lunch. A stubborn piece of pastrami had wedged itself between two of my molars, and I was using the tip of my tongue to try in vain to work it free.

Jen was telling Patrick about some remodeling ideas she saw on HGTV.

"Everything on there is crap," I said.

"Not all of it," she said.

"Are you kidding? Those shows where they have to race to get everything done in time for the big finish?"

"They're not all like that."

"Maybe not, but they've always got to come up with some fake bullshit conflict to liven things up two-thirds of the way through. I wouldn't trust any of those guys with my house."

"You don't have a house. And you can't compare everybody to Norm."

"Who's Norm?" Patrick asked.

"From *This Old House*," Jen and I said almost simultaneously.

"Oh," he said. "Of course."

I added, "Don't forget *New Yankee Workshop*. Norm's amazing."

"Nobody watches those shows anymore," Jen said.

"It's not my fault the world's going to shit," I said. "You don't need all that fake HGTV tension to make things compelling. It drives me up the wall. Just show us how to do quality work the right way. Don't give us a bunch of bullshit over-the-top drama."

Patrick took a long drink of his iced tea. "Think maybe you're getting a little too worked up over this?"

"No, I don't. You should be on my side, Patrick. This is all about authenticity. That's totally a hipster thing."

He and Jen just looked at me.

"No offense," I said.

"None taken," he said. I think that was true, too, which was a shame. We'd been giving him crap about being a hipster for years. If his skin had finally gotten thick enough that it didn't bug him anymore, then we'd have to come up with something else to needle him with. He was still the newest member of the squad. Until someone else transferred in and moved him up a notch on the totem pole, letting him off the hook simply wasn't an option.

Jen got a call. It was quick. When she hung up, she said, "That was Stan—he came up with something on the canvass."

8

Three CDs: *Fairytale*, Donovan; *The Deer Hunter: Original Motion Picture Soundtrack*, Various Artists; *Remain in Light*, Talking Heads.

Julia Rice was a photographer with a background in sociology. She'd worked for the city for several years and had even taught in the MSW program at CSULB for a few semesters. According to her website, she'd given up the day jobs to focus full time on her photography. She'd had half a dozen shows in the last three years all over Southern California. Her name came up during Stan Burke's canvass of the shelters. She'd done a lot of social work with the homeless in her old job, and recently, according to one of the food-bank administrators, she had started a photography project taking portraits of street people in an effort to raise awareness and, ultimately, of course, money. The man running the shelter had said he thought she was there on one of the rare days he'd seen Bishop.

When Jen had called her earlier to arrange a meeting, Julia had told her to stop by her studio—which was actually a loft in one of the newish buildings that had opened on the Promenade downtown with the most recent spurt of redevelopment.

We walked into the lobby and ogled the concrete and glass and metal. "Seems upscale for a social worker," I said.

Jen corrected me. "A *former* social worker. Now an artiste."

I was never comfortable around people with lots of money, especially if they felt the need to be hip and cool about it. Something felt off about going to one of the trendiest and most expensive buildings in town to investigate the murder of a destitute victim. I tried to swallow my disdain.

Before we had the chance to find Julia's number on the intercom system, the elevator opened and two young women with enormous breasts, carrying yoga mats rolled up in earth-toned tote bags, passed us in the lobby and went out the gray-glazed glass door into the heat. I was still watching them walk away when Jen said, "Hey."

She stood in the elevator with her hand extended so it wouldn't close, until I boarded too.

"You know the apartment number?"

"Yeah. Fourth floor."

We rode up and found ourselves wandering the halls in order to figure out which way the unit numbers ran. Two wrong turns later, we found Julia Rice's apartment and, out of courtesy and general niceness, gave the door a normal civilian knock. It's rare that we do this when we're on the clock. We're so conditioned to pounding on every door with the heels of our hands—and the resultant booming echoes—that it feels anticlimactic to just to give a door a run-of-the-mill tap. But that's what I did.

From behind the door, we heard a muffled voice. "Yes?"

Jen held her badge up to the peephole and said, "Ms. Rice? I'm Detective Jennifer Tanaka. We spoke on the phone earlier."

We heard the sound of the deadbolt and the door opened.

"Hello, Detective." Then she realized Jen wasn't alone and said, "I beg your pardon, Detectives." She smiled at me, and, without thinking, I smiled back. "Won't you come in?"

She wore old-school Levi's and an olive-colored T-shirt. Her light-brown hair was pulled back into a loose ponytail. It looked like she'd done it that way for convenience rather than for style. "Let's sit in here." She led us into a living area with a large brown sofa and two matching chairs that faced each other in front of a floor-to-ceiling window that overlooked Alta Way and the square. Jen and I took the sofa, and Julia sat in the chair closest to the window.

"This is a very nice view," Jen said.

"It's okay. I'm looking for a new place."

"Why?" I asked. "This place looks great."

"The apartment's nice enough. But the people here are all pretentious assholes." I must have smiled again, because she looked at me in a curious way. "How can I help you?"

"We're investigating a murder," Jen said.

"Is this about the man who was burned to death by the river?"

"Yes," I said.

"That's horrible. What can I do?"

I let Jen answer.

"We don't know who he was. The director of the Rescue Mission said you have a lot of photos."

"I do. If you don't know who he was, how do you think we might find him in the pictures?"

"We believe he went by the name of Bishop, but we suspect that's not his real name."

"That doesn't ring any bells. Can you give me a physical description?"

We did. "Doesn't sound too unusual, but I can start looking through what I have. I get names whenever I can, but a lot of my photos are just faces."

"How many do you have?" I asked.

"Thousands. Only about a dozen of the portrait series I'm working on, but I've been taking pictures of the homeless for years, trying to document the conditions on the streets. I used to be a social worker."

Jen nodded. "We have someone who used to play chess occasionally with the victim. So far he's the only person who would be able to recognize his face."

"I know what I can do," Julia said. "I'll put together a catalogue of everything I have that matches the description you gave me."

"That would be very helpful," Jen said.

"We'd only need photos that would be a good likeness, that might help us identify him."

"Well," she said, "that shouldn't be too tough, then. I think I can have something for you in the next day or two."

"Thank you." I handed her my card. "Just let us know when you have it ready for us. We appreciate your help."

"I'm glad to do whatever I can, Detective Beckett."

She showed us out, and in the hallway while we waited for the elevator, I said, "She wasn't really what I expected."

"You know," Jen said, "she already had my number."

I had no idea why she was suddenly so amused.

• • •

There was a message from Kyle waiting for me when we got back to our desks. "You said to give you a heads-up when we were done processing everything from the John Doe's cart. We've got everything finished. Let me know if you want to check it again before we put it into storage."

I headed downstairs to Evidence Control. The clerk told me where to find Kyle. He was in a processing room double-checking his inventory sheet against all the tagged and bagged evidence on a large worktable in front of him.

"That everything?" I asked.

"Except the clothes he was wearing. What the ME could save of them."

He handed me his clipboard so I could look at the list. "Anything new?"

"Nothing substantial," he said. "We've got more detail and description. Confirmed the count of socks and things. But it's basically what you've already seen."

I read through the list again, item by item. The man's whole life was there in that dry, clinical list of a few dozen possessions. Would they add up into any kind of cohesive narrative, or would Bishop remain a mystery with nothing but a random assortment of accumulated belongings to mark his passage?

One thing on the inventory caught my attention. I'd noticed it on the preliminary list but hadn't taken a look at it in person yet. A copy of John Steinbeck's *The Grapes of Wrath*. There were three other books on the list as well—a mystery novel from a few years ago, the title of which sounded vaguely familiar, and two others that didn't ring any bells at all. I knew the Steinbeck book, though. How could I not? If I hadn't already read it, I certainly would have the first time I heard Springsteen sing "The Ghost of Tom Joad."

I took a pair of latex gloves out of my pocket and opened the evidence bag. The book was a trade paperback Viking Critical Library edition that included a lengthy introduction and a bunch of other academic addenda. As I thumbed through the pages, I saw that someone had annotated the margins throughout the novel. Reading a few of the penciled notes, it was clear that the person who made the comments knew what they were doing. I looked inside the front cover to see if there might be a name. No luck.

"You think there's any chance this might be Bishop's handwriting?"

"Bishop? I didn't know we had a name. You got an ID?"

"Nothing solid yet. We have a witness who thinks he went by that. Probably an alias."

"You ever watch that show *Fringe*?"

"Yeah, why?"

"When you said that name I thought of the character."

There were two characters with that name, a father and a son. "Walter or Peter?"

"The father."

I imagined John Noble, the actor from the series, scribbling in the margins of *The Grapes of Wrath.*

"What about the handwriting?" I asked.

"We didn't find anything else to compare the notes to, but they seem more grad-studenty than homeless guy."

"You're right. I'd like to read them. Any chance we can scan the pages?"

"We could. But it's probably better to go through by hand, unless we need them for a trial. Do less damage to the book that way."

I would have liked to have a copy I could take with me, because the evidentiary chain of custody would be much stronger if the book stayed in the evidence room.

"I'll be back to look at it," I said. I wasn't sure when, but I knew the chance to hold the book in my hands and read the same words Bishop presumably had read wouldn't be an opportunity I'd be able to let go of until I had done it.

• • •

That evening a marine layer drifted in and overcast the sky, and the heat backed off by a few degrees. The air, though, was filled with a muggy thickness that drained even more energy out of me than had the dry Santa Ana conditions of the last few days.

Things were beginning to slow down on the case, as they normally do after the first surges of evidence come pouring in with the wide sweep of new investigation. Once the crime scene is processed, the witnesses interviewed, and the obvious connections explored, the pace lets up. There are always more strands to tug at and more leads to follow, but the initial momentum begins to fade and the intensity, if you're not careful, diminishes. I always fought against that tendency, against the idea of *The First Forty-Eight*—the mistaken popular notion that if a murder case isn't closed in the first two days, then it's unlikely to be closed at all. Like so many other misconceptions about homicide that media of all types love to perpetuate, it's simply not true. There are a good number of cases closed in that time frame, but they're the slam dunks, the cases where we find a husband weeping over the body of the wife he just killed, or those incidents in which "it just went off," or those times when the witnesses line up around the block and tell us that guy had been talking about killing his father for years. The truth is that we work a lot of cases like that. People forget the definition of "homicide." It simply means the death of one person at the hands of another. Those cases are how we spend most of our time. But *murder*, especially first-degree murder, killing with intention and forethought, was where our energy and our intellect went. We spent a lot of time filling out paperwork, dotting i's and crossing t's. But it was on cases like Bishop's that we really earned our keep.

I brought copies of the case files home as I always do, but the pain was shooting up my neck, and I'd been in chairs or car seats for most of the day, so I decided to take a walk before I settled in for the night, hoping the exercise would alleviate some of the tension and stress I could feel settling in my spine.

The sky was still banded with gray in the west as I set out toward Belmont Shore. I lived near Warren High School, and one of the routes I liked to walk took me south and east to Naples Island, which had been built at the mouth of the San Gabriel River around the turn of the twentieth century in emulation of Abbot Kinney's Venice development on the coast near Los Angeles. Depending on my pace and how many spontaneous diversions I made along the way, I could count on anywhere between one and two hours on my feet.

I was damp with sweat by the time I was three blocks from home, but once I settled into an easy pace, I began to relax and let my thoughts drift away from the motivations of Omar, Francisco, and Pedro, and I began to think about Bishop. Whenever I work a case with an unidentified victim, I feel a strong need to discover not only the circumstances of the crime itself, but to also unravel the mystery of who that person was. This isn't unusual—most homicide detectives I know feel the same way. Typically, though, the process is enmeshed in the investigation itself—determining the victim's identity is central to understanding the circumstances of the murder and vital to making the case. This one was different. While I'd closed investigations with unidentified victims in the past, I'd never had so tight a case for a John Doe. We could close this with what we already had on the record. Of course it would be even more solid if we could tell Bishop's story to more fully humanize him, and it would tighten the noose even more to have a real picture of the motives behind the teenagers' acts, but those weren't necessities from a legal perspective. There are always unanswered questions in any investigation. The difference now was that I was becoming obsessed with finding the answers I wanted, rather than the ones I needed.

By the time I reached the stretch of million-dollar houses along the waterfront and stopped at the end of Appian Way on the tip of Naples Island, the sky was dark, and a nearly full moon was rising above Alamitos Bay and ghosting its way through the marine layer. I thought of Bishop walking along the Los Angeles River on the other edge of the city. I couldn't quite see it from where I was standing, but I knew the San Gabriel met the Pacific Ocean on the other side of the marina. I wondered if Bishop had walked along this river, too, separated as it was not just by six miles of Long Beach coastline, but by a socioeconomic divide that seemed unimaginable even to me.

• • •

Walking home, I decided to head west on Second Street and get something to eat. In the past I would have gone to the ShoreHouse Café, an old nautically themed diner that I'd first gone to when I was a student at Cal State Long Beach that had a long tradition of making up for its bad food by being open all night. Thus it was one of the few places in Belmont Shore where you could find some hot food to help sober you up after the bars closed. But the ShoreHouse, like so many other local neighborhood businesses, had closed up shop to make way for a new, upscale gastropub called Simmzy's. I'd heard the place was good, though I hadn't eaten there yet. The quality of the food had never really been the point.

At the other end of the commercial stretch of Second Street, I stopped at Super Mex and put in a takeout order for a carne asada burrito.

While I waited for my dinner, I crossed the street and went into Apostrophe Books looking for a new copy of *The Grapes of Wrath*. I knew I had one buried somewhere in my garage, but I didn't want to spend the time digging through the storage boxes to find it. The bookstore was small, really just one wall of books and another of cards and gifts. I was hoping the Steinbeck novel was enough of a perennial that they'd have it in stock.

I walked up and down the shelves, and when I didn't see it, I inquired at the counter.

"I'm sorry, we don't have that in stock," the young woman said. "Would you like me to order it for you?"

"No, that's okay. Thanks."

"We do have *Of Mice and Men*."

"I don't think that one's thick enough."

She smiled politely but didn't say anything.

"For some reason," I said, "that sounded funny in my head."

She kept smiling, and I thanked her and left the store before I could make things any more awkward.

Rereading the book wasn't going to solve the case. But still it felt necessary, as if the story itself might somehow pull me closer to Bishop and help me understand him.

I picked up my food and walked home. A light harbor breeze had blown some of the humidity away but brought with it vague traces of the stewing scent of industrial runoff and stagnant water.

• • •

Without Steinbeck to keep me company, I decided to practice for a while. The Online Banjo School with Tony Trischka was probably as good as any music lessons on the Internet could possibly be. I'd been working at it for months, but I'd only worked my way through about a third of the beginner's section. I'd made the leap from forward rolls on "Boil Them Cabbage Down" and second-guessing my readiness for the same song with mixed rolls when I decided to throw in the towel for the night. I wiped the Saratoga Star down with my gray Deering Care Cloth and put it back on the oak stand in front of the picture window in my living room. I pulled the curtains closed, turned off the lamp, and sank into the couch.

My copies of the case files were spread out on the dining-room table. I could see them stacked in piles around my MacBook from where I sat. I wanted to go back to them and keep reviewing and analyzing them, but I knew from experience that no matter what my impulse was, my mind needed some downtime occupied with something else—anything else, really—if I was going to be able to maintain any kind of perspective. So I fought the urge and stayed where I was.

Thumbing the remote through the entire channel rotation on the cable box, I gave up on finding anything interesting to watch and settled on the KABC 7 *Eyewitness News*. I remembered believing, as a child, that the "Eyewitness" in the name of the broadcast somehow distinguished it from the other local news shows. They couldn't call it that if it wasn't different, right? I dozed off thinking of Jerry Dunphy and trying to remember Dr. George's last name.

I managed about two hours before I woke up to Dr. Oz spewing unsubstantiated bullshit for people uninformed enough to get medical advice from a talk show. I turned off the TV, brushed my teeth, popped a Vicodin, and went to bed, where I stared at the ceiling in the dark, listened to radio news from the BBC, thought about Bishop and Jesús, and didn't sleep.

• • •

Usually the second or third night after I catch a big case brings with it enough exhaustion for a good five or six hours of sleep, but that night it didn't. I was still awake at four in the morning when

KPCC broadcast Garrison Keillor's *The Writer's Almanac.* It was the birthday of two writers I'd never heard of and the anniversary of the date *On the Road* was published. I remembered being annoyed by the book in college, but my recollections were cut short by the poem Keillor read—"Wrong Turn" by another writer I'd never heard of named Luci Shaw. I spent one more hour in bed thinking about my dead father who'd been shot responding to a routine domestic disturbance call and my dead wife who may or may not have known she was pregnant at the time of her accident and the way life is really just a series of losses, one after another after another, and how the moment we realize that is the moment we begin to die.

I fucking hate poetry.

• • •

When the first light of morning glowed in the window, I got out of bed and took a hot shower. The water rinsed away some of the thoughts that had kept me awake, and I wallowed in the few moments of relaxation it brought me. Over the years, I'd learned how to relax through my insomnia, to breathe deep and let go of my tension and worry and find some degree of restfulness in the dark hours of the night. Most of the time I was pretty good at it. That night, though, I hadn't been able to will myself into that state of mind. I'd have to make do with the shower and a few gallons of coffee.

As I toweled off, I reminded myself to call the landlord and ask him not to switch out my showerhead.

I put on a pair of shorts and thought about going out into the garage and searching through the boxes of books on the shelves along the back wall, but I thought better of it. I got out my Kindle and downloaded the e-book instead. At the dining-room table, I sat down with a freshly filled Smith & Wesson mug and started reading.

To the red country and part of the gray country of Oklahoma, the last rains came gently, and they did not cut the scarred earth . . .

9

ZIPLOC BAG, QUART-SIZED, CONTAINING: ORAL-B TOOTHBRUSH, ONE; COLGATE TOTAL TOOTHPASTE, THREE-OUNCE, NEARLY EMPTY.

I was at my desk in the squad room planning my schedule for the day when Patrick came in. He was halfway across the room when Ruiz leaned out his office door and said to him, "Don't sit down."

Patrick dropped a bike helmet and courier bag on his chair and headed straight into the lieutenant's office. Somebody got killed and he was next up in the rotation. Patrick was still new enough to the squad to feel the rush of excitement that came with being the lead detective on a fresh case. He'd been doing excellent work all around, but the murder rate was down in Long Beach this year, so this was only his fourth time in the driver's seat.

When he came out I said, "What did you catch?"

"Drive-by in Cambodia Town." I could tell he was experiencing that odd mix of emotions that only a homicide cop can understand and identify with. No one without sociopathic or psychotic tendencies can be glad at the news of another person's death, but there is a kind of surge of adrenaline and sense of purpose that can be very powerful. It is without doubt a dark and complicated feeling, shared with firemen and soldiers and paramedics and emergency-room workers, that comes from knowing that you can only be at your best and only really achieve any kind of fulfillment when what is at stake is literally life and death. I know I'm better at investigating murders than I have ever been or will ever be at anything else. It's the only thing I've ever been good enough at to make me forget my chronic pain and my grief and to engage me so fully and completely that I'm lost to anything else. It's the only thing I've ever done that's truly allowed me to achieve that transcendent mental and emotional state that athletes and artists sometimes refer to as "flow." I get there often when I'm working a case. Especially in the early stages. A lot of cops don't like to think about this obsessive aspect of our work, but it's a fact of life for many of us. It's also why we drink and why we divorce and why we search for a higher power and why we eat our gun barrels. It's why my father, just a few months before my sixth birthday and his own death in the line of duty, told my mother, "Don't ever let him be a cop." It's why whenever I hear someone quote Joseph Campbell's admonition to follow your bliss, I shudder.

Patrick, though, hadn't thought as much about all of that. He just tried to contain his enthusiasm beneath a respectful countenance and got to work.

"Good luck," I said.

"Thanks."

"Marty going to meet you there?"

He nodded and slung his courier bag over his shoulder. I'd partnered with Marty myself on my first rollout as primary. Patrick could do a lot worse. Marty was the most senior member of the squad. His regular partner, Dave Zepeda, was out on medical leave with a broken foot. Supposedly, he injured himself when he was climbing off the small sailboat he kept in Alamitos Bay. When he'd been in the station a week earlier, everyone old enough to remember *Jaws* had hit him with "This was no boating accident!" jokes. I thought he'd appreciate it when I told him everyone was misquoting the line. Richard Dreyfuss actually says, "This was not a boat accident." People always get that one wrong. That fact didn't lighten Dave's mood, though. He just grumbled some about assholes and crutched his way back to the elevator. Most people don't sweat the details the way I do.

So Marty was, for the time being, partnering with Patrick.

As I watched Patrick leave, I wasn't sure if the emotion I felt was envy or sorrow.

• • •

It wasn't long after nine when the phone on my desk rang.

"Homicide," I said in the voice I had honed to a dull edge over the years. "This is Beckett."

"Hello, Detective. This is Julia Rice."

I paused.

"We spoke yesterday?"

"Of course, Ms. Rice. I didn't expect you to call so soon."

"I wanted to get the photos to you as quickly as I could."

"We appreciate that."

"They're all in the file. I'm afraid it's too big to e-mail. I have them on a flash drive, or I can upload them to a website that—"

"Are you at home? I'm only two blocks away. I could come by and pick them up."

"Oh, no," she said. "I'll bring them to you. I'm going to be staring at a computer screen all day anyway. It'll do me good to get out."

Twenty minutes later, I met her downstairs and she handed me a small beige envelope with the flash drive inside.

"I hope there's not too many there. The description wasn't terribly specific, so I erred on the side of inclusiveness."

"That's good. We're glad to have anything that might be even a remote possibility."

"I really do hope it helps." She used the word "hope" a lot. I wondered if I should infer anything from that.

"So do I. Thank you for your help, Ms. Rice."

"Please," she said. "Call me Julia."

"I will," I said.

• • •

"What's that?" Jen asked as I inserted the drive into my computer.

"Julia Rice dropped it off. It's the pictures she mentioned to us yesterday."

"She made a special trip?"

"Yeah. Why?"

Jen didn't answer. She just grinned and shook her head.

It was early still, especially for someone working nights, but I dialed Henry Nichols's number anyway. When his voice mail picked up, I assumed he was still asleep and left a message asking him to call me back as soon as he could. With luck, we'd be able to get him into the station that day to look at Julia's photos and see if he could find a shot of Bishop anywhere in the batch. I felt hopeful, but I assumed it was Julia's attitude affecting me. Generally, I agree with Stephen King that hope is a dangerous thing. And also that the road to hell is paved with adverbs.

"You want to bring him in or take the photos to him?" Jen asked.

"Bring him in," I said. "I think the change of location might help him focus."

"Get him lunch and set him up in the conference room. Give him the VIP treatment."

"That's a good idea."

"Want me to do the talking?"

"You've got a rapport going with him," I said. "You mind?"

"Not at all."

When he called me back, I explained what we wanted to do and asked if he could come in around noon. Then I went over to Modica's Deli and brought back five different kinds of sandwiches and a bunch of sides. Nichols would get a good lunch and so would the rest of the squad.

Jen met him when he arrived and led him to one of the nice administrative conference rooms. I brought the food.

"What kind of sandwich would you like? Turkey, roast beef, ham, pastrami, or vegetarian?"

"Wow. That's a good selection," he said. He seemed to be in much better shape than he had been the last time we talked to him. He was understandably more awake and alert, but he seemed somehow sharper, too. The khakis and white long-sleeved button-down he was wearing helped. "How about the roast beef?"

"You got it."

I dug through the bag and found the wrapper with the big black "RB" written in Sharpie on top. I slid the sandwich, a Coke, a bag of chips, and a stack of napkins across the table to him. Then I let Jen take over.

"Thanks for coming, Henry," she said. "We really appreciate it."

"Sure. I'd really like to help if I can."

"How are you doing today?" she said. It was a little late in the conversation for that question, but she'd picked up on the change in his demeanor too.

"Good," he said. "I'm having a good day."

"They're not all good, are they?"

"No, ma'am, they're not."

She took a bite of her sandwich so he'd feel comfortable taking one of his. When he was almost done chewing, she asked, "Was it a good one when we talked to you last time?"

"No, and it got worse after I saw you. No offense."

"None taken." She gave him a warm smile. "Everything going okay with work and the new place?"

"It is. I'm just trying not to get too comfortable."

"Why?"

"Just worried that something might still go wrong, you know?"

"You don't need to worry about that," she said with an authority in her voice that even convinced me.

"I hope not."

She kept smiling and he took another bite of his roast beef. "Is that good?"

"Yeah, really good, thanks again."

She chatted a bit more as we worked our way through lunch. We both paced ourselves against Nichols, and when the food was nearly gone, she explained what we wanted him to do.

"So just look at all the pictures and look for Bishop?"

"That's right."

Jen slid the laptop in front of him and showed him where to click to advance to the next photo. We moved in closer to him, Jen on his right and me on his left, so we could watch the faces as he clicked through them. He took his time with each one and studied it intently before moving on. Occasionally he'd give his head a little shake or mutter a soft "no" or "uh-uh" under his breath. When he got to the end and hadn't seen Bishop's face, he said, "Could I go through one more time?"

"Of course," Jen said. I could tell that she was glad that he volunteered without having to be asked.

He clicked through all of the pictures again, and when he finished, his shoulders rounded and he lowered his head. "I'm sorry," he said.

"It's okay." Jen put her hand on his forearm. "Don't worry."

He looked up at her, a realization dawning in his eyes. "Wait. Oh, man. I don't know why I didn't think of this before."

Henry had a story, and thanks to Jen, he was comfortable enough to tell it.

• • •

Things had gone well at the VA, and for the first time in weeks, Henry felt that his luck might be changing for the better. The first check had been issued to him for the back pay and the Wounded Warrior benefits he was supposed to have received after his injury in Afghanistan. A stupid clerical mistake had denied him his due for more than a year. But things were looking up. He'd been able to get a shower at the shelter and had gone to a good laundromat by the hospital to wash his clothes. The VA had also confirmed his spot on the waiting list for transitional housing. In group, everyone had congratulated him and smacked his shoulders. Good news went a long way these days. He might even be out of the van by the end of the month.

After he'd finished cleaning everything he owned—he even washed the van at the coin-operated car wash on Broadway—he put almost all of the rest of the money in his Wells Fargo account. He had more than enough to cover the deposit at Century Villages. He thought again about the sixty extra dollars he'd kept out of the check for a new phone. Before he came home from active duty, he'd never been much of a second-guesser. He followed his instincts when that seemed appropriate, made a plan when necessary, but either way, once he committed he was all in.

Not anymore, though. Now every decision, even the smallest, was an ordeal. Especially every purchase. But he reassured himself. He'd even run the idea past Dr. Winston, the VA psychiatrist, who'd reassured him.

But he couldn't help feeling that a cell phone was a luxury. An indulgence he couldn't afford.

He'd only been living in the van for a few months, but everything about him had changed.

No, he thought. That's not right. Everything changed before the van, before he came home. He remembered the desert, the heat, the smell of the baked dust.

But he stopped himself. Thought of the plan again. Focused on his goal and started the van and headed north on Bellflower.

Inside Target, he purchased the cheapest prepaid cell phone they carried—an LG TracFone—and the phone card to go with it. He sat in the parked Chrysler, in the back corner of the parking lot by the McDonald's, where he allowed himself the further indulgence of a strawberry shake, and he counted his breaths. He got to thirty before he felt calm and centered enough to dial the number.

His mother didn't answer. He heard the same answering-machine message that he'd helped her record when he was still in high school. That was okay, though, it felt good to make the connection. He left a message, told her he was sorry it had been so long since he'd called and that things were looking up. He told her he loved her.

Then he wondered how to spend the afternoon. A kind of low-grade satisfaction that he remembered from years ago filled him, left him with a warmth that he struggled to recognize. It wasn't contentment—he didn't feel that secure yet, he knew he'd need to save that for a roof and a job—but it was something good.

At the Jack in the Box drive-through, he got three of the one-dollar chicken sandwiches, two tacos, and a large Dr Pepper. With the soda in the cup holder and the fast-food bag in the passenger's seat, he thought about where to go. It didn't take long to decide.

He took PCH to Redondo, hung a left, and drove all the way to Ocean. Before long, he'd made it through downtown and had parked the clean but aging Town & Country in the lot at Palm Beach Park and was sitting in the shade watching the Catalina Express cruise under the Queensway Bridge heading for Avalon.

The Dr Pepper had been drained down to the ice, but he'd only eaten one of the sandwiches. He thought that maybe the most valuable skill he'd learned in the army was how to save food for later. The circle of shade he'd been sitting in had moved left, leaving him in the sun. He stretched his legs out in front of himself, leaned back on his hands, and looked up at the sky.

The time seemed to soften and elongate, and he wouldn't have been able to say how long he'd been there before Bishop approached him. He wouldn't even have been able to say that that was exactly who he'd been hoping to see when he came to the park. But when Henry saw him, he was glad. That much he was sure of.

"Bishop," he said. "Pull up some grass."

"I don't mind if I do," the older man said. "Not at all."

"I got some lunch for you. Tacos or chicken sandwich?"

Bishop looked baffled.

Henry smiled at him and said, "How about one of each?"

"You sure?"

"Yeah, I am."

The two men set up the chessboard and ate as they played. When Bishop had claimed both of Henry's knights, one of his rooks, and a quartet of his pawns, he looked at the young man and said, "Good day, is it?"

Henry was confused for a moment, thinking he meant the game, but then he realized it was him, his mood, that Bishop was commenting on. It must have been as apparent to everyone else as it was to Henry himself. "Yes," he finally said. "It is."

He told Bishop about everything, the VA benefits, the waiting list for transitional housing, even the cell phone.

"Phone has a camera on it, right?" Bishop asked.

"Yeah, I'm sure it does. Didn't try it yet."

"Well, get it out. It's a good day for a picture."

• • •

"This was in July?" Jen asked.

"Yes," Nichols answered. "Just a day or two after the fourth."

He held the flip phone open for us and we leaned in and got our first look at Bishop. I was completely unprepared for what I saw.

Bishop was happy.

I'm not sure why it came as such a shock to me. The possibility of his mirthful smile, of the cheerful exuberance shining in his eyes, of his whole face crinkled into such an expression of felicity, had not ever entered into the realm of my imagination. It seemed to me a failure of imagination on my part that made my stomach knot with sorrow.

In all of my consideration of Bishop, the only thing I had been able to imagine was pain.

"You okay?" Jen said to me. Nichols was looking at me too.

"Yeah, I'm fine. I just, I didn't expect him to seem so—" I stopped midsentence, searching for the right word. "Could you excuse me for a minute?" I got up without waiting for an answer.

In the men's room, I splashed cold water on my face in the vain hope that if anyone else came in, they wouldn't be able to tell I had been crying.

10

Plastic poncho: blue and gold, w/ UCLA logo.

“What happened in there?” Jen asked when we were back at our desks.

“They looked happy in that picture,” I said. “Didn’t they?”

“Yes. Why is that upsetting?”

“I don’t know. Have you been imagining Bishop happy?”

“No.” Jen shook her head.

“Neither have I.”

“I still don’t get it.”

“Neither do I, really.”

“Maybe,” she said, “it’s because if we think of him having been happy, then it seems like a greater loss.”

“No, I can’t accept that.”

“Why?” she asked.

“You know why. We can’t think like that. We can’t let ourselves think like that.”

“Every victim is created equal?”

“Yes,” I said. “Do you work harder for happy victims?”

“You know the answer to that.”

“But that’s what you’re suggesting.”

“No, it’s not.”

“You sure about that?”

"What the fuck, Danny? You've been doing this even longer than I have. You know the job. Sometimes they hit you harder. But you work the case just the same."

I didn't say anything. She was right, of course. I wasn't just behaving like someone who'd never worked a murder before, I was acting like I'd never even been a cop. My ability to compartmentalize had vanished. I was identifying too strongly with Bishop, and it was beginning to interfere with my objectivity.

I tried to forget about it and got back to work. Now that we had a photo, the Media Relations Detail would reach out to the public with press releases and an update on the LBPD asking for assistance with the identification. They'd set up a tip line and e-mail account to handle the incoming info. It could lead to a break.

Just as I hung up, Marty came into the squad room and plopped himself down in his chair.

"How's Patrick doing?" I asked.

"Great," he said. "He's still working the scene. Kid's got the bug. He's gonna be fine."

"You hungry?" Jen asked. "We've got some leftovers from Modica's."

"No, thanks. We were right around the corner from Joe Jost's, so I grabbed a salami sandwich."

That was Zaferia, not Cambodia Town. "Where's your scene?" I said.

"Tenth and Ohio. Why?"

"One of our suspects lives right there. Trying to get his brother to talk to us," Jen said.

"What's the address?" I asked.

Marty leaned forward. "1072 Ohio."

"Shit," I said, looking at Jen. "That's the front house."

We peppered Marty with questions, and we found out that early in the morning four Latinos in a stolen Yukon had pulled over in front of the gray Craftsman, and the two on the passenger's side had leaned out of their windows and opened fire, one with an AK and the other with an AR. On the driver's side, another shooter climbed up and sat on the windowsill behind the driver so he could reach up and over and use the roof as a rest for his own weapon. They all had multiple jungle-clipped magazines, and the three of them kept at it long enough to fire more than two hundred rounds into the house.

Five people lived there. A husband and wife and their three children. The mother and children were in the bedrooms in the back of the house, and even though dozens of the bullets penetrated the three or four walls between them and the street, they all managed to survive. One of the little girls suffered minor injuries from either bullet fragments or some other kind of shrapnel-like debris. The father had been in the living room, just off of the porch, drinking a cup of coffee and watching a morning news show. He'd reportedly been in a good mood because his kitchen-remodeling business was finally beginning to pick up again after bottoming out with the housing crisis. Later that morning he had been scheduled to begin work on a mid-six-figure job over in Belmont Shore. It would have really turned things around for him, and he was looking forward to moving his girls into their own house again and finally being able to stop worrying about the crappy neighborhood where his daughters were spending what should have been the happiest years of their childhood.

Instead, he was shot eleven times and bled out on the living room floor in front of the flickering and slowly fading image of Matt Lauer.

"Did you talk to the people in the back house?" I asked.

"Of course," Marty said. "Drunk woman and her little girl. How are they connected?"

"The woman has two older sons," I said. "High-school students. One of them is in custody on the burning. The other we think was supposed to be there but got smart just in time. We're trying to flip him."

"Patrick didn't make the connection yet?" Jen said. "He's been helping us with some background."

"Not before I left."

I was sure I knew the answer, but I asked anyway. "You have any motive on the drive-by? Any gang connections for the contractor?"

"Nothing yet."

"This is too much of a coincidence. I think they were gunning for Jesús. The addresses are screwed up on the houses. From the street, you can't tell which one's 1070 and which one is 1072. They've got both numbers on the front. You can't tell which is which until you get to the back and see the numbers on the porch. I only knew because I checked it out on Google Maps before we rolled."

Marty thought about it. "So you think somebody wants to be sure this Jesús kid keeps his mouth shut?"

"If they do, this goes deeper than we thought," Jen said. "Had to be somebody with some serious juice to call in a hit like that."

I said what we were all thinking. "We've got to find Jesús."

• • •

Patrick was still processing the murder scene when we arrived. It would take a long time to process everything. The crime-scene technicians would attempt to account for every bullet. And it was likely that they would. A scene like that takes time and patience.

The neighborhood, too, was so densely packed with residents that the canvass would be daunting as well. That's what never shows up in the movies and on the TV shows: the hours and hours spent with a laser pointer and hundreds of feet of string, calculating bullet trajectories. Or the days spent knocking on each door in a three-block radius and hearing everything from the unanswered echoes of your door-pounding fist to "I don't know" and "Fuck you" and the unfathomable digressions about lost loves and dying puppies and that time on spring break in Mexico to push the day into unapproved overtime. Or the repetition and the mundanity and the endless details, each of which must be entertained and examined because of the very real possibility of some minute bit of information buried in all of the other noise that might be the one that makes all the difference, the one that breaks the case open, and the one that brings with it that fleeting sense of closure that is the nearest we ever really get to anything resembling justice.

Ohio Avenue was still cordoned off, so we parked on Eleventh, made our way to the corner, and badged the uniforms, and they lifted the yellow tape so we could duck underneath it. The house was four doors down.

I walked out into the middle of the street and looked at the front house again. There was a fence in front with a gate on each edge of the property and a driveway on each side. The curb numbers were next to each one—1070, the back house, on the right, and 1072, the front house, on the left. As I studied the addresses and the fence and the driveways, I tried to imagine that I'd never seen the property before. With the victim's work truck parked on one side and obscuring the garage, it was impossible to tell which driveway and address number went with which house.

We stopped on the porch and looked inside. Patrick was in the living room talking to a crime-scene tech who was examining a bullet hole in the wall.

"Hey, guys," he said as he turned and came to the door. "What's up?"

"We think we might have a motive for you," I said. We told him about Jesús and his family.

"Shit," he said.

"Did you talk to the mother?" I asked.

"I took a statement from her."

"You didn't catch the name?"

"Solano?"

"Yeah."

"No. That's not the name she gave me." He pulled a notepad out of his shirt pocket and thumbed through the pages. "Felicia Gonzales is what's on the lease."

I looked at Jen. "We know if she was married before?"

"No." Jen thought about it. "Maybe the kids have different fathers. There's almost a ten-year gap between Jesús and Maria."

"I wonder if she'd have any reason to use an alias. If she was undocumented you think she might use another name to help hide the tracks?"

"Give me a few minutes." Jen was already dialing her phone when she went out the front door.

I turned back to Patrick. "Marty gave us the rundown. Anything new come up after he left?"

"No. Just lots and lots of bullet holes."

"How much do you have on the victim?"

"Basic background," Patrick said. "No known gang affiliations. Neighbors all apparently liked him. He did handyman stuff for the old couple next door for free."

"I think they were gunning for Jesús."

He considered that. "Makes sense. You didn't know this place, it would be easy to get the addresses confused."

"I'll talk to Ruiz. We should be working these together."

"You're right." He held his laser pointer out to me. "Want to help me record bullet trajectories?"

I looked at the device in his hand. It didn't look like any I'd seen before. "Is that a miniature lightsaber?"

His face fell in disappointment. "If you have to ask," he said with a sigh worthy of an exasperated Wookiee.

• • •

As soon as I got outside, I dialed Jesús's number, but the call went straight to his voice mail. I left a message asking him to call as soon as he could and then sent a text saying the same thing.

Jen was on her phone too, searching for information on Mrs. Solano/Gonzales.

I made three more calls, all requests. The first, for a BOLO to be put out on Jesús; the second, for a meeting with Pedro Solano; and the last to get the ball rolling for a court order to obtain Jesús's cell-phone records.

• • •

"They're all documented," Jen told me in the car a few minutes later. "And Solano is her first ex-husband's name. Gonzales is the second husband. Apparently, they're still legally married, but she's gone back to "Solano" to match the kids' name. And she's the only one who has official standing with the school district. He's not allowed to pick up the kids."

I'd been talking to the uniforms while she was on the phone. "Nobody knows where she went. She was told it would probably be a day or two before she could get back in the house."

"We have a cell number for her?"

"Not yet."

Jen made another call.

I took us down Long Beach Boulevard and turned west on Third. But instead of turning into the LBPD lot, I continued to Ocean.

Jen pulled the phone away from her ear. "We're not going back to the squad?"

"I want to look at something."

She had seen enough of my spur-of-the-moment distractions and digressions to give me some slack, and she went back to her conversation.

A few minutes later, we pulled into Palm Beach Park, the place where Nichols and Bishop used to meet to play chess.

Jen finished her call and said, "This is why you never drive." She hadn't been paying attention to the passing scenery, and it took her a moment to get her bearings and figure out where we were.

"Have you been here before?" She caught herself and added, "Before the case."

"I've walked around the path a bunch of times and out on the little pier there." I gestured toward the concrete quay that jutted out into the Catalina Express marina. "But this is the first time I've ever parked here."

Palm Beach Park really wasn't much of a park at all. There was more parking lot than there was green space. The trees and grass made a band around the white-gridded asphalt taking up the center of the small peninsula upon which the park was situated. The peninsula separated Golden Shore Marine Biological Reserve, at the mouth of the Los Angeles River, from the rest of Rainbow Harbor and Shoreline Village. It was a small transitional blip of land that divided the industrialized harbor area to the west and the downtown tourist-centric waterfront.

There were a dozen other cars in the lot, but no one else in the "park" itself except a lone man in a dark suit at the end of the concrete jetty, facing away from us and looking out at the water.

Jen and I walked over to the strip of grass and stopped in the shade of a tall palm tree. I thought I could understand the appeal the place had for Bishop. It wasn't hard to feel alone here. With the Long Beach skyline at our backs and a giant container ship slowly drifting across the horizon, it was impossible not to feel the urban world surrounding me, but there seemed to be a stillness here in the center of everything that made me feel an almost overwhelming sense of solitude somehow comingled with a sense of connection to the city around me.

"You still with me?" Jen asked.

"I think I get it," I said to her.

"What?"

"Why Bishop liked it here."

"Why?"

I explained it to her as well as I could, but I knew I wasn't able to satisfactorily translate what I was feeling into words.

She surprised me with her response. "I think I know what you mean."

"You do?"

"Yeah. It's kind of what *randori* feels like."

I'd watched her train and teach many times. I knew *randori* was a form of sparring, and I'd seen her, in front of a dojo full of students, being attacked simultaneously by four or five other black belts. In all honesty, those sessions were some of the most impressive physical displays I'd ever seen. There was a violence in them, to be sure, but there was a fluid and powerful kind of grace as well.

"What does it actually mean? I know I've seen you do it, and it's a form of sparring, but what does the word actually mean?"

"I've heard it translated different ways. The one I've always liked best was 'seizing chaos.'"

"That's good."

"It was, until I heard an MMA douchebag visiting one of my classes tell an orange belt that's what his kanji tattoo meant. I looked at it and told him he had it wrong. It really translated as 'egg drop soup.'"

"It did?"

"I don't have the slightest idea what it meant. But he started to tear up. And later, on the mat, that same orange belt had him tapping out."

The laugh that escaped me then felt like the first genuine sound I'd made in a long time.

11

RALPHS PLASTIC SHOPPING BAG CONTAINING THREE USED PAPERBACK BOOKS: LONESOME DOVE, BY LARRY MCMURTRY; TRUNK MUSIC, BY MICHAEL CONNELLY; SLAUGHTERHOUSE-FIVE, BY KURT VONNEGUT.

Roberto Solano, father of Jesús and Pedro, lived in Riverside.

"Think a shot in the dark is worth a three-hour round trip on a Friday night?" I asked Patrick and Jen.

"We could just call it a night," Jen said.

"I'm worried about Jesús." I tapped the eraser of a pencil on a yellow writing pad on the desk in front of me.

"I know." She looked at Patrick. "What do you think?"

"You've got dinner with your folks, right?" he asked.

She nodded. "They'll get over it if I cancel."

"They have all seventeen thousand other times," I said. That had sounded funnier in my head.

But Patrick stepped up and rescued me from my own awkwardness. "I'll go. Let's do it."

"You sure?"

"Yeah. I'm waiting on forensics and ballistics results anyway. Why not?"

We knocked on Ruiz's office door and told him what we were planning.

"You think it's worth the drive? A phone call won't do it?"

I said, "I thought about that. Not sure it's a good idea to give them a heads-up. If Jesús is there, he might spook. Don't want to lose him."

"Well, it's your Friday night. If you two want to spend it on the freeway, be my guest."

On the way back to our desks, Patrick said, "That means no overtime, right?"

• • •

By the time we hit the 91, rush hour had peaked. We'd done rock-paper-scissors to figure out who would drive each way. I'd won, so Patrick got stuck behind the wheel in the bad traffic. It would be a breeze on the way back to Long Beach. I wondered how we'd manage if we ever partnered regularly. We must have been the only two cops in Long Beach who never wanted to drive.

"I might have to move," I told him.

"Why?"

"My landlord decided to sell the duplex. Every other one they've sold on the street in the last two years has been converted into a single-family house. So he'll probably want to do that to mine."

"Sorry, man. That's a cool place."

"I know. I really like it there."

"You always lived there by yourself, right?"

"I moved in a couple of months after Megan died." A twinge of anxious sadness curdled in my stomach. "I chose it because I knew she would have loved it there. Kind of weird."

"Not weird at all. How long do you have?"

"Don't know. The only thing he's talked about doing so far is changing out all the old fixtures for new low-flow stuff. Seems like an odd way to renovate. Maybe he's just trying to get the ball rolling."

"You going to stay in the same neighborhood?"

"I don't know."

Patrick had moved last year as well. He'd lived in one of the few authentic lofts in Long Beach, an old mixed-use industrial building he'd converted himself. It was an impressive place, hipster living at its best.

"You miss your old place?" I asked.

"Sometimes. It was a bitch to keep up, though. You know how hard it is to vacuum a two-thousand-square-foot concrete floor?"

I laughed.

"How about the condo?" He'd moved into a bland townhouse on the edge of Signal Hill. It had a great view of the harbor and the sunset, but in every other way it was a virtual clone of thousands of others just like it all across the city.

"It's okay. Nice to blend in. I don't feel the same need to make a statement with my living arrangements that I used to."

He'd never told me the reason for the change, but he'd been attacked in his old place in the course of one of our previous investigations, a disturbing multiple murder that involved a congressman, a dirty FBI agent, and a trio of Eastern European thugs. Whenever I thought about it that way, I thought it sounded like one of the absurd cop thrillers that Patrick and I had so much fun mocking. In reality, though, there was nothing funny about it. Patrick had spent several days in intensive care while the rest of us waited anxiously to find out if he'd ever regain consciousness. I understood changing your living arrangements to escape the trauma of violence and loss.

"You thought about buying something?" he asked.

"Jen loves her place," I said. "Looks like I missed the window on that, though. The prices and interest rates are already going back up. And I don't have the nest egg she did. If I was going to buy, I'd have to look at either condos or a crappy neighborhood."

"Don't knock condos. It's not nearly as soul crushing as you think it will be."

"I just don't want to move."

A few miles later, he said, "Did you ever check out that link I sent you?"

"No, not yet. It got pushed way down in my e-mail and I forgot about it." I was never as good at managing my personal e-mail as I was with my work account. It happened a lot, and I was always apologizing to people. "Sorry."

"You should be sorry. It's going to change your life."

"Really? Must be quite a link."

"Remember who you're talking to. How many shitty links have I ever sent you?"

"Good point."

• • •

It seemed like hours of toll roads and carpool lanes, but we made it to Roberto Solano's address in ninety-two minutes. He lived in a bad neighborhood in an old two-level, eight-unit apartment complex.

We drove past, turned right at the end of the block, and cut down the alley behind the building. It was a simple rectangle, four apartments on each level stacked one right above the other. There was an exposed walkway on the second floor that each upstairs unit opened onto. They probably had identical floor plans. While we were in back, Patrick slowed the car and looked up through the windshield.

"Can you see the number by the door up there?"

I squinted into the darkness. "It looks like 2D."

"Well, that's it," he said.

The building was perpendicular to the street, and Solano's apartment was all the way at the back, farthest from both the street and the stairway to the upper landing. If anyone saw us coming, the only escape route would be a jump from the second story to the ground and a climb over the six-foot barbed-wire-topped concrete block wall.

Our unmarked Police Interceptor wouldn't fool anyone, especially in this part of town. So Patrick had pulled into half a space along the curb and didn't worry about the front end in the red zone. We could have tried to hide the car by parking up the street or on the next block, but we decided the advantage of having the car closer outweighed any stealth we might gain. Besides, no one in the vicinity would be surprised by the presence of a cop car.

Before he got out, Patrick slipped his iPhone out of his jacket pocket and pulled up a copy of Roberto Solano's driver's-license photo. "Want to take one more look?"

"I had plenty of time to memorize it on the drive."

The sign mounted on the front wall of the building identified it as the "el Ray." The first letter was missing. "What do you suppose it used to say?"

Patrick examined the cracked yellow stucco where the missing letter should have been. "Been gone so long you can't even see the fade marks. I bet it was a *D*."

"Why?"

"Because slumlords in the desert an hour away from the beach think they can trick people into imagining an ocean breeze."

"Marina Del Rey is spelled with an *e*."

"Illiteracy just supports my theory," he said with a grin.

There was a locking front gate, but it had been propped open with half of a broken concrete block. We started up the stairs. "Be careful," I said. "The railing's loose."

Patrick shook it and the wobble was visible all the way up to the second-floor landing. "Nice," he said.

In apartment 2A, someone peeked out from behind the curtain covering the front window next to the door as we passed. The heavy fabric moved back to its original position, and the light behind it went out.

Apartments 2B and 2C were both dark. As we walked slowly toward Solano's door, the floor below us creaked and the railing rattled. We stopped before the last window and listened. The curtains there were closed as well. Nobody lived in the el Ray for the view.

The only sound coming from the apartment was a dull monotone that sounded like someone talking on the TV or the radio. It wasn't loud enough to tell for sure which it was.

At the end of the landing, there was a good five feet between Solano's door and the railing. The doorknob was on the right, so if someone cracked the door or used a safety chain, one of us could hide against the wall on the other side of the door. I gestured for Patrick to move into that space. He did and I knocked.

"Mr. Solano!" I said, rapping on the door. "Police. We need to talk to you." I gave it a few seconds and knocked again. "Mr. Solano, it's the police. We need to talk to you." After the second round, I heard someone moving inside, and a shadow partially blocked the sliver of light along the curtain's edge.

The door cracked open about an inch. An eye peered around the edge of the jamb. There was a solid safety latch, the sort that hotels use, spanning the small gap.

"Mr. Solano?" I asked, holding open my badge holder so he could see my ID.

On the other side of the doorway, Patrick had his back to the wall and his hand under his coat on the grip of his Glock. I was careful not to look directly at him and give away his presence and position, but in my peripheral vision I could see him give his head a single shake.

"Sir, I need to ask you a few questions about Jesús."

The man in the apartment said, "Okay. What?" His voice was soft and flat, and I couldn't see enough of his face to get a read on his expression.

"Sir, can I come inside?"

He took a quick look at something behind him inside the apartment, then looked back at me. "I'll come out," he said.

The door closed, and we heard him flip the latch back against the doorjamb. I moved my hand inside my jacket to where the grip of my pistol hung under my left shoulder, and I very briefly made eye contact with Patrick. I relaxed slightly as the door opened, knowing he had me covered.

The man who stepped out in front of me was thickly muscled and tall. He had a goatee and a shaved head and wore a long-sleeved black dress shirt buttoned all the way up. I took a few steps backward, and he moved with me. The light from the window hit the side of his head, and, though I couldn't be sure in the dim light, there appeared to be some neck ink peeking out of the top edge of his collar.

"What's going on with Jesús?" he asked. "Is he in some kind of trouble?"

"Honestly, Mr. Solano, we don't know. We need to talk to him about his brother."

"His brother." The big man pondered that for a moment. "Pedro?"

"Yes, Pedro. You looked like you had to think about that name."

"He has other brothers. And I haven't seen those two in years."

"Other brothers with different mothers?"

"Yeah. So?"

"I'm just asking for the record, sir. These details could be important. You say it's been years since you've seen Jesús? Have you had any contact with him at all?"

"No, nothing."

"Well, then, thank you, sir. Would you give me a call if you hear anything at all from him?"

"Yes, of course." He exhaled and his posture softened. He thought he'd made it.

He started to turn toward the door.

"Just one other thing, Mr. Solano."

The man's jaw clenched, and he transferred his weight to the balls of his feet. The look on his face was one I'd seen a thousand times before. He was trying to figure out if I believed he was the man he was pretending to be.

"Could I see some ID?"

I was able to set my feet and get my left arm up to block the punch, but he still connected with enough force to knock me off balance and drive my guard into my side hard enough that I lost some wind.

Patrick moved in with a kick to the back of his calf that dropped him to one knee.

I threw a hard right cross downward into his face, which seemed to have little effect.

Patrick moved in to take him to the ground with an arm bar, but the big man muscled his way out of the hold and thrust himself up and back.

The move startled Patrick and caught him off guard. He reached around the man's neck and locked his forearm into a solid choke, but the two of them had built so much momentum that they were going to hit the railing.

I was afraid they were so tall that they'd topple over it, so I rushed forward to try to stop them.

I never had the chance.

The railing gave way as if it had been made of balsa wood, and then they were gone.

12

Ziploc bag, quart-sized, containing: comb, nail clippers, Advil (four individual-dose packets).

When I got to the edge of the landing and looked down, I was surprised to see Patrick alone on the ground. He saw me above him and yelled "That way!" He gestured toward the back of the building, and I turned just quickly enough to see a dark shape turn the corner and move out of view.

Patrick looked up at me and said, "I'm okay! Go!"

I took off as fast as I could to the front of the building. As I reached the top of the stairs, I saw the black shirt run out the front gate. Taking the steps three at a time, I gave chase. He turned the corner at the end of the block, and by the time I got there, he was gone. I ran in the direction he had gone and stood in the middle of the intersection looking down each street for a flash of movement or a shape, but there was nothing to see except oncoming traffic. On the sidewalk, two teenagers put their heads down and pretended I wasn't there.

Gasping for breath, I called in a 911-officer-needs-assistance and turned around to run back to Patrick.

To my surprise, he was standing up. Wincing, but up on both feet.

"Help's on the way," I said. "How bad is it?"

"Ankle's messed up, but I can stand on it. Shoulder hurts worse."

I had watched him go over and knew he'd gotten lucky when his hand found the railing and caught it with a grip strong enough to slow his fall and to peel the big man off of him. Before the railing gave way completely, it had provided enough support for him to flip himself completely over and drop to the ground feetfirst.

"That fucker, though, the only thing that broke his fall was the wall. Just grunted and got up and ran."

We heard the approaching sirens, so we headed to the front of the building with our hands up and our badges held high.

Patrick's left arm was bent at the elbow, though, and his fingertips barely reached above his shoulder. It hurt too much to go any higher.

I said, "On a scale of one to ten, with ten—" I stopped midsentence when the headlights of a Riverside Police cruiser lit us up.

Two uniforms popped out and pointed their guns at us over the opened car doors. "Stop!" the driver yelled.

We did. They saw our badges.

"I'm Danny Beckett. I made the 911 call. This is my partner, Patrick Glenn."

They relaxed, but not completely. The cop on the passenger's side holstered his pistol and came toward us. "Can I see your IDs?"

We held them out for him to take a look at. More units were pulling up outside. An ambulance rounded the corner.

I told the responding officer that a suspect was fleeing on foot in the area, and he called it in. By the time the paramedics were examining Patrick, a helicopter was circling the neighborhood and making pass after pass with its spotlight.

"We need to check out the apartment," I said. "The man we came to see could be bleeding on the floor inside."

"The sergeant's on his way. We'll let him decide how to handle it."

I didn't agree, but we were out of our jurisdiction and had no authority. "What's your name?"

"Rosales."

"I'm Beckett." I held out my hand and he shook it.

Patrick was sitting in the back of the ambulance. "They don't think anything's broken, but my shoulder's dislocated and my ankle's starting to swell up. I'm trying to talk them out of taking me to the ER."

"You should go," I said. "Don't take any chances."

"What's going on upstairs?"

I told him.

"Well, I'll go to the hospital, but not until we see what's inside."

The next five minutes felt like fifty. When the sergeant arrived, he got the rundown from the first responders, went upstairs to talk to the two uniforms watching the door, and then called someone on his cell phone before he decided to check in with Patrick and me.

He was short and wiry, and his hair and mustache were so dark and monochromatic that they must have been dyed. The brass nametag on his chest read *F. Berry.*

"You're Long Beach?" he said to us.

"Yes, sir, sergeant," I said. "We are Long Beach."

"That's quite a drive just to take a shit in someone else's yard."

"That wasn't our intention. We just wanted to ask a guy some questions."

"Sure, if you say so." He eyeballed us so hard that Patrick and I deliberately avoided making eye contact with each other. If we had, one or both of us would have laughed in his face. Berry was the kind of cop you can find in significant quantities in any large police department. They get used to people doing what they say because they somehow managed to pass a test that put some stripes on their sleeve, and they confuse the deference that comes to them by way of their rank with some kind of genuine respect or earned authority, and most often they remain completely oblivious to the mockery and derision that always surround them, lurking just out of earshot.

"What are we going to find inside?" he asked.

"I don't have any idea."

"We're going to wait for SWAT."

"Don't. The man who attacked us was an imposter. Roberto Solano could be bleeding out on the floor of his apartment. If you don't want to take responsibility, I'll go in right now."

"Oh," Berry said, his voice thick with condescension. "You'd like that, wouldn't you?"

"Yes," I said with as much earnestness as I could muster, "I would."

"I'll back him up," Patrick said.

"Great, that's just great."

"Please, go in. If there was another suspect inside we'd know by now."

"Sarge," Rosales said, "I don't think we should wait." He spoke with an edge of experience in his voice that his sergeant would never lay claim to because it was the voice Berry mistakenly believed he already possessed.

Berry looked at the officer, then back at me, and then once more at the officer. Then he spoke as if he had made the decision himself. "Take whoever you need and go check it out."

Rosales looked at me. "You guys are Homicide?"

I nodded.

"Looking for a missing kid?"

"Yeah."

"Come on upstairs." Rosales rounded up two more uniforms and led us up to Solano's apartment.

"Let us go in," he said to me. "Soon as we clear it, you can check it out."

"Thanks," I said.

It took them all of about ninety seconds, and then they were back out on the landing. I moved toward the door and looked inside.

The man I assumed to be Solano was in the middle of the living room strapped to a dining chair with heavy-duty plastic cable ties and duct tape. He was slumped over, and his face was bruised and swollen and dripping blood onto the worn rust-colored carpet.

I looked at Rosales. There were small dots of blood on the index and middle fingers of his right hand from checking for Solano's pulse. He wiped them on his pant leg and shook his head.

"Still warm?"

He nodded.

I fought the urge to cross the threshold. But if there's one thing every homicide cop knows, it's that you never violate someone else's scene.

• • •

The Riverside detective who caught the case was a long-timer named McDermott. After he apologized for Berry, I gave him a detailed statement about our case and told him I'd copy him on all the reports.

"You have any other leads on Jesús?"

"None yet. I'm hoping he ran. If there's an upside to this, it's that if they had anything solid on him, they wouldn't be torturing his father."

"That's true. I'll let you know if we come up with anything about the Solano boy. Might come across someone who knows something about him."

A uniform approached us. "Detective McDermott?" she said.

"Yeah?"

"We think we might have the suspect's car. A witness on the next block saw a man run across the street and get into a Ford Fusion. We got a description and a partial plate. It was reported stolen from Long Beach Airport this morning."

"Well," McDermott said, "looks like the ball's back in your court."

• • •

While I was waiting for Patrick at the ER, I called Ruiz and Jen to update them.

Ruiz had already heard from the Riverside PD brass and was more concerned about Patrick's condition than anything else. I told him it didn't look bad and that I'd update him when we were on the way home.

Jen didn't take the news as well.

"Fuck," she said when I told her how the incident outside Solano's apartment had gone down.

"It's okay," I said to her.

"No, it's not. I knew I should have gone with you."

"Why? So you could have gone over the railing, too?"

The silence that greeted that comment caused me to regret my choice of words.

I said, "I just meant that I don't like to think about something like that happening to you."

She was still quiet. I wasn't sure if I'd insulted her by suggesting that she wouldn't have handled the altercation any better than we had, or if it was something else.

"I know it probably wouldn't have," I said, "but thinking about you getting hurt bothers me."

"It's okay, Danny."

"It is?"

"Yeah. But you know I wouldn't have gone over that railing, right?"

• • •

A nurse wheeled Patrick out into the loading zone outside the ER, his arm in a sling and his ankle wrapped with an elastic bandage. He had a large ice pack slung over his shoulder.

I opened the passenger door and heard Patrick say, "Thanks for everything, Kelly."

"You're welcome. Now get in the car," she said as she squeezed his shoulder and smiled at him. "You've got a long drive."

When he closed the door, I said, "She's cute."

"She's a really good nurse."

"Call Jen," I said. "She thinks it's her fault you went over the railing."

"How could it be her fault?"

"She said if she had been here, she could have handled him."

"When the two of us couldn't?"

The traffic light at the hospital's exit was red, and it gave us the time to exchange a glance in which we both acknowledged silently that, in all likelihood, she was right.

• • •

When I parked the unmarked cruiser in the alley behind my duplex, the clock on the dash read 4:15. It was Saturday, so on the off chance that I was able to sleep, I wouldn't have to get up early. At that point, though, the likelihood of a restful early morning seemed remote. I was wired from the events of the night before, and my mind was racing with the implications of the murder of Jesús and Pedro's father and the man who killed him.

The stolen car almost surely meant that the man Patrick and I had fought on the walkway outside of Solano's apartment was from Long Beach. Honestly, I would have assumed that even without the evidence. The murders on Ohio and in Riverside were too much to be a coincidence. They were related, and the connection was Jesús.

I tried his cell phone again, but it went straight to his voice mail.

"Jesús," I said. "This is Detective Danny Beckett again. I know you need help. You're not in any trouble. You did the right thing. Call me. Wherever you are. I'll come to you. Maria needs you. Let me help."

When I cut the connection, I felt like I'd just drunk-dialed someone after a bad date. I'd meant to be reassuring, to give him the sense that calling us was his best and safest option. Instead, I sounded desperate, as if I needed him more than he needed me. For all I knew, that was true. And whoever was gunning for him had a strong enough desire to keep him quiet when there was no evidence at all that he'd said anything to us. Would he really be safer if he contacted me? Or would that put him even more at risk?

That morning I felt as lost as I had at any time since we first responded to Bishop's murder. Our first instincts, that the three boys had burned the homeless man in some kind of twisted attempt to gain notoriety and street cred, seemed to be more and more off base. I'd wanted to understand what motivated them and to know if there was something at work beyond their sociopathic urges.

Now that it seemed that there was more to the case than we had initially suspected and that they were not the only ones responsible for the immolation, I felt no sense of relief.

Very few murders are purely the result of psychopathy or sociopathy. Most are committed because of money, because of power, or because of sex. There's almost always a motivation that can be tied back to one of those basic desires or to some combination of them.

It was only just now striking me that my initial drive to find some baser cause for the three boys' actions was the wrong thing to hope for. I wanted this crime to make sense, and now that it seemed that there might very well be something more complicated at work, I knew that what I should have wished for was that simple, original instinct—that this was an act of violent insanity and that to try to make any more of it would only lead to more suffering.

But there was more to it, and I knew that I had to figure out what it was. I decided then to see if I could get anyone from Gang Enforcement to come in to the station the next day and help me try to identify Roberto Solano's killer.

My shoulder felt like it was being slowly tightened in a vise, and I couldn't help thinking about Patrick's injured rotator cuff. Maybe I was experiencing some sort of sympathy pain. Or maybe, as always, I was trying to make sense of something that was ultimately inscrutable. David Foster Wallace once wrote, simply, that "pain is pain." One of the great challenges of my life was attempting to subvert my own deep desire to figure certain things out. Most of the unhappiness and the sometimes-severe depression I've dealt with throughout my life have come not from the losses and injuries I have suffered but rather from my incessant, bone-deep need to make sense of the suffering. I knew that the very quality that made me a good detective also made me an unhappy person. A therapist asked me once, matter-of-factly, if I would be willing to trade my compulsive desire to ferret out fact and truth for a life of markedly less suffering and discontentment. I told her that I wouldn't because I believed then, as I still believe, that my job, and really my purpose, was not to solve crimes or render justice but to face reality and to examine the brutality and senselessness of our world so that others might be spared the experience. When she asked me if I thought that might be a little grandiose, I told her that it was. But I also told her that it didn't make it any less true.

I turned on the radio and listened to *Morning Edition* in an attempt to distract myself from the freight train of thoughts barreling though my head. Maybe it worked, or maybe exhaustion just caught up with me. Whatever the reason, sleep came quickly.

If I dreamed, I didn't remember. I woke to the sound of my phone at a quarter past nine, feeling as if it had been only moments since I'd put my head down on the pillow. The impulse to ignore the call was strong, but I fought it, and it was a good thing that I did because the name on the display was Jesús Solano. And he needed to talk.

13

ONE BOX DIXIE MEDIUM-WEIGHT PLASTIC FORKS, ONE HUNDRED COUNT. TWENTY-SEVEN FORKS REMAINING.

The nightmares had come again, as they had every time Jesús had tried to sleep since he'd abandoned Pedro and the other two that night. He couldn't remember any of the nightmares clearly, but when he woke from them he was covered in sweat, and it would take several minutes for the images of flames and the echoes of screams to clear out of his consciousness and allow him to return to the small back bedroom he shared with his brother and little sister. When he was once again aware of the quiet darkness enveloping him, the first thing he thought about was Maria. He worried that his dreams would somehow spill over onto her, and that even if she should be spared, he would make some kind of noise in his sleep, that he would convulse in his bed or moan loudly enough to wake her. There was nothing he hated more than to see fear in her eyes. She'd had too much of that already, and he knew that if he didn't keep her safe, no one would. His mother was receding farther into her alcoholism every day, and Pedro had come up with his insane notion that somehow the solutions to all their problems could be found with the steady and reliable income he believed he would receive once he'd made it into Omar's set.

Jesús knew that he was all Maria had anymore. He had to take care of her, and to do that he had to take care of himself.

Even though he'd barely slept that night, when he heard the gunshots, he thought he was dreaming. He wasn't sure how long it took to understand what was really happening. When he did, when the realization washed over him, time seemed to slow down and stretch out before him.

He threw himself across the room, rolled both of them down onto the floor, and shielded Maria's body with his own.

Her screams didn't even register in his ears until the vicious roar of the bullets ceased. He felt the silence even more than he heard it.

Was that the squeal of tires from the street or Maria's shrieks? He couldn't tell. He just held her in his arms and tried to comfort her.

His mother was screaming too. "Maria! Jesús!" He couldn't remember the last time he'd heard her say their names.

In that moment, with his family wailing and terrified on the cold hardwood floor of his bedroom, Jesús knew what he had to do.

He dressed as quickly as he could. He grabbed his jacket and his school bag. He kissed his mother and his sister goodbye.

He was out the back door and over the concrete block wall in the backyard a full thirty seconds before the first siren stopped in the street in front of the house.

• • •

Five blocks away from home, on Seventh and Redondo, he finally stopped walking and tried to figure out where to go. School wasn't an option. That was the first place they'd look.

He didn't even know who "they" were. The cops? The gang Omar and the others were trying to get into?

He wondered if he should call that detective who came to see him. What was his name? Jesús checked his phone. Beckett. Daniel

Beckett. Maybe that was his best bet. It wasn't the police who had opened fire into the front house.

A realization overtook him and he stopped. The people in the front house had taken the heat for him. He didn't even know their last name. Only that one of the girls was called Mary. "That's the same almost as my name!" Maria had exclaimed when she'd met their neighbor.

Jesús wondered if they were okay. There were so many gunshots. More than he'd ever heard before. Those must have been assault rifles. What else could have made a noise like that? He tried to think of a way to find out if anyone had been hurt. But someone must have been. So many gunshots. They could all be dead. Was it his fault? Were they looking for him? Did someone think he would snitch about Omar's plans? What did he even know that could hurt anyone? Only that the killing was to keep someone quiet. Jesús didn't know why. But the fire was all Omar's idea. "We've got to make this large," he said. "Only way to get noticed."

They got noticed, all right. But by whom? Who was after him?

He looked at the cop's name on the small screen of his flip phone again. Should he call? Then he thought about the battery. Did he have the charger in his backpack? He crossed the street and stood next to one of the outside tables behind Starbucks and rummaged through his bag.

Shit. The charger wasn't there. He knew that if he wasn't careful, he'd only have a couple of hours before the battery was dead. Who might call him? His mom, the detective. He thought that was it. Did anyone else have his number? Only a few friends from school. Pedro. Would he have given it to anybody? Could the gang have it? Probably.

He texted his mom to tell her he was okay and that he'd call as soon as he could, and then he powered the phone off. He'd check it for messages later. But first he had to figure out where to go and what to do.

Instead of taking the bus, he decided to walk the three miles down Pacific Coast Highway to the Marina Pacifica, thinking he'd spend the day in the movie theater and in the Barnes & Noble. Maybe even the Best Buy. On the way, he stopped at a Jack in the Box to kill time. If he went straight to the mall, he'd still be too early and the bookstore wouldn't even be open. He got himself a medium drink and an order of hash browns and sat and thought. The only other person inside the dining area was an old guy in a dirty flannel shirt. Jesús wondered if the man was homeless. There were so many more people who lived like that than he'd ever noticed before. They were all over the place. He got two refills of Dr Pepper before continuing his walk down PCH. It still took him another half hour, and as he walked he could already feel how hot the day would be.

Maybe it was his lack of sleep or even the morning exercise, but his agitation and anxiety had worn themselves down and he didn't feel the same panic in his gut that had driven him out of the house and onto the street. He planned the time out in his head. Two hours at the bookstore, three hours in the movie theater, then it wouldn't be that long before school would be out and he could call David.

He knew his friend would put him up for at least one night. His mom was a nurse and worked twelve-hour night shifts at Long Beach Memorial. Jesús had crashed at David's a few times before. It would definitely be okay. They'd been friends since elementary school, though, and Jesús was sure that David would know something really bad was wrong. He'd probably know about Pedro and maybe even about the shooting that morning. Would that be too much risk? Would he be putting someone else in danger?

His mind was starting to race again.

Back to the plan, he told himself.

David would be okay with not knowing what was going on. He wouldn't like it, and he wouldn't stop asking, but he'd still help. Jesús knew this was true because he'd do the same for David.

He started to feel like he could maybe make it through the day.

But what then? What about Maria? His mom? He walked faster. That helped. Concentrating on walking and not stumbling or taking a wrong step forced him to focus at least some of his attention on something other than his problems. He thought about jogging but decided against it. That would make him too sweaty. He might start to smell like he always did after gym class back in middle school, and he knew he had to try to keep from being noticed. When someone stank, he thought, people remembered him. That, he knew, was what he had to focus on.

Don't be noticed.

Don't be remembered.

Get to David's house.

Figure it out then.

That basic plan gave him enough of a sense of focus that he thought he could make it through the day. He could do it. He just had to stay calm.

He stopped at the fancy Ralphs in the shopping center and got a couple of Snickers bars and a bunch of peanut M&Ms. The regular-sized candies were three for a dollar. He took them to the self-checkout and punched in his home phone number to get the club-card special. Even after the fast food and the snacks, he still had almost sixty dollars in his wallet. It was grocery money his mom had managed to scrape together, but this was an emergency, so he tried not to feel guilty about spending it.

Barnes & Noble still wouldn't be open for almost half an hour, so he cut in between Buffalo Wild Wings and Chipotle and stood at the back edge of the shopping center, looking out over the small arm of Alamitos Bay that flowed between the shops and restaurants and the condo complex on the other side. There were rows of docks along the bottom edge of the building, and Jesús wondered if every condo had its own boat slip. He thought about how often the people there were woken by noises that might have been gunshots. There wasn't a night he could remember that he hadn't heard a sharp bang somewhere in the neighborhood and wondered if it was a gun or if someone had just gotten his hands on an M-80 or some other illegal fireworks. He figured that didn't happen very often here on the bay.

The last time he'd been here, with Pedro and Francisco, they'd stood in almost the same spot and watched some old white guys drive a sleek little speedboat up to the small dock on this side of the water, tie it up, and use a key to let themselves into the gate down below. One of them said something about a golf game, and the others laughed as they walked into the Indian place, Kamal Palace. Jesús had never had Indian food. He wondered what it tasted like.

• • •

During the movie, he kept looking at the screen and wondering what was happening. Over and over, he'd find himself lost in his thoughts, and when he focused on the giant robots on the screen again, it would be like he hadn't been there at all. Like he'd gone to the bathroom and just come back into the theater. And then before he'd be able to figure anything out again, he was thinking about Maria or his mom or Pedro. Or the people in the front house. Was it wrong for him to leave? What if someone got hurt because of him? The guilt and the regret would overpower him, and then something would explode on the screen in front of him, and for just a moment he'd be pulled out of his head and back into the movie.

At least it was better than the bookstore had been. He usually liked to read, but that morning he couldn't focus on anything, so instead of sitting down with a book or a graphic novel, he just wandered up and down the aisles, occasionally pulling something off the shelf and pretending to read the back or the flap inside the front cover. He must have looked at a hundred books that way, with none of them registering or leaving any impression on him at all.

The worst part of it all was how slow the time seemed to pass. It was worse than geometry class. He wondered if it would ever feel normal again.

He wasn't sure what he was thinking when he bought the movie ticket, why he picked the one film he'd been wanting to see for weeks. He hardly ever got to see a real movie, and halfway through the running time, he felt like coming there had been a mistake, that sitting in the dark with a Snickers and a Dr Pepper would never be the same again.

And even as miserable as he had been, he was sorry when it ended. Going back outside into the light and the heat of the day seemed impossible. He should have gone to the Edwards at Long Beach Towne Center or even to the Pike. In those places there were so many screens he could have theater-hopped all day. Now, he knew that the dark of the theater was just one more thing he didn't know he'd miss until it was gone.

Last week he'd thought things were so awful, with his mom and with Pedro hanging out with those fucking losers and with feeling like he had to take care of Maria all by himself. He'd give anything if he could just go back to that.

Anything.

But even then he'd known he couldn't. That what had gone wrong had gone so wrong that things would never be the same.

It wouldn't be long, he thought, until he could go over to David's house, and that would be better, at least a little. He sat down at the bus stop and got an idea.

He didn't know why he hadn't thought of it before.

Jesús called his father.

• • •

They were in David's living room in Rose Park. It was less than a mile from the small back house that Jesús shared with his family, but it felt like a whole other city. Trees all up and down the street, the houses all fixed up and painted with lawns. And no apartment buildings. It was a nice place. David's father didn't live with him either, but at least David got to see him most weekends and he helped out with child support for David and his little brother. And David's mom had a good job, too.

"You just got his voice mail?" David asked.

"Yeah. Maybe he'll call back."

"You know what he does for a job now?"

"No," Jesús said. "It's been like six years and all he ever did was send a birthday card like twice."

Jesús had been right. Of course David was cool with him staying. And his mom wouldn't be back until like seven in the morning, so she'd probably never even know he'd stayed all night. He used to think sometimes how much he liked it there. He'd spent the night many times when they were younger, and often Jesús would feel envious of his friend. And not just because he got all the new Xbox games and they had a big-screen TV with all the cable channels. It was nice there. David's mom was kind to him, and he never had to be the one to clean up everybody else's mess.

"You think I should call the cop?" Jesús asked David.

"I don't know. If Omar's gang is the one that shot up the front house, they must think you're already talking to the police, right?"

"I guess they must. Why else would they do that?"

"You want to try your dad again?" It was almost five.

Jesús did. He heard the same message as before: "This is Roberto. Leave a message and I'll call you back." It felt weird to hear his father's voice. It seemed familiar to him in a way that didn't make him feel good. Like when you go to the dentist and hear the drill in another room and wonder how you could have possibly forgotten that sound, how it wasn't the only thing you remembered at all.

"Just the message again. Can I use your charger?"

"Sure." David looked like he didn't know what to say. "You want to have something for dinner?"

They microwaved Stouffer's lasagna while Jesús's phone charged.

Jesús tried to pretend everything was normal, and a few times, for a few minutes, he succeeded. They watched TV and played *Black Ops II* for a while. He tried to read while David worked on a paper that was due the next day. Jesús thought he should have been working on it too since they were in the same English class, but he hadn't been to school all week and really couldn't imagine when he'd be able to go back. David didn't get very far, though—because, he said, "I can't just leave you sitting there worrying."

The night was almost as hard as the day had been, but Jesús felt better not to be alone. He actually felt less alone than he had all week. But there was another worry tugging at the corners of his awareness. It took hours for him to realize it, but once he thought of it, he couldn't rid himself of the notion that he was somehow putting David at risk, too. That was why he ran when he heard the shots—he thought he'd put Maria and his mom in danger if he stayed. And now he was thinking the same about David. But it was different, wasn't it? They knew where he lived. There'd be no way they could find him here, though. He kept telling himself that.

Then he wondered who might guess where he was. His mom, maybe. Pedro for sure. But his brother wouldn't say anything. Could he even tell anyone anything while he was in jail? He asked himself if there was anyone else. He didn't think so. But the worry wouldn't go away.

Even after they went to bed, with Jesús on the floor of David's room on top of an unrolled sleeping bag, he listened to his friend's soft snoring and thought about them pulling up outside this house and unloading just as they had at his home that morning.

Jesús's breathing accelerated, and he felt a kind of pressure on his chest. It seemed like there wasn't enough air in the room, and he imagined himself inside the sleeping bag and feeling it constrict around him, tighter and tighter, until he could barely breathe at all.

He closed his eyes and tried to force himself to slow down his inhalations, but he couldn't. It kept getting worse and worse, and he became certain that he was dying.

The next thing he knew, David was holding him by the shoulders and telling him to be quiet, that it was okay, everything was all right.

Slowly, he began to calm down. His breathing returned to a more normal rhythm, and he started to cry.

"It's okay," David said again. How many times had he said it? Ten? Twenty?

Jesús was embarrassed because of the tears and wiped his face on his hand and then found himself not knowing what to do with his fistful of snot. David went into the bathroom and brought back a box of Kleenex.

"You okay?"

Jesús nodded.

"I think maybe I should call my mom."

"No, don't. I'll just go, okay? You'll get in trouble."

"I won't. She'll be cool, I swear."

Jesús didn't say anything, and David took that as acceptance.

When she got there, less than an hour later, she held Jesús in her arms and let him cry and cry.

He couldn't remember ever feeling that safe before.

14

DUCT TAPE, 3M BRAND, ONE ROLL: PARTIALLY USED, APPROX. 1/3 REMAINING.

Jesús told Jen and me the story in the car on the way to the station.

"You hungry?" I asked him. He and I were both in the backseat of Jen's RAV4.

"No," he said. "David's mom made bacon and pancakes."

"She seemed really nice."

"Yeah," he said. "Have you talked to my mom?"

"No, not yet. We've been trying to get her on her cell phone, but she hasn't returned any of my calls."

He looked out the window without answering.

"Do you know where she is?" I asked.

"No."

"She disappeared with your sister after the shooting."

"You didn't keep track of her or something?" he said. "Aren't you guys supposed to do that?"

I could see the smile in Jen's eyes in the rearview mirror.

"Yeah, we are. That was somebody else's case, though. We didn't know it might be connected to the thing with Pedro until last night."

"What if they shot them too?" He pulled the seat-belt strap across his chest away from his body and twisted it in his hands.

"They didn't."

"How do you know?"

"We're homicide cops. We know about everybody who gets shot in Long Beach."

"Is there a lot of people who do?"

"Yeah. But we know about all of them."

That seemed to relax him. I hadn't been dishonest with him, but I still felt my conscience nagging at me. *We do know about all of them*, I thought, *eventually.*

"When we get to the police station, there are going to be other people who need to talk to you, but we'll be there, too, okay?"

He looked at me as if he wanted to say something, but he pinched his mouth into a slit and just nodded.

"What's on your mind, Jesús?" I said.

"I'm scared."

"It's going to be okay."

Jen's eyes caught mine again and I knew she was thinking the same thing that I was. We were both hoping I hadn't lied to a frightened teenage boy whose father's murderer was, in all likelihood, at that very moment hoping to kill him too.

• • •

Patrick met us in the squad room. He had a trace of a limp that I probably wouldn't have noticed if I hadn't been looking for it, but his left arm was still in the sling he'd left the hospital with the night before.

Jen gave him a sympathetic wince when she saw it. "I'm sorry I wasn't there."

"It's okay," he said. "It wasn't your fault. We're two fully grown detectives. We can handle things." It was clear from the tone in his voice that he didn't find any more veracity in that statement than she did.

Ruiz was in his office with a social worker from Child Protective Services who was there to help break the news to Jesús about his father and to evaluate any other needs he might have.

The lieutenant came out and I introduced him to Jesús.

"How are you, son?" He still had faint traces of the Rio Grande in his voice from his days as a Texas Ranger. Otherwise he never would have been able to get away with that "son" appellation in his greeting.

"Okay," Jesús said.

Ruiz spoke with a warmth in his voice that I'd only heard him use on rare occasions when talking to a victim's next of kin. "I need you to come into my office for a minute, okay?"

Jesús hesitated.

"You want me to come with you?" I asked.

He looked at Ruiz, then at me. He shook his head, and Ruiz led him across the room and into the office, gently closing the door behind them.

With all the activity, it didn't seem much like a Saturday after all.

When they came out of the office, Jesús didn't seem too shaken with the news of his father. "You okay?" I asked.

"Yeah." He lifted his shoulders slightly in half a shrug. "I barely remember him. He hasn't talked to us in years."

"But you tried to call him yesterday."

"I didn't know what else to do."

"I'm sorry," I said to him.

"Thanks. Now what do we do?"

• • •

Jesús, Jen, Patrick, and I set things up in the same conference room where we'd talked to Henry Nichols. We wanted to make the boy as comfortable as possible.

"What happened to your arm?" Jesús asked Patrick.

"I got in a fight," Patrick said.

"Did you win?"

"Not this time, but there's going to be a rematch."

We spent a long time talking. Jesús took us back several months to his initial meeting with Omar and Francisco.

"I thought they were bad news the first time I saw them. They think they're all big time with their sleeves and everything. But I knew they were going to get Pedro in trouble. Guess I was right."

He wanted to talk. It had been building up in him since before Bishop's murder. He had watched his brother going off the rails and felt powerless to help him and afraid to reach out to anyone else. Now that he knew he'd been correct in his predictions, his inaction was troubling him.

Jen said, "There is no way this is your fault. No way at all."

That seemed to comfort him for a little while, so we tried to nudge him in the direction of talking more about the buildup to the murder.

"I didn't really know what was going on, right up to the day it was supposed to happen. Pedro told me the other guys wanted me to hang out with them and help them with something, but he didn't say what they wanted me to do. I didn't want to do it, but Pedro kept saying that it would be really good for us—the family, he meant. I was worried about how things were going with Maria and my mom, but Pedro kept saying that this would set us up."

"What did you think they were going to do?"

"I don't know. I knew it would be bad. Maybe breaking in someplace or something."

"When did you get out?"

"Not until it was almost time to go. We were at Omar's house. They have a fancy place, kind of by the beach? Pedro said they wanted me to film something on this cool new Galaxy he got. I like to make videos sometimes. My phone won't do them, but last year Pedro got a pretty good Android that had video. Sometimes he'd let me use it."

"And that's what he wanted you to do on Tuesday?"

"Yeah, but I didn't know what they wanted me to shoot."

"How did you find out?"

"I was in the bathroom. I was in there for a while, and when I came back, I heard them talking about how were they going to carry the gas. So I knew they were going to burn something."

"But you didn't know what?"

Jesús shook his head.

"What happened then?"

"I asked what they needed gas for. 'You'll see,' Omar said. That scared me even more."

• • •

Omar told him they'd planned on taking two cars to wherever they were going. Omar was going to take Francisco in his Mustang, and Pedro was going to drive Francisco's Scion with Jesús. Why this was all so complicated, Jesús could only guess.

They were already on the way when Jesús asked Pedro what was really going on.

"This is a really big deal," Pedro said. "Don't screw this up. It's gonna be really good for us."

"What are we going to do?" Jesús was almost crying, and he knew Pedro could hear it in his voice.

"We're gonna do a favor for somebody Omar knows. It's a really big favor."

"It's bad, isn't it?"

"Somebody saw something they shouldn't have. We're gonna fix it."

"What are you going to do, Pedro?"

"We're gonna fix it."

"With gas?"

Pedro stared through the windshield at the taillights of the BMW in front of them.

"I don't want to do this."

"Don't be a pussy."

"You shouldn't do it either."

"We don't got no other choice."

"Mom's going to get a new job."

Pedro looked at him with the saddest expression he'd ever seen on his big brother's face.

"Please, Pedro, let's just go home, okay?"

"Too late for that."

Jesús asked again. But Pedro did that thing he always did when he was done talking. His face became a stone-like mask, unmoving and emotionless.

Jesús knew his brother had said all he would, and if he kept trying, Pedro would just get pissed off. And that would make things even worse.

They were getting close to downtown. Jesús knew what he had to do. When Pedro slowed down at the red light at Ocean and Alamitos, Jesús put one hand on his seat-belt buckle and one on the passenger's side door handle. As soon as they rolled to a stop, he released the seat belt and flung open the door. Before Pedro could do anything, Jesús was already running past the gas pumps at the 7-Eleven on the corner.

He kept going until he couldn't run any longer. Around the corner and halfway up the block on First, he stopped and leaned over with his hands on his knees to catch his breath. He looked behind him to see if Pedro was following. It didn't look like it. Just in case, though, he cut back to Ocean at the corner, figuring that if Pedro went looking for him, he'd guess that Jesús would head straight for home. He wouldn't go back to Ocean. Pedro wasn't smart enough for that.

• • •

"What did you do then?" I asked.

"I walked up Ocean, then cut over on Junipero and walked home."

We pressed him for more details. But he wasn't able to add much to what he'd already given us. We now had confirmation that Bishop's murder was more than just three kids with sociopathic tendencies. We knew that Omar, Francisco, and Pedro were out to make their bones killing a man who'd witnessed something he shouldn't have. Another answer that led us to another question. That's the nature of police work. You keep answering the questions until there aren't any more to ask. Then your case is either closed or it's cold. We had Bishop's killers. We could close the case with what we already had on our plates. People would start pressing us to do that before too long. But that wasn't enough. Those three teenage wannabes didn't kill Bishop. They were just the weapon. I wouldn't be able to rest until I knew who aimed them at him and pulled the trigger.

• • •

"What's going on with his mother?" I asked Ruiz.

"When we try to call, it goes straight to voice mail."

"Battery's dead. Wherever she is, she can't find a charger."

"That's what I figured."

I called Patrick over. It was hard to tell if his limp was almost gone or if he just wanted us to think it was.

"Can we get a GPS location on a cell phone with a dead battery?"

"Probably. A phone usually shuts down before the battery's completely drained. You know the carrier? Depending on which company it is, we should at least be able to get the location of the phone when it died."

"Want to see if you can get the info on Felicia Solano's phone?"

"Does it need to be admissible?" Patrick always asked because after spending six years in Computer Crimes, he was usually able to hack his way into just about any information anywhere online. But there was always the question of how much we were able to do without a court order. It wasn't as clear-cut as most of our procedures. The technology changed so rapidly that we had to work to keep on top of the latest rulings. One misstep with the wrong digital information could derail a case. Something that was fair game one day might be illegal the next.

Because the lieutenant was standing right next me, I answered, "Yes?"

Ruiz nodded and Patrick headed back to his desk.

"Is Jesús going to stay with the CPS woman?"

"She's agreed to keep him here for a few hours, while we try to find his mom."

If I hadn't been worried about Jesús's little sister, I probably would have recommended that she get him into the system as soon as she could. But I didn't want to risk him being separated from Maria for any longer than he had to be. I knew being apart wasn't doing either one of them any good.

• • •

Ruiz managed to convince the lieutenant of the Gang Enforcement section to authorize OT for one of the detectives to come in and help me try to identify the man who'd killed Roberto Solano. Brad Hynes was one of the oldest members of the detail. I didn't know him well, but we'd been in uniform at roughly the same time and had worked a few cases that were tangentially connected. He was one of the many department cops I knew well enough for a wave or a how's-it-going in the hallway, but our conversation never went much deeper than that.

"How's it going?" I said even though we weren't in the hallway.

"Well, it's Saturday and I'm at a desk, but otherwise I can't complain." The tone in his voice told me he didn't mind being here. I wasn't sure if it was just because of the overtime or because he, like me, didn't have anything better to do on a weekend afternoon. "What do you need?"

"I'm looking to ID someone from a murder last night."

"We had a murder last night? Surprised I didn't hear about it."

"Not Long Beach. Different jurisdiction."

"Where?"

"Riverside."

"But you think he's local?"

"Found a vehicle stolen from Long Beach Airport, figure it's our guy."

"And you got a solid description?"

"Oh, yeah."

"Who's your wit?"

"Me. Saw him myself. Had a few words with him before we knew what he did."

"Let me fire up the computer. What did he look like?"

"Latino. Midthirties. Big. Six-four, two-fifty. All muscle. Bald with a Fu Manchu and I think some neck tats. At least one on the right side."

"Could you see what the design was?" His fingers were clicking on the keyboard.

"No. He had a collared shirt. I only saw a bit of it. Looked pointy, like the top of a triangle. Couldn't tell if it was words or an image. Just the dark ink."

I waited for him to finish typing and for the computer to pull up possible matches.

"Sound like anybody you know?" I asked.

"Could be a lot of guys," he said. "Bald's in these days." A few more seconds, and the database kicked back a list of names. "Looks like about three dozen. How do you want it? Go straight to the photos?"

"Sure," I said.

"Here," he said, rolling to the right in his desk chair. "You go ahead and advance them yourself."

I moved into the place he'd just moved out of and leaned in. The killer's face was in my head, but I'd worked with enough eyewitnesses to know that memory is rarely as reliable as we believe it to be. I clicked through the photos quickly to see if anything would be an instant match for the image I remembered. I gave each photo two or three seconds before I moved on to the next. I'd take each one in as quickly as possible. They were so similar that it often seemed like I was looking at different pictures of the same face, until some difference would register—the spacing of the eyes, the curve of the nose, the squareness of the chin—and I'd click through to the next. I made it through all thirty-seven possibles without any of the faces setting off alarm bells in my head.

Hynes knew what I was doing, and he seemed as disappointed as I did when I got to the last one and shook my head.

"Take it slower this time," he said.

I did. The second time through I found five possibilities. We made a list of them with their known gang affiliations, and Hynes added his own thoughts about the three he'd had direct experience with.

I studied the list and the photos. At that point, though, I knew I'd be doing calculations about the likelihood of each suspect and that would be influencing my perceptions. Hector Salazar, for instance, with his bounces for second-degree murder and aggravated assault and ties to MS-13, seemed more likely than David Escalante, who'd only gone down once for less than a year on an intent-to-distribute charge. And, of course, it might have been none of them at all.

Still, I had a list of names, so that was something.

• • •

By the time I got back upstairs to the squad room, I had a message from the detective from Riverside, Mike McDermott. I called him back.

"Just finished with the autopsy," he said.

"Find out anything interesting?"

"It doesn't look like our guy meant to kill Solano. At least not as soon as he did. You remember the duct-tape gag?"

"Yes," I said.

"Well, at some point, he popped Solano in the nose hard enough to break it."

"Solano suffocated?"

"Yeah."

I'd actually seen it before. If an assailant does too good a job and makes a gag airtight, the victim can only breathe through their nose. A broken nose will cause the sinuses to swell and fill with mucus and blood, cutting off the airways. With the mouth blocked, asphyxiation can occur in only a few minutes. Sometimes the assailant figures out what's happening, sometimes they don't.

"Fuck."

"Don't go there," McDermott said. He knew what I was thinking. Any decent cop would. I wondered if Solano had suffocated after we decided to interrupt the interrogation. Would he have just been given a solid but relatively minor beat-down if we hadn't showed up?

"Beckett, you still there?"

"Yeah."

"Don't blame yourself."

"I'm not. Solano was a douchebag who deserted his kids. He didn't deserve what he got, but he wasn't an angel."

"What is it then?"

"His son."

"Not the one in jail. The other one?" He paused long enough to check his notes. "Jesús?"

"He's just a decent high-school student trying to take care of his little sister, and his world's falling apart around him."

"Sometimes I wonder," he said. "Give a kid a name like that, you're just asking for trouble."

• • •

Jesús's mother finally returned our calls and told us that her phone had died and she wasn't able to charge it, just as we had hypothesized. She also sounded half-drunk, so the phone may have been lower on the priority list than she wanted us to believe. She'd spent the night at an acquaintance's house. We sent a unit to pick her up.

Ruiz had left Jesús and the social worker in the conference room. I went in and sat down next to him. He was reading a blue-and-black hardcover.

"What are you reading?" I asked.

"It's called *The Fault in Our Stars*," he said. "We have to read it for our one-book-one-school thing that we have to do over winter break."

"You're starting early."

"Yeah."

"Is it any good?"

"It's about some kids with cancer," he said, as if that answered the question.

"Sounds sad," I said.

"It is, but it's funny too."

"You like to read?"

He nodded. "My English teacher said I might be able to go into AP next year."

"That's good." I gave him a minute to go on or to change the subject, but he waited for me. He was sharp enough to know I wouldn't have come in if I didn't have something to tell him. "Your mom's on the way," I said. "She's okay, and Maria is fine."

He tried to play it cool, but he was clearly relieved.

"What's going to happen to us now?"

"We're going to find someplace safe for you until we can figure out who took those shots yesterday. We want to make sure everything's okay before you go back home."

"Where is it safe?" he asked.

I didn't know how to answer.

• • •

Jesús had an aunt who lived in Oceanside. She agreed to let the family stay with her for a few days. I worried that that wouldn't be long enough. And I worried that it wasn't far enough away. Oceanside wasn't much farther than Riverside, and Roberto Solano had been out of touch with the family for years. Apparently, the aunt checked in with her sister fairly regularly.

When Ruiz called Jen, Patrick, and me into the conference room with Jesús and told us the plan, I kept my misgivings to myself. But I followed him out into the squad room and said, "Can I have a minute?"

He led me into his office, and I closed the door behind us. "They'll find him," I said.

"Why do you think that?"

"They found his old man."

"That's different."

"How?"

"A parent is a lot easier to track down. It's harder to find out someone's aunt than it is their father."

"It's not much harder. Besides, what if Pedro is talking?"

Ruiz didn't say anything.

"They might be tracking his cell. The hitter went to Riverside a few hours after Jesús's first call to his dad in years."

"Can you prove there's a connection?"

"No."

"Then I don't know what else we can do. This is the best option we have."

"We can't give them some kind of protection?"

"There's no actual threat. It's just guesswork at this point. You're assuming it's some big conspiracy when you don't have anything solid to even connect the Ohio shooting and the Solano killing. You just told me that the autopsy showed that his death likely wasn't even intentional. They haven't even been approving protection for witnesses testifying in gang murder trials. You know it's a stretch."

"But you'll still ask, right?"

"Yeah, I'll try, but we both know the brass won't approve it."

"Thanks."

"Leave it open," he said as I walked back into the squad room.

I always kept a cheap prepaid cell phone in my desk drawer in case I needed to give someone a way to contact me.

"Take out your phone," I said to Jesús. He did. "Who do you have in the contacts that you might need to talk to in an emergency?"

"My mom. David. Not Pedro anymore."

I slid a notepad and a pen across the desk to him. "Write their numbers down."

"Okay," he said.

While he did that I popped open the plastic packaging for the TracFone LG and programmed my number into it.

"Trade me," I said.

Jesús looked at the new phone and wasn't impressed.

"I know," I said. "It's a piece of crap, but it will get the job done. I promise I'll take good care of yours, okay?"

He nodded.

"Don't add any other contacts. Just dial from your list if you need to."

He nodded again. "All right," he said.

"And the same rule's still good," I said. "You call me any time for anything. You remember that."

• • •

Mrs. Solano seemed sober, and as much as I wanted to force a Breathalyzer test on her before she got into her old Hyundai with her children and headed south on the 405 to her sister's house, I fought the urge. Instead, I emptied my wallet and gave Jesús seven twenty-dollar bills and another one of my cards.

"Check in with me every day or two, let me know you're okay," I said.

"I will." He made sure Maria was secured in her car seat and got in the front, next to his mother. He closed the door and rolled down the window. "Detective Beckett?"

"Yeah?"

"Thanks."

I wished that there was something else I could do for him, but Ruiz had been right. "You're welcome," I said, reaching through the window to put my hand on his shoulder. "Remember, you can call or text anytime, okay?"

He nodded, I pulled my hand back, and as the window began to close, Mrs. Solano said, "How much he give you?"

Jesús watched me through the window as they pulled away. He looked small there in the passenger's seat, small and alone.

15

WOOL GLOVES, ONE PAIR: GRAY, HOLES IN LEFT THUMB AND MIDDLE FINGER.

After the shooting on Ohio Avenue, I had called Siguenza to arrange a meeting with Pedro. I wanted to see how he reacted to the news that someone had tried to kill his brother. Because of Siguenza's court schedule, that afternoon was the soonest he could accommodate the request.

Jen and I sat in the jail's small concrete interview room with Siguenza and waited for the guards to escort Pedro in. We'd exchanged pleasantries with him, and in the silence that followed, I studied him. I made his age at forty-five or so, about the same as Benny, but he had little of the other man's authority or presence. The most notable thing about him was his suit—not the same one he'd worn the first time I met him, but just as expensive and finely tailored. It looked like charcoal-gray money.

When they brought Pedro in, he looked weary and frightened. Part of the effect came from the orange jumpsuit and handcuffs. He looked out of place and in over his head, as kids almost always do in his situation.

When he sat down next to his lawyer across the table from us, I said, "How are you, Pedro?"

He looked at Siguenza, who nodded back at him.

"Okay." His voice sounded far away.

"We're here because we need to tell you something," I said.

"What?"

"Somebody tried to kill Jesús."

His eyes widened and he again looked at Siguenza, who sat motionless with a neutral expression on his face.

"Jesús is okay. So are Maria and your mom. But they killed your neighbor by mistake."

We watched him trying to process the information, and as he did, the confusion in his eyes slowly disappeared and was replaced by fear.

"Is there anything you'd like to tell us?"

Siguenza leaned forward and said, "I'll need a few moments to confer with my client."

Outside in the hallway, Jen said, "You think he'll tell us anything?"

"Not now. Maybe after he sits with it for a while."

When we sat down again, Pedro looked as if he might have been crying. I wondered what Siguenza had told him and repeated my last question.

"No," Pedro said, his voice barely above a whisper. "I don't have anything to say."

Siguenza put his hands together and said, "I believe we're done here."

• • •

On the way back to the station, I asked Jen if she wanted to get some dinner, and she reminded me that she'd already invited Patrick and me to her house for a barbecue.

"Shit," I said. "That's tonight?"

At least she laughed at that.

"What can I bring?"

"Something to drink."

"Who's going to be there?"

"Just you and Patrick, if he can get away from the drive-by."

"Okay."

"You look relieved."

"I'm just not feeling like I'd do well with a big crowd tonight."

"When have you ever not felt like that?"

She had a point. I've never been much of a socializer. But I was worried about Jesús, and I knew I'd be thinking about work. With Jen and Patrick I wouldn't have to worry about bringing it up.

I went home and changed into cargo shorts and a T-shirt, tucked my Glock into an inside-the-waistband holster, and put on a plaid seersucker button-up to cover it while I stopped at Ralphs to buy Sam Adams and Diet Coke.

The sun was low in the sky and beginning to color the altocumulus clouds orange when I parked on Colorado outside Jen's Craftsman. Patrick's VW was outside too, and there was an unfamiliar Honda Accord in the driveway behind Jen's RAV4. I figured they'd already be out in the backyard, so I went through the gate in front of the cars and around the house.

Jen was under the pergola with a pair of tongs in her hand, flipping chicken breasts on the grill, while Patrick sat at the teak table and sipped from a Blue Moon bottle.

"Hey, guys," I said, dropping the two six-packs on the table. "Whose Honda is that?"

Jen laughed and Patrick shook his head and muttered, "Shit." He slipped a twenty out of his wallet and held it up for her. She folded it in half with one hand and stuck it in the back pocket of her jeans.

"What?" I said.

"She bet me that the first thing you'd say after 'Hello' was 'Whose car is that?'"

"Seriously? You two don't have anything better to do?"

"Not really," she said, still happy from her win.

"Really, though, whose is it?"

This time they both laughed.

• • •

Less than ten minutes later, Lauren Terrones, the rookie from Bishop's murder scene who'd been assisting with the case, came through the gate, put a paper grocery bag on the table, and began to unload it.

"Hello," I said.

"Hi, Detective Beckett," she said, opening a bag of tortilla chips and pouring them into a large orange bowl.

"Call him Danny," Jen said without turning away from the grill.

Lauren looked uncertainly at me and I nodded. "Sure, call me Danny."

"I just ran down the street to that little store."

"Ma N Pa's?"

"Yeah. Seems cool."

She was right. It was a little hole-in-the-wall market that also made sandwiches and other to-go items. It was the only business in the residential area and had a kind of quaint charm that's hard to find in any city, especially one as big as Long Beach. And they had fantastic homemade beef jerky.

"I got some potato salad, too," Lauren said.

"Oh, thanks." Jen was still turning over the chicken on the grill. The last time I'd been here for a barbecue, I'd tried to tell her not to flip it so much. I was half-convinced she was only doing it to mess with me.

"What do you want to drink?" Patrick asked me.

I wanted a beer, so I said, "Diet Coke."

He went inside and came back out with a Blue Moon and a can for me.

"No glass?"

"Seriously?"

"I just wanted to see if you'd go back for one."

Lauren smiled at me, and I thought about what Jen had said about it sounding like I was flirting with her at the crime scene. That idea had honestly never entered my mind. I had just been trying to get her to feel comfortable. But now I didn't know what to say. Why had Jen invited her here? She couldn't actually think I was interested in a rookie, could she? I knew I could be an asshat sometimes, but she didn't think I'd be a big enough douche to hit on someone just out of the academy, did she?

Jen still had her back to us, so I couldn't read her expression.

"Jesús made it to Oceanside," I said. "He texted me when they got there."

"That's good." Jen turned around and looked me in the eye. "He'll be okay."

"I hope so."

"That's the fourth boy?" Lauren said. "The one whose house got hit by the drive-by."

"Yeah. Do all the uniforms know about the connection?"

"I don't think so," she said.

Patrick dipped a chip into the salsa. "I told Lauren about it before you got here."

"Don't spread it around," I told her. "Okay?"

"I won't."

Jen was using the tongs to take the chicken off the grill and load it onto a plate. "There was no way we could have kept that quiet." She put the plate on the table.

"I know, but the fewer people who are talking about it the better."

"I won't say anything," Lauren said. She seemed nervous. Probably thought I was accusing her of something.

"Jesús is going to be all right," Patrick said.

"I'm just being paranoid." I looked at Lauren. "I didn't mean anything by it."

"Didn't think you did." She served herself two kinds of salad—the potato she'd just bought at Ma N Pa's, and a bunch of spring mix Jen put out in the middle of the table. We all filled our plates.

"Good," I said, wondering if I sounded as awkward as I felt.

What was Lauren doing there? I looked quizzically at Jen but she just looked right back at me, pretending to be oblivious.

"So you've been on the job, what, like a month now?" Patrick asked Lauren.

"A little over."

"What do you think?"

"Pretty much what I expected."

"Yeah?" Patrick seemed surprised.

"Just like on *CSI*," Lauren said without a trace of irony or sarcasm in her voice.

He laughed. "You had me there for a second."

"Honestly," she said, "I've got cops in the family, so there weren't any big surprises. And I'm a little older than most of the other rookies. So I knew what I was in for."

"What did you do before the academy?" Jen asked.

"Law school," she said.

I wondered if that was a joke too. She had the same deadpan expression on her face as she'd had a minute earlier.

"No shit?" I said. "Why aren't you a lawyer?" As soon as I'd said it, the thought occurred to me that she might not have passed the bar exam or that something else might have derailed her plans.

"Since the recession hit, there are three lawyers for every decent job. The LBPD sounded a lot better than ninety hours of contracts a week in a windowless cubicle for the same money."

"No prosecution work available?" I asked.

"Have to get in line behind all the people who've been laid off in the last few years. And it didn't look like I'd be able to pay off the loans with a public defender's salary."

"You must not have told anybody," Jen said.

"Only Stan Burke. How'd you know that?"

"Haven't heard any jokes about rookie lawyers," Jen said.

"You think you would have?"

"Are you kidding?" Jen said. "You're the first new recruits in five years. Everybody hears everything about you guys."

"That's good to know," Lauren said. "Could you all forget I told you that?"

"We'll try," Patrick said. He took another bite of chicken and washed it down with the last of his beer.

• • •

Lauren was the first to leave. When she was gone and Patrick went inside to the bathroom, I asked Jen, "Why'd you invite Lauren?"

"So you could hit on her again."

"Really."

"Because I knew it would make you uncomfortable."

"Come on." I gave her my serious face.

"You know you're taking all the fun out of it, right?"

More of the face.

"She might rent the guesthouse."

I felt relieved. Then I started to worry about why I had been uptight about it in the first place. "Can she afford it? She was just talking about paying back her loans."

"If she wants it, I'll give her a good deal."

"How much?"

"I was thinking a thousand a month."

Patrick came back outside with a fresh beer. "A thousand a month for what?"

"The guesthouse."

"That's a hell of deal," I said.

"You know you could get almost twice that much, right?" Patrick said.

"Yeah," she said. "I'd rather get less and get somebody I wouldn't mind being neighbors with."

"But that much less?" he said.

"It'll be worth it."

"You think she's okay?" I asked.

"Yes, I do." She started clearing the table.

• • •

When I got home, I opened the windows and turned on the ceiling fans. The temperature didn't drop, but the stuffiness gradually dissipated. I sat in the lamplight of the living room and reviewed the case file again. After an hour, I felt myself skimming through the familiar information and realized it was becoming nothing more than a rote exercise and that I was unable to bring anything new to my reading, as if I was simply repeating the same thought processes

I'd gone through dozens of times before. There was nothing to be gained while I was in that frame of mind, so I put the file away and wondered what would be the best way to take my mind off of Bishop and get some distance from the work.

I hadn't checked my personal e-mail in days, and I remembered Patrick mentioning the e-mail he'd sent me. Once I'd powered up my MacBook, I opened my Gmail account and found Patrick's message. It was a YouTube link with a note that said, "Danny—You're going to like this."

When I clicked on it, a window opened on a channel belonging to someone calling himself Banjo Boog. The video opened to a blue background with title graphics that looked like they'd been created on someone's Commodore 64 and read, in a primitive pseudocursive font, "Hallelujah by Leonard Cohen." I was almost too apprehensive to keep watching. But I did watch.

A white-haired man with glasses and a Colonel Sanders facial-hair arrangement began picking out the opening chords of the song. As soon as he began to play, I felt a twinge of guilt for my prejudiced reaction.

He was good.

The image was grainy and the sound thin and tinny, but his skill with banjo was more than enough to overpower the technical limitations of the video, and after only a few seconds, I was pulled into the melody and felt myself connecting to the music in a way I wouldn't have thought possible only a few minutes earlier. I've always been a Cohen fan, and I had at least five covers of this song in my collection, but this one struck me with its simplicity—no singing, just the perfectly picked notes singing out of the man's open-back instrument.

I'd always loved the song, especially the original version. Ever since Jeff Buckley had gotten a hold of it, it seemed everyone who did their own cover went over the top with it, using it to display a kind of gymnastic vocal virtuosity that, while often impressive, always seemed to me to be much more about the singer than the song.

Boog's straightforward arrangement, though, reminded me of the relative simplicity of Cohen's original, and the dissonance from hearing the melody on the banjo, surely one of the last instruments most people would think of when calling the song to mind, somehow became a surprisingly effective substitute for the ever-present irony of Cohen's voice.

I replayed the video several times and bookmarked it in the browser. Halfway through the first viewing, I knew I now had a very specific goal. I had to learn how to play "Hallelujah" on the Saratoga Star.

By the fifth or sixth replay, though, I was thinking about my difficulties with the fingering of even the most basic of chords, my virtually nonexistent sense of rhythm, and my inability to get my Saratoga Star anywhere near proper tuning even with multiple electronic aids. My ambition began to wane, and the hopeful optimism I'd been feeling slipped away.

Why even bother? After months of practice I was still struggling with the most basic lessons on Tony Trischka's website.

No. There wouldn't be any practicing that night. Instead, I cued up *The Essential Leonard Cohen* in iTunes, reclined on the couch, and stared up at the spinning ceiling fan. My weariness caught up to me, and I was nodding off when track eleven—"Who by Fire"—began to play, and with a cruel inevitability I should have foreseen, I found myself doing exactly what I had been doing two hours earlier. Thinking about Bishop.

16

LEATHERMAN MULTI-TOOL: WELL USED, IN BLACK NYLON SHEATH.

I woke to a deep, slicing pain running down my neck and into my arm. On the shelf at the bottom of my nightstand was an industrial-strength heating pad of the type that athletic trainers use for professional sports teams. My physical therapist special-ordered it for me. It felt like a smaller version of one of those protective lead aprons they put over you when they x-ray your teeth at the dentist's office. It was always plugged in and ready to go. I turned it on in the dark, making an educated guess at the temperature setting because I couldn't see the LCD display in the dark. The maximum was 165 degrees. Hot enough to give me a burn if I wasn't careful. I didn't care about that then, only about getting the pad as hot as I could as quickly as I could. While I waited, I popped a Vicodin.

I tucked one corner of the pad between my shoulder and the bed, and then pulled the opposite corner up alongside my neck and held it there. After about five minutes, the pain at the edge of my trapezius had dulled somewhat, but the sharp tendrils slicing up into my neck and down into my arm and back were even worse than they had been when I woke up.

The heating pad wasn't going to be enough. I got out of bed, went into the bathroom, and opened the hot-water faucet in the shower all the way. When the mirror began to fog, I added just enough cold to the mix to prevent any actual skin damage, stepped inside, and let the scalding water wash over me.

The heat and the pressure and the opioid analgesic slowly began to relieve the pain. I knew it wouldn't go away. It never did. That had long ago stopped being the point of any of the treatments I employed. The best I could ever hope for was a lessening, an easing, a tempering of the hurt.

As the hot water supply began to diminish and the flow began to cool, I thought again about my landlord and his impending plumbing improvements. If he really thought he was going to replace my old high-pressure showerhead with one of those useless low-flow models, he could go fuck himself.

I was still sweating when I put on a pair of cargo shorts and a seersucker shirt and walked out the door for breakfast at Egg Heaven.

Harlan Gibbs was an early riser, too, so I sent him a text message asking if he'd like to join me.

I walked slowly, hoping to cool off, but it was clearly going to be another torturously hot day, and I knew the layer of perspiration that had been present since my shower would remain either until late that night or until I decided to settle in somewhere with air-conditioning.

Halfway through my corned-beef-and-bacon omelet, Harlan came in. He surveyed the other diners. Only two tables were occupied, as were three seats at the counter. Then he saw me in the back corner.

"You really need the gunfighter's seat at seven thirty on a Sunday morning?" he said.

"Can't be too careful."

He sat down and the server brought over another menu. "Coffee?" she asked.

"A bucket if you have it."

She smiled at him and he smiled back.

"You know she's only being nice because you're old and sad, right?" I said. When I first became acquainted with him, Harlan had already added five years of retirement to the thirty he'd spent with the LA Sheriff's Department.

"So what? I'll take it. Would have thought you'd understand that."

"Why?"

"Because you're older and sadder than anybody I've ever met." He chuckled at his own joke.

I took too long with a rejoinder, and I could see that he was worried that he might have crossed a line with his quip. So I looked down wearily into my half-empty cup and let him think he had. After he had a few seconds to stew, I brought my napkin up to the corner of my eye and began delicately dabbing at it.

"Asshole," he said.

"Come on, you were asking for that one."

"It's early. I'm not at full alert yet."

The server brought his coffee—in a perfectly regular cup—and asked, "Need a little more time?"

He shook his head and ordered scrambled eggs, bacon, and an English muffin.

"You back on the regular diet?"

"Doctor says anything that doesn't make me puke is okay."

"Really? The doctor said that?"

"More or less."

"Is it working okay for you?"

"Yeah, as long as I don't overdo it, I'm eating pretty normal again."

"That's good."

"Taste keeps getting better, too." For months after his stomach-cancer surgery and chemo he couldn't taste anything. Nobody could tell him definitively if he'd regain the ability.

"It's funny," he said, sipping his black coffee. "In some ways that was the worst part of the whole mess. It's the stuff you don't anticipate that's the toughest. I was ready for everything else. No one ever said anything about not being able to taste."

I clenched and unclenched my fist and looked at the scar on my wrist. "Nobody expects the Spanish Inquisition."

He paused long enough for me to wonder if he got the Monty Python reference, and then he looked right at me and the corner of his mouth curled into a quarter of a grin. "It's good that you can turn everything into a joke."

Three cups of coffee and forty-five minutes of conversation later, I still didn't know how to take that.

• • •

At home after breakfast I tried to call Jesús. After several rings, I got his voice mail. Rather than leaving a message, I sent him a text: *Jesús, how's it going? Everything okay? Let me know.*

He didn't reply for a few minutes, and I started worrying. I knew it was silly. He was, after all, a teenager. How many other texts was he getting? How many tweets was he reading? Maybe he even had the good sense to put his phone down for a while. But before I could get too worked up, he replied.

everythings ok. its weird here. hope we can come home soon

I hope so, too. Do me a favor--don't mention where you are to anyone. Especially on the phone or in text messages, okay?

Ok

Good. Let me know if you need anything.

As I typed, I felt self-conscious for properly capitalizing and punctuating.

i will
thank you for helping us

You're welcome.

He signed off with a happy-face emoticon.

• • •

Instead of going back to the case file, I picked up *The Grapes of Wrath.* I'd been working my way through it five or ten pages at a time, whenever I had a few minutes to spare or when I wanted to get a bit of distance from the investigation. With the empty day stretched out in front of me, I settled in on the couch and really dug in.

Kyle had photocopied the pages of Bishop's edition of the book so I could study the marginal notations. But the text of the novel itself was difficult to read in the photocopy, so in addition to the Kindle version, I'd found online a copy of the same Viking edition that Bishop had owned and paid triple the price to have it shipped overnight.

There were three versions of Steinbeck's novel in front of me.

As I read, I was spurred on by the marginal notations, which, because of their depth and the close reading they demonstrated, reminded me of the first time I'd read the book—in an American literature seminar in college—and how boring I had found it then, how much of a struggle it was to slog through it.

I read for most of the day. I was surprised at how caught up I got in the book. Ever since Springsteen's *The Ghost of Tom Joad* came out, I'd meant to go back to it, but I never had. After two decades, though, it had taken on a new weight. This time through, I felt like I got it. So much of the thematic material that resonated with me now had just gone over my head when I was still in college. It made me wonder how many of the multitudinous other books that I hadn't liked in college would strike me differently today with so much more life behind me. And I thought, too, about the degree to which my response was due to Bishop and the case. Was I really that much more mature than I had been in college, or was I only more bleak and weary and desperate to understand a man who I could never really know?

• • •

I didn't quite make it all the way through the book. There were still about a hundred pages left when I put it down and decided it was time to figure out what I was going to do for dinner. Having eaten with Jen and Patrick the evening before and with Harlan that morning, I had already exhausted all the people I might conceivably share a meal with, so all I had to decide was whether to stay in or go out. A quick examination of the refrigerator told me my only dine-in options were frozen Stouffer's lasagna, Frosted Cheerios, string cheese, or overripe bananas.

I decided to walk around the corner to Mosher's for a corned-beef sandwich. The food wasn't great, but what it lacked in quality it made up for in convenience. The small Seventh Street shop was only half a block away from my duplex. I'd have to hurry, though. For some unfathomable reason they closed at five on Sundays.

My upstairs neighbors, Keith and Kim, were just walking up the street as I locked the front door. Since their son had graduated from Warren High School and matriculated at San Diego State, they'd been talking about moving south. I hadn't seen them since I'd gotten the notice about the landlord selling the building.

"You get the notice from the owner?" Keith asked.

I nodded. "Haven't heard anything else yet. Think they'll remodel? Go single on us?"

"I don't know," he said. "Hope not."

"That wouldn't be so bad," Kim said. "It would finally give us the motivation we need to start looking for a house." She was obviously more enthusiastic than he was, but I knew better than to say anything about that.

I said, "I'm more worried about the plumber they've got coming. They're going to install low-flow toilets and showerheads."

Keith's face fell. "They are?"

"I'm sure that's what they meant about the 'upgrades.'"

"Shit," he said.

Kim frowned. "It's not that bad," she said. "This is a desert and we're in a drought. It'll be good for the environment."

He raised his eyebrows at me as if to apologize for her.

"Don't look at him like that," she said.

"You're all eco-friendly now," he said, "but wait until the first time you try to wash the conditioner out of your hair."

I laughed as they walked up the stairs.

In the few minutes since I'd decided on dinner, the idea of a mediocre corned-beef sandwich had really grown on me. But the neighbors had slowed me down. I looked at my watch, muttered "Shit" more loudly than I meant to, and looked over my shoulder to make sure no one had heard me.

Unless I wanted to walk for several blocks, which in the late afternoon heat I really didn't, the choices were limited. So I strolled past the Chute Boxe Vale Tudo martial-arts school and momentarily considered something from FroGurtz for dinner, then remembered that the frozen-yogurt vendor had been replaced by a taco shop that hadn't lasted long either. Something called Seoulfood was coming but wasn't there yet.

All that was left was Starbucks. I got a ham-and-Swiss panini and a venti vanilla latte and took it back home to eat. I sat at the dining-room table, opened Bishop's file, and reviewed it while I ate.

Among the items on the inventory of his possessions that had slipped from my mind were a single can of creamed corn and a few dozen plastic forks.

• • •

That night I dreamed that I was on the bank of the Los Angeles River with Bishop. He stood thigh-deep in the dark water while I sat on the rocks above him.

"Danny?"

"Yeah?"

"Danny, I'm not going on."

"What do you mean?"

"Danny, I'm not going to leave this water. I'm going to walk on down the river here."

"You're crazy," I said. "There's nothing there but the harbor."

"I'll catch fish. You can't starve beside a nice river."

I said, "This isn't a nice river."

"I can't help it. I can't leave this water." Bishop's blue eyes were half-closed. "You know how it is, Danny. You know how people are nice to me. But they don't really care for me."

"You're crazy."

"No, I'm not. I know how I am. I know they're sorry. But—well, I'm not going. You tell Jen."

"Look now—"

"No. It's no use. I'm in this water. And I'm not going to leave it. I'm going on now, Danny, down the river. I'll catch fish and stuff, but I can't leave it. I can't." He turned downstream.

"You tell Jen, Danny."

He stepped up onto the rocks and headed toward the harbor.

I followed after him. "Listen, you goddamn fool—"

"It's no use," Bishop said. "I'm sad, but I can't help it. I have to go." He turned abruptly and walked downstream along the shore. I started to follow, and then I stopped. Bishop disappeared behind the chain-link enclosure of a storm drain outlet, and then appeared again, following the edge of the river. I watched him growing smaller on the edge of the river until he disappeared at last around the bend at the edge of the biological reserve.

I walked back up the bank and found Jen waiting for me beneath the Ocean Boulevard overpass.

"I have something to tell you," I said to her.

"What?"

"Bishop. He went on down the river. He's not going on."

It took a moment for her to understand. "Why?" she asked softly.

"I don't know. Said he has to. Said he has to go. Said for me to tell you."

"How will he eat?" she asked.

"I don't know. Says he'll catch fish."

• • •

When I got out of bed, the sun hadn't yet risen. It wasn't hot yet, but I had tossed and turned all night with a sharp pain running up the back of my arm into my neck. I took another long, hot shower, wondering about the new plumbing that was on the way. Surely the owner would be reasonable, I thought. He'd let me keep my old showerhead.

I had a big cup of coffee and scrolled through the *LA Times* and the *Press-Telegram* online and then decided to head in to work early.

Before I left, though, an idea occurred to me. Why take a chance on a landlord's reasonableness? I got a crescent wrench and went into the bathroom. With a washcloth wrapped around the flats where the showerhead attached to the pipe, I used the wrench to loosen and remove the showerhead. I dropped it into my courier bag and took it with me.

Fight the power.

• • •

The squadroom was empty, as it usually was early on mornings after no one got murdered. I had the place to myself for more than an hour. The quiet helped me get the piles of paperwork on my desk sorted out. Just as I was about to turn my attention back toward Bishop's case, Patrick rushed into the room. "We got prints on some of the brass we found at the Ohio shooting," he said. He looked expectantly at Ruiz's office.

"Not yet," I said. "Tell me more."

"Two sets. One of them we've got on file."

"Who?"

"Guy with three arrests, but no convictions. Robert Medina."

"What were the arrests?"

"One car theft, one battery, one ADW."

"Know who he runs with?"

"No. File says 'undetermined.'"

"Talked to anyone in the gang detail?"

"No one's there yet."

"You know Hynes? He came in on Saturday to help ID our guy from Riverside. I'll give him a call."

• • •

"You're gonna owe me, Beckett," Hynes said.

Patrick and I met him in the Organized Crime Detail's squad room. "It's only forty-five minutes before the start of your shift."

"Early is early."

"Okay," I said. "Lunch is on me. What do you want?"

"A pizza from Michael's."

Michael's was an upscale pizza joint that Zagat had recently rated the best in Los Angeles. It was okay, but as far as I was concerned, any place that didn't actually have pepperoni on the menu had no business claiming to make pizza. "You got it."

Patrick said, "You have anything on our guy?"

"I don't recognize the name offhand," Hynes said. "But he shows up in the database."

"He have any affiliations?" I asked.

"There are a few known connections with a couple of different sets, but they're thin, nothing definitive."

Patrick was looking over his shoulder. "What's the program you're running?"

Brad said, "It's new. Based on stuff the military was using in Iraq and Afghanistan to track insurgents. Collects metadata, social media, cell phones, anything digital we can get. We're trying to get it to mesh with our old-school intel."

Patrick leaned in closer to the screen. "Is that ORCA?"

"No," Hynes said. "But it's the same basic concept."

"What's that?" I asked.

"An acronym," Patrick said to me. "Organizational, Relationship, and Contact Analyzer."

He turned back to Hynes. "Any chance I could get access to it?"

"I'll have to run it by the lieutenant. It's a pilot program, so they're being pretty tight with who they'll let play with it."

"Should I get Ruiz to ask?"

"Let me try first." On the screen in front of him, Hynes was clicking on little diagrams that connected dots in increasingly complex patterns. Patrick's eyes were glued to the images, but I wasn't sure what I was seeing. I wanted to ask more about it, but I didn't. He was absorbed in the data, so I just watched and let him go with it. My curiosity could wait.

I left them to the program and headed back to my desk.

When Patrick came back twenty minutes later, he was clearly excited.

"Get anything?" I asked.

"Not yet, but this could be huge for the case."

"How is that different from what you were doing with the Facebook and Twitter stuff?"

"It's the same basic idea, but I was doing everything manually," Patrick said. "With the program's processing power it'll crunch all the data thousands of times faster than I could. And find more connections."

"So we can figure out who Medina and the other shooters from Ohio Avenue were working with."

"And a lot more."

"Think they'll let you use it?" I asked.

"No idea," he said. "I hope so."

"What's your next move?"

"Find Medina."

17

UNDERWEAR: THREE PAIRS HANES MEN'S BRIEFS; TWO PAIRS WHITE, SIZE LARGE, FRUIT OF THE LOOM BOXER SHORTS; THREE PAIRS ASSORTED PLAID.

My phone rang, and I was surprised to see Julia Rice's name on the screen. I wondered why she was calling. The message I'd left for her said that, unfortunately, Bishop wasn't in any of the photos she had prepared for us. I thanked her and thought that would be that. But maybe she had found something else. More photos to look at. While I was trying to decide if I should answer it, the call went to my voice mail. As soon as it was complete, I listened.

"Hello, Detective Beckett. I got your message. I'm sorry the photos didn't help. I . . . would you call me back if you have a chance? There's something I'd like to ask you. It's not related to the case. Thanks."

I listened to it again. The pause made it sound like she was uncertain about something. What could it have been? If she'd found more photos, she wouldn't have said it was unrelated to the case.

When Jen sat down at her desk, I played it for her. "What do you think that's about?" I asked.

She looked at me before answering. "What do *you* think it's about?"

"I don't know." Or maybe I just didn't *want* to know. "That's why I'm asking."

"Why didn't you just call her back?"

"What do you mean?"

"How many calls do you return in a day? Thirty? Forty?"

"Depends on the day." I didn't see what she was getting at. "You do just as many as I do. What's your point?"

"How many of them do you listen to five times and analyze before getting back to the person?"

The answer was, of course, none. "Every once in a while, when a suspect or a witness calls, you know. Trying to figure out the subtext."

"She's a suspect now?" Jen raised her eyebrows.

"No."

"Just a person of interest."

"Would you please just say what you mean?" I said, hoping that my suspicions about Julia's reason for calling might be mistaken.

She studied me, trying to see if I did in fact know what she was talking about or whether I really was dense enough to miss her implication. I wasn't, not quite. But I wasn't going to admit it, not to her and especially not to myself.

"She wants to ask you out," Jen said, trying hard to make it sound like a simple matter of fact.

"That's what I was afraid of."

"Why?"

"Because it would be inappropriate. She's involved in the case."

"No, she's not. She tried to help. She couldn't. She's done with it."

"We don't know that for sure," I said. We didn't. It was very unlikely that she'd have any further involvement with the case, but we couldn't be positive.

"If she hadn't been involved at all, what would you do?"

"But she was involved." I thought about what Jen was saying. It had been twenty years since I'd been on a date. And I hadn't even considered becoming involved with anyone since my wife's death. There'd been a single one-night stand with a patrol sergeant from Garden Grove after a retirement party more than a year earlier, but my most vivid memory of that incident was the relief I felt when she didn't return my call the next day.

"Would you go out with her if she wasn't?"

I didn't know how to answer that question. Julia Rice was attractive and smart. I liked her. But the thought of dating her or anyone made me feel uneasy. It was difficult to imagine myself in that situation. "Fuck if I know," I said.

"You should just call her back and talk to her."

"Why?"

"Because everyone who cares about you is afraid you're going to wind up old and alone and depressed, sitting in a dark room thinking about putting the barrel of your gun in your mouth."

When she saw the expression on my face she said, "Too on the nose?"

"Maybe," I said. "A little bit."

• • •

When Marty came in, Patrick filled him in on the developments in the case. "We know where to find Medina?" Marty asked.

His first thought, like mine, was to get out on the street and track him down.

But Patrick said, "I'm waiting on his phone records. I already started looking at his location tags on Facebook, so that should help us narrow his movements."

"How about knocking on his door?" Marty said.

"Of course," Patrick said. "But shouldn't we try to figure out if he's there first?"

"Yes," I said. "If he's not, we could give him a heads-up."

"Okay," Marty said. "Have a warrant yet?"

Patrick nodded. "And a BOLO."

"You have anything so far?" Marty asked.

"Last thing he posted on Facebook was after two this morning. A status update. 'Long-ass day good night.' Gives his location as 'Near Compton.' That fits the address we have for him. North of the 91 off of Atlantic. Waiting on cell-phone records. Should be here soon."

"He have a job?" Marty asked.

"Not that we know of. Gang Enforcement thinks he's banging full time."

Marty seemed skeptical. "So we're just going to watch him online?"

"For today. He usually posts a status update or tweets when he's done for the day. I think we wait for his signoff and then bust his front door down."

I understood Marty's doubts. He had spent a career hunting suspects on the street and was dubious of technology. Things had been advancing so fast in the last few years with cell phones and other connected technology that it often seemed like we had a new playbook every week. But I trusted Patrick. And I realized what I'm sure was one of his primary motivations for his plan: if we waited until that night to pick up Medina, Patrick would have another day's worth of metadata to add to his investigation.

• • •

Jen was meeting with an ADA about a trial in which she had to testify, so I went to the Potholder Too by myself for lunch. The lunch crowd was light, and there was a table open by the window that looked out over a small patio and onto Broadway. If I leaned a little bit to the left, I could see the LBPD headquarters across the street. So I made it a point to sit straight up.

An older server who usually worked at the original location in Belmont Heights came over to the table. Her nametag read *Fullerton*. I'd always wondered about the story behind that, but never asked. She recognized me too, but we'd never established a relationship that went deeper than casual remarks about the weather. I kind of liked it that way, and I assumed that she did, too.

"Coffee or Diet Coke?" she asked.

"Let's go with the soda."

"And a Rancher?"

"Let's go with the chicken-fried steak." I wasn't sure where the spontaneous order came from. It was as much of a surprise to me as it was to her.

She looked out through the window and up at the sky, then back at me. "Just had to see if any pigs were flying out there."

I laughed and tried to remember when I'd had anything other than the Rancher. Years ago, when Megan and I would fight the weekend breakfast crowds at the original café, I dabbled occasionally in French toast and waffles, but before too long, I settled into a routine. That's been my standard MO for as long as I can remember. Find a restaurant I like and a dish I like and just keep ordering it forever. Back then, once I'd figured things out, it was always chicken-fried steak.

I hadn't thought about that when Fullerton took my order. I'd been planning on the usual corned-beef-and-bacon omelet. Why had I changed my order?

The obvious answer, I thought, shifting into my armchair psychologist self-diagnosis mode, was that my subconscious was trying to hang onto the past. Julia Rice wanted to go out with me. For years, I'd been doing my best to deflect any romantic interest that came my way. Is that what I was doing now? I'd already allowed myself to go further down that road than I ever had before, but I was trying to talk myself out of meeting her.

Why? I didn't know.

• • •

"Bingo!" Patrick shouted on the other side of the squad room.

"What?" Jen asked.

"We've got a number that links Medina to Bishop's killing."

"Links him how?" I said, crossing over to Patrick's desk. Jen beat me there.

On his MacBook screen was a simple diagram with a few dozen points interconnected by a complicated series of lines. It looked like the diagram Hynes had shown us when he'd demonstrated the program based on the military ORCA system.

"They give you access to the database?"

"Not at first, but Ruiz had a talk with someone."

"What are we looking at?" Jen asked.

"A program that tracks digital connections." He moved his cursor over various points on the diagram and showed her how small boxes would pop up each time he touched one of the dots. "These red dots are suspects. Medina and the three who killed Bishop." He rolled over each of the four in turn and their names appeared with their DOB and a list of sources for the connections. "This is just the overview. There's a lot more here. But watch." As the cursor hit each dot in turn, Patrick highlighted it. First Medina, whose dot was by itself in the top right corner of the image, then Omar, Francisco, and Pedro, whose dots were clustered separately below Medina's. Each of their names remained displayed on the screen. There were multiple lines connecting our three killers, but nothing between any of them and Medina.

"But there's no connection," Jen said.

"Hang on." Patrick hit a few keys on the keyboard and another dot appeared in the upper left corner of the diagram. He clicked on it and a box with the word "unknown" popped up. "Now watch," he said. He tapped the return key, and bright red lines appeared linking the mystery number to both Omar and Medina.

"Find that phone," Patrick said.

Jen completed his thought. "And we find the connection."

• • •

"You call her yet?" Jen asked me.

"No."

"You should."

"I don't think you're right about what she wants. I think it's got to be something to do with work. Maybe she found some more pictures for us to look at."

"Call her and find out."

18

ZIPLOC BAG, QUART-SIZED, CONTAINING: IRISH SPRING SOAP, ONE BAR.

There were half a dozen new voice mails on the Bishop tip line. I followed up with quick calls on five of them that didn't provide any new or useful information. But the sixth call, from the owner of a coin-operated laundromat near the intersection of Anaheim and Cedar, sounded more promising.

The man was at work, and I didn't have anything pressing on my desk, so I arranged to meet him as soon as I could get there. Thirty minutes later, we were standing in the parking lot he shared with a bodega and a liquor store.

His name was Jae Lee and he'd owned the coin-op for ten years. He stood about five-four and had a weathered look and lean frame that at first glance made me think he would be harder than he was. I wondered whether he'd felt the need to Americanize his name.

"I was sad to see the news article," he said to me. "He was a good man, not like a lot of the other ones."

"What other ones?"

"The other homeless people."

"How was Bishop different?"

"He was friendly and nice to people. He didn't scare away the customers like some of the other ones do."

"No?"

• • •

The first time Lee saw Bishop loitering outside the laundry, he worried about having to ask him to leave. He always hated to do that. Lee knew what it was like to have no place to live, and he hated to remember the days before he'd made it to Long Beach.

So he watched the man outside, hoping he would move on of his own accord. But he didn't. He stood outside and carefully removed the cover from his shopping cart by unhooking a couple of bungee cords. He placed them in the top child seat part of the cart and took off a folded blue blanket that covered the contents, folding it one more time and laying it neatly on top of the cords.

Lee kept watching. He was surprised by the slow and methodical movements of the tall man outside. It was clear to Lee that the man was being very meticulous as he went through his belongings. Lee watched as he sorted his clothes into two folded piles on top of the blanket. After a few minutes of this, he had selected eight or nine pieces of clothing—shirts, socks, underwear—and put them into a reusable Ralphs shopping bag. Then he put the other clothes back into the cart, covered them again with the blanket, and reattached the cords. Then he pushed his cart up close to the window and came inside.

Instead of going straight to a washing machine, the man approached Lee.

"Excuse me, sir," he said. "Would it be all right if I did a bit of laundry?"

Lee was surprised. He couldn't remember anyone ever asking his permission before. "Of course," he said. "Why not?"

The tall man looked down at his feet. "Sometimes people such as yourself prefer not to do business with people like me."

Lee felt bad for the thoughts he'd had when he first spotted the shopping cart outside the window. How he'd assumed this man would quickly become a nuisance. But he wasn't. The tall man wasn't drunk or on drugs, he wasn't rude, he didn't even smell very bad. Instead he was respectful and even seemed embarrassed about feeling the need to ask to use the machines.

"No," Lee said. "It's okay."

"Thank you," the man said. "I won't be too long."

Lee watched as he went to the machine closest to the window and loaded his laundry inside. The man carefully counted out his quarters and checked the prices posted on both the washer and the dryer before he began feeding them into the machine. Once the load was in progress, the man went back out to his cart, took a book out of the top of the cart, and sat down on the concrete to read.

It was a slow morning and only two other customers were doing their laundry. Lee went through the unmarked door in back that led to his small office. He tried to go through some paperwork but instead decided to read the *Press-Telegram*. There was a two-way mirror that looked out into the other room, and Lee would frequently look out to see the progress of the homeless man's wash. If he sat up straight, he could just make out the top of the man's head and the handle of his shopping cart through the front window. After several minutes, the washer he was using buzzed to signal the end of the cycle. Lee looked out. It didn't seem as if the man had heard it, so he got up and went outside.

"Excuse me, sir?" Lee said.

The man didn't answer, so Lee stepped closer to him and repeated himself. "Sir?"

The man looked up. "Oh," he said, standing up. "I'm sorry. It's been a long time since anybody called me 'sir.'"

Lee said quietly, "Your wash is over. Time for the dryer."

"Thank you," the man said.

Later, when the tall man was folding his still-warm clothes, Lee approached him again. The man looked up and smiled kindly at him.

Lee said, "You can come here anytime you want."

"I appreciate that," the man said. "I'll be back as soon as I get some more money."

"No," Lee said. "That's not what I mean. Anytime you need to do washing, come in. From now on, it's on the house for you." Lee extended his hand. "My name is Lee. What's yours?"

"Everybody just calls me Bishop," he said.

• • •

"He came in almost every week after that." There was a palpable sadness in Lee's voice. "Every time, before he came in, he would pick up all the trash in the parking lot. I told him he didn't have to. He said, 'I want to.'"

"How long ago did that happen?" I asked.

"Maybe a year and a half, almost two?"

"And he'd been coming here ever since?"

Lee nodded.

Bishop was becoming less and less of a mystery to me.

When I told Jen about my conversation with Mr. Lee, she said, "That explains a lot about how he kept his cart. He worked hard at keeping himself together. Maintaining what little sense of order he could. You're getting solid background. Did you get anything else?"

"No, nothing that connects directly to the murder."

"But you're putting a face on him. That's good."

• • •

Jen was almost surely correct about Julia Rice. I knew that. And if I could have been certain of it, I would have ignored her message and not returned her call. Kind of dickish, I know, but the idea of a date with anyone at all filled me with trepidation. But really, if I was being honest with myself, some part of me refused to believe she could be interested in any way other than professionally. I was a morose insomniac with chronic pain who was obsessed with dead people and who was trying to learn to play the banjo. That couldn't have been on anybody's Match.com wish list. No. The only reason any woman could possibly want to talk to me was because I was good at my job. Whatever Julia wanted to talk about had to be related to the case.

So I called her back.

"Hey," I said when she answered. "It's Danny." As soon as I spoke, I realized I'd done two things I never did on a work-related phone call. I never used the word "hey" as a greeting, and I never used my first name. Why had Jen said what she did? There would be no way I could continue the call without wallowing in self-consciousness.

Shit.

"I got your message," I said. "What can I help you with?" Seriously? *What can I help you with?* Had I actually said that?

"Hi," she said. "I wasn't sure if you'd call back."

"Of course I'd call back. Why would you think I wouldn't?"

"Well," she said. "I wasn't sure if it was appropriate."

"Oh." Jen was right. Of course Jen was right.

I'm not sure how long I was silent, but it was long enough for her to say, "Are you still there?"

"Yes," I said. "Yes, I am."

"Would you like to get a cup of coffee?"

No, I thought. No, I wouldn't. "Yes, I'd like that."

"Oh, good," she said. "Are you free after work tonight?"

"Sure."

Shit. Shit shit shit.

19

CHARMIN BASIC TOILET PAPER, ONE PARTIAL ROLL.

I told Julia I'd text her when I left the station, and I planned to walk over and meet her outside of her building. The day had been as hot as every other for the last two weeks, and I lost count of the times I felt myself sweating through my shirt. For the last two hours I'd been at my desk in the air-conditioning. When I smelled my armpits, the body odor had faded into a stale trace smell of perspiration and deodorant. I didn't have time for a shower, so I went into the men's room and tried to clean my underarms with paper towels and hand soap. Fortunately, I kept a spare deodorant in my desk. I put too much on and then washed my face and looked at myself in the mirror. There were bags under my eyes and I needed a shave and a haircut.

Great.

It was still over ninety at a quarter to seven when I walked out onto Broadway toward Julia's apartment. Fifty feet later, I took off my tie, folded it, and put it in the side pocket of my suit jacket. My Glock was in its shoulder holster under the coat, so I couldn't go much further in removing layers. Opening the collar button of my white dress shirt was all the relief I was going to get. If I hadn't already texted her, I would have gone back to the locker room and changed into jeans and a T-shirt.

Julia was waiting on the corner of Broadway and the Promenade. I spotted her a block away, and I'm reasonably sure that she saw me but pretended not to until I was only about ten yards down the street. Then she looked at me and smiled.

The day had been easier on her. She was wearing a pair of jeans under a white cotton blouse and a pale-blue tank top. Her hair was pulled back, and I was guessing that it had taken her a while to look like she had no makeup on at all.

As I got closer, I saw a hint of happiness in her eyes that made me nervous.

"Hi," I said. "How are you?"

"Good." She raised her eyebrows. "What about you? Long day?"

"Is it that obvious?"

"No, I didn't mean that. Just that it's almost seven. What time did you get to work this morning?"

"I'm not sure." I didn't want to tell her that it was still dark when I had first sat down at my desk, so I changed the subject. "Where were you thinking of going? There's Starbucks right around the corner."

"How about the GreenHouse? It's just a few blocks down the street. I thought we might walk."

"Oh, okay."

"It's a bit warm," she said. "You don't need to keep your jacket on, not on my account."

"Well, uh . . ." I lifted my lapel just enough to show her the Glock hanging in its holster.

"Oh," she said with a little laugh. "I didn't think of that."

For a moment, the awkwardness was more uncomfortable than the heat. "The GreenHouse? That's the place that used to be Sipology, right?"

"Yes. It's a lot better now."

"Oh, okay. Good." I didn't feel like walking that far, but she seemed enthusiastic about it, so I went along. As we walked, I asked how the preparations for her show were going, and she humored me by going into detail about all the arrangements that had to be made with the studio to get everything set up properly and how tough it was to get the word out.

"It's a good city for art, though, isn't it?" I didn't really know anything about the art scene other than that small galleries were always springing up downtown and around the East Village. There was even an organization that put on shows in vacant storefronts. And there had been a lot of those since the recession bottomed out a few years earlier. The businesses were coming back slowly, but it seemed like there was always another show popping up somewhere.

"It is," she said. "Sometimes a little too good. Most weekends have more than one opening, so the core group of art aficionados gets split up."

"Wow."

"What?"

"You just used 'aficionados' unironically in a sentence."

She smiled at me. I think I smiled back.

• • •

"It hurts all the time?" she asked.

We were sitting at a table on the second floor by the window looking out over Linden Avenue. I had just finished a chicken panini and was working on an iced mocha. She'd ordered a salad that she hardly touched because, I suspected, she'd already eaten and was too thoughtful to admit it and let me eat alone.

"Yes," I said. "It's always there. Sometimes it's worse and sometimes it's better, but it never really goes away completely. You get used to it. Learn to manage it, ignore it."

"I'm sorry," she said. "It must be awful."

It was. "You deal with it. I see people every day who deal with harder things." I wondered if she knew about Megan. Had I mentioned that to her? No, I hadn't. At what point in the date do you tell the woman you're with about your dead wife? I hadn't thought twice about revealing it to a rookie at a murder scene. But I wanted something then—I wanted Lauren to trust me and to open up. She did. What did I want from Julia?

"I know." I thought she was referring to Megan. But then I remembered my last statement. Of course she knew about people dealing with difficulties. Maybe even more than me. As a homicide detective, I studied the wreckage of human misfortune. Social workers actually have to put it back together.

She took a sip of her green tea, put her cup down, and wiped a finger at the corner of her mouth. I thought about asking her something about her time on the job, but decided against it. Looking at her, I knew we shared an understanding, not unlike the unspoken shared knowledge that many cops have with one another, that there's a darkness in the world, and that sometimes we know that our only real purpose is just to bear witness to it so that no one else has to.

I thought I understood something about her in that moment, something about her art. Raising awareness wasn't the point, as the food-bank administrator had suggested. The point, I thought, was to make people really see the things those of us who gaze into the abyss always try to shield them from. At least that's what I wanted to think.

"Tell me about your art," I said.

• • •

The conversation fell into an easy rhythm. We talked about our jobs, about movies, about music, about a bunch of things. I'm never entirely comfortable in a conversation with someone I don't know well unless it's an interview or an interrogation. In a social situation that requires me to talk to normal people, I'm always hyperconscious of my exchanges. So I fought the urge to analyze each statement either of us made, to try to figure out the angles, to determine who wanted what. And surprisingly, little by little, my self-awareness began to fade and I found myself relaxing and maybe even enjoying the conversation.

And then Julia asked me if I'd ever been married. It was a fair question—she'd worked her divorce into the conversation so smoothly I'd barely even noticed it.

"I was," I said. "She died in a car accident a few years ago."

"I'm sorry," she said.

"It's okay." Immediately I regretted my choice of words. "I don't mean that it's okay that she died like that, just that—"

"I know what you meant." She reached out across the small table and touched my hand.

Something in my stomach tightened with the contact, and I hoped she hadn't noticed. Did she think I flinched?

I said, "There hasn't been anyone serious since then." The self-consciousness was growing. How would she interpret that statement? Would she think I was difficult? Withdrawn? That I couldn't let go of the past? Once that last thought reared its evil little head, it was all I could think of. It was a good question. Could I let go of the past? I didn't know.

At that point, one of the baristas came upstairs and told us they'd be closing soon. "But you don't need to rush."

Julia smiled at her and said, "We won't be long."

I wondered what she meant. Had she noticed me clenching up and getting uncomfortable? Probably. She'd been a social worker for years. She was likely as comfortable in this context as I was in an interrogation. Surely she could read me as well as I could read a suspect. That must have been what she meant by *We won't be long.* She was done.

Honestly, I thought, that was kind of a relief. Of course I was attracted to her. But it wasn't supposed to be so hard. Was it?

Julia finished her tea and excused herself to go to the bathroom. I watched her walk away and then took out my phone to check for messages. There was a text from Jen that consisted of only a solitary question mark. I sent one back: *???*

"Ready?" Julia said, returning to the table.

I slipped my phone back in my jacket pocket and got up.

Outside, it had cooled off a bit, but it was still warm enough that I wondered if I would start sweating again, and of course as soon as I thought that, I felt the first drop of sweat lingering in my hairline above my forehead.

It was a quarter past ten, and the traffic both on the street and on the sidewalk had thinned out considerably from the steady flow that had crowded the street on our way there.

Had it really been three hours? I was struck by the amount of time that had passed. It seemed to me that I'd been uncomfortable most of the evening. But had I? Was it just my own self-involvement that made me feel that way?

At the intersection of Broadway and Long Beach Boulevard, the little white silhouette was still telling us it was safe to cross, and I stepped down off the curb. Julia took my hand and said, "It's going to change."

She was right. It did.

• • •

"A little more?" Julia held up the bottle of wine. We were sitting on her couch, illuminated more by the city lights shining in the large window than by the single bulb of the lamp lit in the corner.

"Sure," I said, still surprised to be inside with her. Riding up in the elevator and walking down the hallway toward her door and watching her feel her way to the keys in the bottom of her purse, I'd been rehearsing a goodnight in my head.

She never gave me a chance to use it.

There was no pause in her actions, no lull in the words, no window of opportunity. She took it for granted that I would come inside, and because of that, I did. "Sit down," she'd said, looking at the couch. As I did, she found a bottle of red in the kitchen and brought it and two glasses with her and sat next to me on the couch. "I'm sorry." She put her hand on my knee and I felt all of my anxiety coalesce deep in my gut. "I should have asked if you wanted something to drink."

"Sure." I tried to remember the last time I'd been less sure of anything than I was at that moment.

She said something and I said something back.

My arm was on the back of the couch behind her shoulders.

She touched my leg and said something else.

I think I answered her.

She looked in my eyes and then leaned in and kissed me. She pulled back just enough to look at me again. I don't have any idea what she saw, but the corner of her mouth turned up and the outside edges of her eyes wrinkled and she kissed me again and didn't stop.

I groped clumsily for her breast while she slid her hand along the inside of my thigh. Before it got where it was going, everything let go.

She realized what had happened as soon as I did, and without even pausing to glance at the expression of slack-jawed embarrassment on my face, she pulled my head into her shoulder, held me, and whispered in my ear, "It's okay," her voice warm and tender.

If I could have, I would have hid my face in the crook of her neck for the next few hours, waited for her to fall asleep, and tried to sneak out. That wasn't much of a plan, though.

I lifted my head, looked at her, and saw nothing but pleasant contentment and compassion in her eyes.

"Could you excuse me for a second?"

I fumbled my way into her bathroom, turned on the light, closed the door, and stared at the dark, wet spot in the crotch of my pants, wishing I'd worn my black suit.

After cleaning myself up the best I could, I sat on the toilet and tried to think of something to say to Julia. I thought about calling Jen and asking for advice. I thought about faking a murder callout from the watch commander. I thought about drowning myself in the bathtub. The process of elimination must have taken longer than I realized, because she surprised me by tapping gently on the door and saying, "You okay?"

"Yes," I answered too quickly. "I'll be right out."

I stood up, looked at my withered face in the mirror, ran a hand through my hair trying to make it look a little bit less stupid, and decided what to do. We were both grown-ups. She was a generous and kind woman. We would sit back down on the couch and talk. We would finish our wine and before long we'd be comfortable and laughing and enjoying ourselves. It wouldn't be awkward or embarrassing at all. It wouldn't.

She was still standing by the couch, waiting for me to join her, with what might have been the kindest expression I'd ever seen and her hand held out for me.

All I had to do was cross the room and take her hand.

"I should probably go," I said.

"No, you shouldn't."

When I didn't answer, she came to me.

"I had a nice time tonight," I said.

Her eyes locked on mine, and in the second before I looked away, I thought I saw her make the decision not to try to change my mind.

"So did I." She smiled and seemed resigned to my need to say goodnight. "I really hope we can do this again." She put her hands on my arms and kissed me and I tried to kiss her back.

"You're shaking," she said.

"It was a little cold in the bathroom."

As I went out the door, she caught my hand in hers and I looked back. Her eyes were green with little golden-brown flecks.

Maybe I shouldn't have let go.

In the car on the way home, the midnight British people on KPCC were talking to the tallest man in the world. He was getting married.

20

FLEECE KNIT CAP: NO LABEL OR LOGO, DARK GREEN.

"Did you ask him about the prepaid cell number?" I said. Patrick and Marty were filling me in on Medina's interrogation. A dangerous-warrant team had picked him up at his home address while I'd been out with Julia the night before.

"No," Patrick said. "He was stonewalling on everything. I figured why risk it. If we tipped him off that we knew the number, he'd get word out."

"Good thinking," I said. "Maybe we can keep the number in play. He give up anything?"

"No," Marty said. "He lawyered up."

I thought about that. "Who's schooling these guys?" Anybody who's ever seen a cop show knows the smart thing to do when you're arrested on a murder charge is to invoke your right to counsel. It's surprising, though, the number of suspects who don't. They think they're smarter than we are, or that asking for an attorney will make them look guilty, or that we can't possibly know what we know. We question a lot of innocent people, but we don't arrest too many. If we bring someone in on a murder beef, we've got cause. Most suspects, guilty or innocent, talk to us. But first Omar and now Medina had lawyers, and even Francisco and Pedro had kept their mouths closed. Whoever was pulling their strings was smart enough to plan ahead and to make sure his button men were more afraid of him than they were of us.

"I don't know," Marty said.

Patrick looked at me. "You think it could be Benny War?"

"The only connections so far are his family link to Omar and the fact that Siguenza is his golfing buddy."

"Who's that?" Marty asked.

"That's the guy representing the kids who killed Bishop."

"Send me everything you have on Benny," Patrick said to me.

"What do you mean 'everything'?"

"Contact info, phone numbers, addresses, interview reports, everything."

"Think you can link him to the mystery phone?" I asked.

"I've got all the metadata, calls, texts, locations, all of it. If we can put the phone in the same place as Benny, even once, we've got something."

"Watch your step," Marty said. "You could be getting into dicey territory with privileged attorney-client communications."

"As long as we start with the mystery number and trace direct connections from it to other numbers, we're good," Patrick said. "The warrant clears us for that."

"But isn't it a problem to start with Benny's number and check it against the phone records?"

"It all depends on how I set up the search. If I only search for the mystery number and not Benny's, we should be okay. Same justification the NSA spies on us. Not allowed to look directly, but if they make a connection from a valid source, then it's fair game."

"Really?" Marty said. "You sure about that?"

"This week," Patrick said, "I'm sure. Who knows what will be legal next week?"

He was right. The laws regarding access to digital information were changing every week. The NSA scandal hadn't helped us any either. We had to watch our steps more carefully than ever. Metadata was big news, and that meant that every defense attorney and suspect who'd ever logged on to CNET was taking a shot at a Fourth-Amendment defense.

• • •

When we had the squad room to ourselves, Jen turned to me and said, "So how did it go?"

For a second I thought she was referring to something work related. "How'd what go?"

"Come on," she said. "Don't give me that."

By that time I had figured out what she was asking about. "It was okay," I said. "We just went for coffee. In the East Village."

She waited for me to go on, and when I didn't, she said, "Tell me about it."

"We just talked, got to know each other a little bit."

There was another pause. I wondered if she felt awkward too, or if she was just aware of my discomfort and intentionally drawing out the silences. Probably the latter.

"Do you like her?"

"What? Are we in high school?"

"I'm not. You? Who knows?"

I thought about the way the date ended, and a sudden flush of embarrassment came over me.

Jen saw it. "Uh oh. What?"

"Nothing," I said, too quickly. "We had a nice time."

She studied me. It didn't take her long to figure out something had gone badly and left me flustered and too uncomfortable to talk about it. I knew she'd narrow it down to a few likely possibilities, each as disconcerting as the others.

Her tone softened. "You going to see her again?"

"I don't know." Honestly, I'd been so busy all day that I hadn't thought much about it. Would I see her again? Would she even want to see me? The questions bouncing around in my head made my stomach churn.

• • •

That afternoon, Jesús texted me.

im worried

What's wrong?

theres a guy at jackntehbox. think hes watching me

Are you by yourself?

yea

Are there other people there?

yea

Stay there. Is he staring at you?

no. looked a couple times. i could see his reflection in the window.

Does he know you know he's watching you?

i dont think so.

Good. Keep looking at your phone. Can you describe him without looking at him again?

yea. big, realy big. old. mexican i think

Does he have a mustache? Hair?

no mustache just fuzz on top

Anything else?

got a tatoo on neck

Mother fucker. Jesús was looking at the man who killed his father. He'd obviously shaved and started letting his hair grow back. Ruiz's office door was closed. I didn't bother knocking. He looked up and scowled at me, but his expression changed as soon as he saw mine.

"Solano's killer is tailing Jesús."

"In Oceanside?"

"Yeah. They're both sitting in a Jack in the Box right now."

"Got an address?"

Where are you? Address or cross streets?

vista by town sight

Town Sight's a street?

yea

I told Ruiz and he picked up his phone and dialed. He identified himself and told the operator it was an emergency. He was being transferred to the watch commander when I got back to Jesús.

Stay where you are and just keep staring at your phone, okay? Somebody's going to be there soon to help you out.

ok

Don't worry. It might not be anything at all. And nothing will happen as long as you're with other people. It's going to be okay.

im scared

Don't be. I'm here and help is on the way. Have you ever seen this guy before?

i dont think so is he somebody you know

I doubt it. You eating?

i was. not hungry now

You get tacos? I love their tacos.

those arent tacos!!!

Maybe not, but they're really good.

you never had a real taco?

Where do you get real tacos?

all over its long beach

When you get back, you show me, ok? I'll buy us both tacos.

hes getting up

Dont look at him

watching reflection threw his trash away going out

Just let him go.

got in a white mustang

Can you see the license plate?

6fgr274

I told Ruiz the make and tag number. He relayed it to the watch commander in Oceanside.

That's good. Is he gone?

yea

I went to my recent calls and tapped Jesús's name on the screen. He picked up before I even heard the ring. "You okay?" I asked.

"Yeah," he said. "I think I overreacted. He just got up and left. Maybe he wasn't really watching me."

"Probably not," I said, wondering how much I should tell him. "He was probably just some guy. But it's good you texted me."

"Are you sure?" he asked.

"Definitely."

Ruiz was watching. I nodded and gave him a thumbs-up sign.

"There's a cop car in front," Jesús said.

"Go meet them, but don't hang up."

"Okay."

There was a rustling static on the other end of the line, and then a woman's voice. "Who is this?" she asked.

"Detective Danny Beckett, Long Beach PD." I gave her a brief rundown of the situation. "My lieutenant's talking to your sergeant now. They're going to be looking for the suspect, but could you stay with Jesús?"

"Of course," she said. I thought I could hear a bit of disappointment in her voice. There was a murderer in the vicinity and she had to babysit.

"Maybe take him back to his aunt's house?"

"Let me just clear it with my supervisor."

She gave the phone back to Jesús.

"She okay?" I asked him.

"Yeah," he said. Then he lowered his voice to a whisper. "But I think I like Detective Tanaka better."

I laughed. "We all do," I said.

• • •

The Oceanside PD issued a BOLO and had four cars in the area searching for the Mustang. Within fifteen minutes they found it abandoned in a neighborhood a little under a mile away from the Jack in the Box where Jesús saw the man who'd killed his father. It took another half hour for them to determine the car had been stolen from the lot of an industrial park two hours before Jesús texted me. The neck tattoo didn't leave prints or any other evidence behind.

"Can we get protection for him now?" I asked Ruiz.

"I'll see what I can do."

Jen, Patrick, and Marty were all back in the squad room by then. After I brought them up to speed, Jen asked, "What now?"

"The lieutenant's going to move him," I said.

"Where to?"

"Don't know yet."

"They must have found him through the aunt," Marty said.

"Yeah," I said. "How else could they have?"

Patrick said, "You kept his phone, right?"

I nodded.

"He have any other electronics?"

"No, and he stayed offline, too."

"He told you that?"

"Yes."

"And you trust him?"

"Yeah," I said. "I do."

Patrick thought for a few seconds. "We thought he might have found Jesús's father by tracking his calls. But there was no way he could have tracked him to Oceanside, because you gave him the burner."

I nodded again.

"So was it just a coincidence that he killed Solano on the same day his son called him for the first time in years?"

"What are you thinking?"

21

COLEMAN SLEEPING BAG: LIGHTWEIGHT, LIME GREEN W/ BEIGE INTERIOR, WELL USED, ZIPPER BROKEN.

Felicia Solano might have been a drunk, but at some point, it looked like she had also been a good Catholic. Along the wall opposite the front door of the small house on Ohio was a pristine white side table with curved legs and scallops carved into the edges under the single wide drawer. There was a lace table-topper on which sat a foot-tall porcelain statue of the Virgin Mary. Directly above the statue, an ornate wooden crucifix with an authentically painted Christ figure was nailed in place. Surrounding him were four small oil paintings of figures I couldn't identify but took for saints.

One of the bullets that had penetrated the front wall had lodged in the plaster near the ceiling, a good four feet away from the crucifix. I tried to impart some significance to that distance. Was it a near miss or a wide one?

I'd been inside waiting for nearly three hours as the sun went down and darkness filled the small house. And I was beginning to think Patrick's idea, a long shot to begin with, was not going to pay off.

If Neck Tattoo had used Jesús's phone to find Roberto Solano, then it was likely he'd still be tracking the activity.

We went to see Jesús's friend David and his mother. With generous bribes—a smartphone for David and the security of a new number for his mother—we were able to convince them to part with his old cell. We took David's phone and Jesús's, which was still in my desk, and a new prepaid phone, and set up a series of text messages that told whoever might be monitoring the activity that Jesús and his family would be moving to a new location but that they'd be stopping by the house to pick up fresh clothing and a few other necessities.

"Why do we need both his old cell and a new burner? I'm not sure I follow," Marty had said.

Patrick explained it as if he were talking to elementary-school students. And of course I'd never admit it to anyone, but I was glad because I didn't get it either. "If someone was following the activity on Jesús's old phone, they'd see that nothing has happened recently."

Marty nodded and I tried not to.

"But our guy saw him on the phone in Oceanside, so he'll know he has another phone."

It finally clicked into place. Patrick sent a message to David's phone from the new burner saying that Jesús and his family would be coming home to pick things up. But he didn't reply from David's phone. He took Jesús's old phone and sent another text. This one said: *im not supposed to use this phone but i don't think you read the text from my new one.* Then he repeated the information from the first text and replied from David's phone.

If anyone was paying attention, they'd think the Solanos would be visiting Ohio Street sometime that night.

"Anything going on out there?" I said into the radio.

Patrick's voice came back. "Nothing." He was on one of the balconies of the apartment building next door. From his vantage point, he could see the driveway, the small house, and most of the backyard. We had an undercover surveillance team on the streets around the house watching for any sign of someone checking out the house.

We'd given them plenty of time to make a move. Or get set up for one.

"Should we send them in?" Patrick asked.

"Yeah," I said. "Let's do it."

Our first hope was that someone would try to get inside to set up an ambush. At this point, that seemed unlikely.

I peeked through the mini-blinds on the front window and watched Felicia Solano's old Hyundai pull up the narrow driveway. The porch light was off and only ambient light filtered down toward the front porch. When Lauren Terrones got out, dressed in sweats and a zip-up hoodie, I could almost believe she was Jesús's mother. Jen, though, in her cap and khaki pants, was much less convincing as a teenage boy.

If anything was going to go down, now would be the time. "Patrick?" I whispered into the mic.

"All clear," he said.

They came up onto the porch, and Lauren slid a key into the deadbolt. Once they got inside, they closed the door behind themselves and turned on the lights. Then Jen went into the back bedroom and loaded up reusable shopping bags with clothes for Jesús and Maria. Lauren went into the front bedroom and did the same.

I watched them, my Glock in my hand pointed at the floor, my ears focused and listening for any unusual sounds outside.

"No movement," Patrick said. "Everything looks clear. Marty?"

"All clear."

Patrick checked in with the rest of the team. Clear all around.

There was one more possibility. When Jen and Lauren loaded up the Hyundai, they'd drive to a predetermined rendezvous point near the LBPD North Patrol Division station. The surveillance team would follow them in three cars. The drive would give them plenty of time to determine if anyone else might be following them.

The headlights of their car shone on the blinds in the front window, illuminating the living room. The glow faded as they backed slowly out of the driveway.

"They're off," Patrick told me. "I'll come down, meet you outside."

We sat on the porch of the Solanos' bungalow and listened to the report from Jen and the team. It took them twenty-six minutes to make it to where they were going. They weren't followed.

"Sorry," I said to him. "Thought we had a chance with this one."

"Me too." We were quiet for a few moments. "I still don't believe that Jesús's father just happened to get killed on the same day he called."

I didn't either. Detectives don't like coincidence. We spend all of our time looking for connections, chains of cause and effect, one thing leading to another. We counted on those connections, and we couldn't do anything without them. Coincidence, though, shits on all of that. When we start accepting coincidence, we stop making cases.

22

T-SHIRTS, SEVEN: ASSORTED BRANDS, COLORS, AND STYLES.

We'd had close to a hundred calls and e-mails since we'd put out the press release with Bishop's photo. Almost all of them were dead ends. A few were legit, people who knew Bishop in passing or had seen him on the street or at one of the shelters. None of them, though, gave us any information more substantial than we already had. After Henry Nichols and Mr. Lee, the best lead we found came not from the media outreach but from pounding the pavement.

Her name was Mary, and like most of the people we'd talked to about Bishop, she'd been homeless for quite some time. She'd been in and out of shelters and transitional housing for almost a decade. Most recently, though, she'd been on the street. Lauren and Stan found her through the Centro Shalom food bank. It was luck, mostly. On their most recent swing by the location to check on the copies of the photos they'd distributed, one of the volunteers mentioned that he had seen Mary earlier and that she had commented on the photo of Bishop. They canvassed the area and found her a few blocks away at a picnic table under a large shade tree in Martin Luther King Jr. Park. She didn't want to come to the station, so I took an unmarked cruiser and met Stan and Lauren there.

The park was fairly large, with a community center and soccer and softball fields. Their unit was in the parking lot about twenty-five yards from where Mary sat. They saw me pull up and park next to their car. Lauren left Stan with the woman and came to meet me. While she was walking toward me, I took several bills out of my wallet and slipped them into my shirt pocket.

"She have something good?" I asked.

"I don't know about evidentiary value, but Stan and I thought you'd want to hear it from her."

That made me curious. So we walked past the bronze statue of MLK and a playground with new multicolored plastic equipment on a gray rubberized ground cover and approached them.

"Mary," Stan said. "This is the detective I told you about. His name is Danny Beckett."

She looked up at me, and the creases spiderwebbing her brown face deepened as she squinted. Even though we were in the shade, she lifted a dirty hand to her brow to shade her eyes.

"Mary has some vision problems," Lauren said.

"I haven't been able to get my glasses fixed," she said. It looked like she was missing all the teeth from the incisors back on the left side.

"Well," I said. "We might be able to help you with that. May I sit down?"

She was facing outward with her back against the edge of the table. She twisted around and hefted a tote bag overflowing with soiled clothing items off of the bench and up onto the table to make room for me. "Please." She smiled politely at me and gestured to the empty space next to her. "Make yourself comfortable."

"Thank you. My friends say you knew a man named Bishop."

"Yes," she said, her gaze drifting toward the playground. "I did. So sad to hear the bad news."

"Me too," I said. "What can you tell me about him?"

• • •

She liked to keep to herself. Tried not to go to the mission unless she had to. Didn't like the way they were always preaching at her. But it was the Fourth of July. She hated the Fourth of July. The sounds of all those fireworks going off, all those little explosions. It reminded her of being a girl in El Salvador and how scared she was when the soldiers came.

Last July she was able to get a bed, and she hoped she'd be able to get one this year too. They gave you seven days. She could get cleaned up and get a few good nights' sleep. It would be good. It had been a long time.

She got there early on the third, before breakfast, hoping that she'd be able to get in ahead of everybody who'd be looking for a place. That one with the beard, the young one, said he'd see what he could do. What was his name? Mike? Matt? Something with an *M*.

After the runny oatmeal, she got cleaned up as much as she could and went back to see Mark.

"I'm sorry, Mary," he said. "I managed to get you up to number eight on the waiting list, so there's a chance, but not a very good one."

Mary nodded. "Thanks," she said.

"You can wait and see, or come back at dinner."

"Okay."

"It's the holiday. We always have more people wanting to be inside."

"I know. Don't like to be out there with all the bombs exploding."

He took his glasses off. Rubbed the bridge of his nose.

"If we can't get you in here, Saint Andrew's is having a dinner and keeping their multipurpose room open late, so you won't have to be outside."

She went back in the late afternoon and found out that she didn't make it to the top of the list, so on the afternoon of the fourth, she made her way to the church and pushed her folding cart across the parking lot and found a place near the door. There was already a line, but it wasn't too long yet. Six people ahead of her, waiting along the wall next to the double doors that led into the church's auxiliary room. They did meals most holidays. Not bad.

Mary was surprised that there weren't more people. She didn't know anybody ahead of her. None of them had a wagon or a cart. Maybe they were staying in cars. Maybe they had places and just couldn't afford food. A woman was reading a book while a little girl sat next to her and played with some kind of a Barbie doll. Some stupid thing with blonde hair that didn't look a thing like the child's long black ponytail. The two of them didn't look street, but they did look hungry. She watched the little girl for a long time and tried not to remember the things that were trying to get into her head.

By the time they opened the doors, there were several dozen people in line. Not as many as Mary expected, but more and more families came. She never used to see so many families. The great recession was what did it. There were some familiar faces. Nobody she'd say anything to, but she nodded at people more than a few times.

Toward the end of the line, she saw Bishop. If he'd been closer, she would have talked to him. Not much, just a "Hi, how are you" or something. He'd given her a whole Subway sandwich once. Turkey and ham and everything. It was on the wheat bread, but she didn't complain about that. Honestly, it was so good she hardly noticed. She'd heard a few other people say things about him. About things like that sandwich. People don't talk like that about other people very much. It's always *Stay away from him* and

Watch out for that one. She made up her mind to say hello to him if she had the chance.

They had hot dogs and burgers and potato salad and baked beans. It was good. She had seconds on the beans and potato salad because they didn't get as many people as they'd expected, and that stuff was easy to chew on the right side of her mouth where she still had a few good teeth.

By the time everyone finished eating, even after the vanilla ice cream they had for dessert, it was getting dark. Firecrackers and bottle rockets and all sorts of other things had been going off sporadically for a few hours. But the frequency was increasing. So was the intensity. Everything was getting louder. Closer. She saw the first flash of light in the windows high up on the wall.

She took her cart and moved across the room into the corner farthest from the door, the wall that backed up against the church itself. She wanted to get as far away from it as she could. She pulled one of the folding chairs away from the table and backed it up against the floor-to-ceiling cupboards. She had put as much distance as she could between herself and the noise and commotion outside. It wasn't enough.

She started digging through her cart, looking for her cube. Sometimes it made her feel better. Spinning the colored squares around. She knew the point was to make each side the same color, to make all those little squares match, but she never really bothered with that. She just liked to twist it around and watch it change. But she couldn't find it. She dug deeper and deeper and tried not to notice the sounds.

That's why she didn't hear him at first. She knew from the way he said her name that he was repeating it. He said it again and she finally looked up.

"Hi, Mary." Bishop looked so tall to her. Was he tall? She tried to remember. Maybe it was just because she was sitting down. "Can I join you?" he said.

She nodded, and he went to the closest table and got a chair for himself.

"How you doing?"

"Okay," she said, knowing he could see the lie.

"You thirsty? They've got some soda pop and some punch."

She didn't say anything.

"I checked it." He grinned at her. "It's just plain punch."

She smiled back. To be polite. Kept her mouth closed so he wouldn't see how many teeth were missing.

He sat there with her. She wasn't quite as scared.

"The sound's the worst part?"

She nodded.

He looked at her for a minute, like he was thinking about something, trying to make a decision.

"Wait right here, okay?" he said. "I'll be right back."

She didn't want him to go.

"Really," he said. "Right back."

As she watched him walk out the door, the flashes in the windows got brighter and the explosions got louder. She looked down at her feet, closed her eyes, and put her hands over her ears.

The touch on her arm startled her. She opened her eyes and looked up. It was Bishop. He was standing in front of her, doing some kind of little dance, shuffling his feet and swaying back and forth. It took her a few seconds to notice the headphones he was wearing. They were the old kind, not those ones the kids use now that stick right in their ears. These ones had the foam earpieces and the wire that goes over your head.

Bishop grinned at her again and motioned for her to stand up.

She didn't want to, so he took her hand and pulled gently. When she stood, he removed the headphones from his own ears and put them on her. She recognized the song immediately. "Moon River" from that old Audrey Hepburn movie. Mary couldn't remember when or where she'd first heard the song, but she knew it.

Bishop took the old Discman out of his vest pocket and put it in her hands. She held it in front of herself, and he took her elbows and swayed back and forth with her. It was almost like they were dancing.

When the song ended, he showed her how to work the controls and told her she could hang onto it until he saw her again.

"You sure?" she said, surprised.

He nodded. "I hardly ever use it anyway."

They sat back down and she listened to the song. She didn't forget about what was going on outside, but for a while, at least, it wasn't quite as frightening as it had been.

She closed her eyes for a few minutes. Did she fall asleep? She must have, because Bishop was gone.

She found one of the volunteers and said, "Have you seen Bishop?"

"I'm sorry," the young woman said. "I don't know anyone by that name."

• • •

She turned on the park bench next to me and looked through the aged tote bag she had put on the table. "I never got to give it back to him," she said, holding it up for us to see.

"You shouldn't worry about that," I said. "He would have wanted you to have it."

"I used up the batteries," she said.

"Here," I said, handing her the four twenties that I had folded into my shirt pocket. "Get some more."

"You're a kind man," she said to me. "Like he was. Gave me a whole Subway sandwich once."

• • •

When we'd left Mary on her bench and walked back to the cars, Stan said, "I didn't know if we should call you. The rookie insisted."

I looked at Lauren. "You did?"

She nodded and looked back at me. I tried to read her expression. She had gotten pretty good at deploying her inscrutable cop face, but I thought I saw a glimmer of pride and confidence there.

"Good work."

She let go of the neutral expression, and the left side of her lip curled up. I wouldn't have seen it if I hadn't been watching for it.

"Don't get cocky," Stan said. "Get in the car."

"How's she doing?" I asked.

"Best rookie I've trained in five years."

"She's the only rookie you've trained in five years."

"Good point," he said.

I sat in the car for a few minutes after they drove away. Lauren had good instincts. She knew I'd want to hear Mary's story. Even though it wouldn't help us crack the case, it told us something about Bishop, it humanized him. Most uniforms would have just taken a statement and forwarded that to me, letting me decide if I wanted to take it further. I tried to remember the conversation we'd had at Jen's house. How much had I talked about Bishop? She was perceptive. I was starting to think she might make a good cop.

23

ENERGIZER LED FLASHLIGHT (NO BATTERIES).

Patrick was hunched over his desk and swiveling his head back and forth between his desktop computer and the open MacBook next to it. We'd been talking about the night before and his decoy plan. I'd thought it was a shot in the dark, but I tried to keep my doubts to myself. As we spoke, his attention, as usual, was divided between our conversation and the two screens in front of him. He was big on multitasking. Slowly his focus drifted and the conversation dwindled down to noncommittal "yeahs" and "uh-huhs," and then I let it fade away completely as he was pulled deeper into whatever he was working on at the moment.

Marty came in, looked at Patrick, and didn't say anything. He turned to me and grinned. "I try not to bother him when he's curating evidence."

"I'm not a hipster," Patrick muttered without looking away from his screens.

Marty and I laughed. Some days the most fun we had was goading Patrick into uttering that line.

When Jen returned from her meeting with the ADA, I told her about Bishop and Mary.

"You get anything solid?" she asked.

"Background. A better sense of who Bishop was. I'm putting together his story."

"Does that mean 'no'?"

Patrick leaned back in his chair and crossed his arms over his chest, sitting still, as if he was trying to get a better perspective on all the information in front of him.

"What did you find?" I asked him.

"Last night wasn't a bust."

"It wasn't?" Jen said, rolling her chair toward his desk. Marty and I did the same.

"No," Patrick said. "We got made, but the mystery phone made a call from a block away two minutes after Jen and Lauren left in the decoy."

"He was there," I said.

Patrick nodded. "But that's not the best part."

"What is?" Marty asked.

"The call he made."

"Who did he call?" I asked.

"I'm not sure. The number is for another burner."

"Then how does that help us?"

"Whoever answered it was in Hector Siguenza's house."

"Really?" I said, surprised that we finally had a viable link to the shot-caller and that it might not be Benny War.

"Siguenza is the original three kids' attorney, right?" Marty asked.

"Yes, but it gets better," Patrick said. "The number from Siguenza's house is the same number the mystery phone called from Riverside before Jesús's father was killed."

• • •

Later that day, we had another surprise. Omar's DNA had been collected when he'd been processed into the system. It was standard procedure to see if arrestees might be involved in other open cases with unidentified DNA evidence. The results showed a familial match. Omar wasn't Benny War's nephew. He was his son.

I'd already planned to have a talk with Benny. The new information just gave me one more reason.

24

SCARF: GRAY/BLUE STRIPED ACRYLIC FABRIC, FRINGE MISSING ON ONE END.

In the parking garage under Benny War's office building downtown, I slipped the attendant fifty dollars to let me back into a space close to the "Monthly Only" exit used by the building's tenants.

Earlier, I had checked out Benicio Guerra's house so I could anticipate the route he might take when he left work. He had a five-million-dollar home on Naples Island that overlooked Alamitos Bay. Its private dock was big enough for a sixty-foot yacht, but the sport fishing boat moored there only measured thirty-seven. Maybe you really can't have it all.

The *Which Way, LA?* evening rebroadcast on KCRW was half-over when I spotted Benny's deep-blue Jaguar XJ drive past me. Following him out of the garage and around the corner onto Ocean, I hoped he'd stop somewhere on his way home.

As we headed east, the last purple glow of the setting sun behind us, I thought again about the DNA results. Somebody involved in this mess had a secret big enough to kill to protect, and I was betting it was Benny. Could the fact that Omar was really his son be it? If so, how could Bishop have found out? How could the three killers have learned about it? Why would he suspect Jesús might know as well? I wondered what the ramifications for Benny might be. Most families wouldn't kill people over something like that, but the Guerras weren't like most families. Benny's brother, Oscar, ran the Mexican Mafia in one of California's biggest prisons. He carried serious weight. What would he do to Benny if he found out he was Omar's father? Murder was nothing to him. I couldn't imagine a week went by in which Oscar Guerra didn't give an order to kill someone. Shit, for all I knew it wasn't even a secret at all.

Benny veered left onto Livingston and then onto Second Street. I kept following him, wondering if he'd stop somewhere along the way. Maybe grab some dinner or a drink. He didn't. His Jag continued all the way over the bridge onto Naples Island. I waited for him to turn, but he didn't. He passed the Toledo, Ravenna Drive, and even Naples Plaza. So he wasn't going home. He crossed the second bridge at the end of the island and finally turned on Marina. Was he going to one of the restaurants on the east side of the bay?

No. He took a left into the Whole Foods Market parking lot. Grocery shopping. I thought of Bishop's shopping cart all the way on the other side of town.

He parked the Jag, and I considered following him inside. I hadn't been very careful tailing him. There'd never been more than one car between us, and a few times I'd been right on his bumper. I wasn't concerned that he'd make me. Only that I'd be able to find a place to talk to him alone.

When he came out, cradling his paper grocery bag to his chest with one arm instead of using the handles, he found me leaning against his driver's side door.

"Detective Beckett," he said with the expression of a constipated man working too hard on a toilet. "What a pleasant surprise."

"Hey, Benny."

"What can I do for you?"

"I just wanted to say hi."

"Hi," he said.

When I didn't say anything, he put the bag down on the trunk of his car, adjusted it carefully, and watched to make sure it wouldn't slide off. "And?"

"Stay away from Jesús."

"What?"

"Jesús Solano. Hands off."

"I don't have any idea what you're talking about."

"Bullshit."

"Okay then. I'll stay away. Anything else, or can I go now?"

"I'm not sure you're being sincere."

"Oh, for fuck's sake. Can you just get to the point?"

"He wasn't involved. He doesn't know anything."

"All right." He was starting to lose his patience.

So I kept pushing. "Keep your goon away from him."

The teardrop scar under his eye twitched. "Or what?"

He didn't realize he'd just crossed the line. "Or everybody's going to know your son's looking at death row."

Anger flashed in his eyes and, just as quickly, disappeared. "So you know about that?" He shrugged, but it wasn't as casual as he wanted me to believe. "It was only a matter of time before the DNA came back."

"How's your brother going to take the news?"

"Like he handles everything else. Exactly the way I tell him to." I could see the tension in his jaw. It wasn't as much as I had hoped for, but it was a start.

Still leaning against his door, I eyeballed him hard and said, "That's not actually the threat anyway."

"No? What is?" He sighed and feigned exasperation. Benny was used to being the one making the threats, not the one receiving them. "I suppose you'll never stop until you find some real dirt on me? You'll never rest until you figure out a way to put me back inside? Something like that?"

"No," I said, knowing I had to raise the stakes if I wanted him to take me seriously.

"What then?"

"If anything happens to Jesús, I'll kill you."

I held his gaze long enough for him to realize that I was serious. He needed to believe that I'd go to any length to protect Jesús. And I needed to believe it too.

His eyes narrowed, and in them I saw the Benny who'd done eight years and broken off a shank in an old man's liver. And even as I saw him, I knew that he saw me.

I stood up, the Jag rocked slightly on its suspension, and the bag of groceries slid down the sheet metal and off the edge of the trunk. Something glass shattered when it hit the pavement.

25

SPEED STICK REGULAR DEODORANT, TWO-PACK, ONE STICK PARTIALLY USED.

It would take two or three days to get everything set up, so in the downtime I went through the shopping-cart inventory again, looking for something I might have missed or that I hadn't given enough thought to before, something that might connect to something else or lead me down a new path. What hadn't I thought of yet? What was there on the list that could help me figure out who Bishop was?

Could any of the clothes tell me anything? There were no logos or any distinguishing marks. They were mostly store brands from Walmart and Target and places even lower on the consumer food chain. The lab hadn't found traces of anything other than Bishop himself on them. The same was true of the grooming and personal-care items. Nothing unusual about any of it.

That left only the other miscellaneous items. I felt like we'd accounted for the CDs and that the books had been a dead end.

What about the keys? Other than one—an ignition key to an old Volkswagen with the VW logo stamped out of the metal head—they were generic. Doorknobs and deadbolts. One padlock key. None with any distinguishing characteristics. The locksmith had confirmed my suspicion that there was really no way to trace them. In that way, they were similar to Bishop's postmortem dental records—useful only if we could find something to test them against. If we had a door, we could match a key to a lock, but without it, they were of no use at all.

I looked again at the photo of the key chain. The fob had a blue design on white background sandwiched between two scratched and chipped clear-plastic panels. When I examined it more closely, I realized what the design was: the silhouette of a bucking horse.

There was nothing in the notes about the design. I might even have been the first person to look closely enough at it to determine what it actually was.

A blue horse. I wondered what it might be connected to, so I started Googling. "Blue horse" got about 544 million hits. That narrowed it down.

Blue Horse was the name of the first album by the Be Good Tanyas. I had a few of their songs in my iTunes, so I started playing them and listened to "Song for R" while I read through the other results.

There was a Blue Horse Saddlery in Los Altos. There was Bluehorse Associates, which was a pioneer in sustainability metrics. There was the Blue Horse Lounge in Ceres, California, which only managed to average two and a half stars on Yelp. There was Blue Horse Charities and Blue Horse Kona Coffee and Blue Horse Rescue and Blue Horse Repertory and the Blue Horse Inn. There was even an episode of *Gunsmoke* called "Blue Horse." I spent forty minutes clicking on links and searching for anything resembling the logo on the key chain and didn't see anything at all that came close.

I switched to images and looked at hundreds of blue horses of every imaginable form, and clicked on the "Show more results" button at the bottom of the page until the results field contained almost no blue horses at all, just random images that seemed completely unrelated to the search term.

The final image on the page was a photograph of a woman with bright-red hair in a white dress on a sad-looking mount that had somehow been painted or dyed a pale blue. I felt bad for that horse.

There was nothing that matched the keychain.

I remembered then that a few months earlier, Patrick had shown me how to use Google image search. I dug around in the menu until I found it. I clicked on the little camera in the search field and then clicked on the button that allowed me to upload the photo of the key chain. When I had it uploaded, I hoped for a break and clicked again. No matches.

Shit.

Did that mean that there were no matches because the blue horse silhouette was nowhere to be found online, or was it only because it was a photo of a keychain when what I really needed to search for was the image itself? I had no idea. I made a note to myself to ask Patrick for help as soon as I had the chance.

I sat there for a few minutes trying unsuccessfully to come up with another strategy. The time displayed in the upper right corner of my MacBook screen told me that it wasn't even two a.m. yet. Fuck it, I thought. Patrick answered on the third ring.

"You up?" I asked.

"No, I'm not up. Who is this? Danny? What's wrong?"

"Nothing. I just need a favor."

"What is it?" He was alert and focused. It doesn't take long, once you're assigned to one of the major detective details, to learn to wake yourself quickly in response to a middle-of-the-night phone call.

"I'm trying to do a Google image search and I need some help."

There was a very long silence.

I said, "Don't hang up."

"You called at two in the morning to get help with a Google search?"

"Yes."

There was another long silence.

"Don't hang up."

He took a deep breath and exhaled slowly and loudly. "What do you need?"

I told him.

"That's just basic image editing. You can't do that?"

"Uh . . ."

"Okay, just send me the photo."

He hung up.

I sent him an e-mail with the picture of the key fob as an attachment. Less than three minutes later he sent me a blank reply with a new attachment titled "seriously?.jpg." I opened it. He'd edited the photo to isolate the image of the blue horse in such a way that it no longer even looked like the photo it had been. Now it resembled nothing so much as a piece of old blue clipart. I saved the file to my desktop, opened the Google image search window again, and uploaded the new file.

There was a hit.

The blue horse was the logo of the Bishop Union High School Broncos.

• • •

"Bishop," Jen said. "I never even thought of the town."

"Neither did I. Ever been there?"

"That's the place where you have to put tire chains on your car when you're going to Mammoth, right?"

Mammoth Mountain was five hours north of LA on the other side of the Sierras from Yosemite and a prime destination for serious Southern California skiers who weren't satisfied with the smaller and less impressive resorts closer to the city. I'd never been much of a skier, but I'd been there on three or four occasions with Megan and her sister and brother-in-law, who'd spend the day on the black diamond runs while I took beginner's lessons on the children's slope for an hour or two before I'd give up and wander around the town or see a movie.

But the town of Bishop was far less memorable. It was one of those places that I only ever think of as being on the way to someplace else. Like Baker or Barstow or Bakersfield. We have a lot of those that start with *B*s.

By eight, I was on the phone with someone named Pam at the Bishop Police Department. The website had told me the PD had fourteen sworn officers and a handful of administrative support staffers. Pam was, apparently, at the top of the civilian employee pecking order.

"So," she said to me, "all you have is the keychain with the high-school logo on it?"

"Yes," I said. "That and the fact that the only name anyone here seemed to know him by was 'Bishop.' Figure that's way too much to be a coincidence."

"I would certainly have to agree with you." From the sound of her voice, I figured her for early fifties, with a long stretch of service to her organization. She seemed to know the procedures cold. "What would you like us to do?"

"I know you're a small department. You have enough manpower up there to stay up to date with MUPS?"

"Oh, yes. Because we are so small, we make sure we're on top of that. Never can tell when we'll need help from the state."

"Do you happen to know if your cold cases are on file as well?"

"Back to 2000. Before that's hit or miss."

I took that as good news. If Bishop was indeed from the town and had gone missing before the turn of the century, his case might never have been entered into the system. If that was the case, it might mean there was useful information and explain why it didn't turn up in the MUPS search.

"Pam, if I were to send you a set of prints, do you think someone could check it against your older files?"

"How far back would you like us to go?"

Until you get a hit, I thought. "As far as you can."

"Well, that could take a bit of work. I'll have to get the chief to approve it."

"Would it help if I got a request from my boss?"

"No, let me just run it past him after he's had his coffee. Get him to sign off on it and expedite it so the request doesn't sit in a pile until we have a slow day."

"I'd really appreciate that."

"Happy to help. You send the prints, and I'll let you know what he says."

I sat at my desk doing paperwork until she called me back at a quarter after ten.

"Oh, he grumbled and went on and on about it like he does, LA this and LA that, but he put Lewis on it, so it'll get done right."

"Thank you, Pam. I owe you one."

• • •

Late that afternoon my iPhone chimed with a new e-mail. At the next stoplight I looked down and saw the notification on my lock screen that told me it had been sent from an e-mail address that

I didn't recognize. When I opened my inbox and looked more closely, though, I realized it was from an @bishoppd.org address. I hadn't been expecting such a quick response.

Before I could open it, the phone rang. It was Pam. I pulled over to the curb and stopped the car just in time to prevent the call from going to my voice mail.

"Beckett," I said.

"Hello, Detective, this is—"

"Pam. How are you?"

"Good. I think I have some good news for you."

"Did you just send me an e-mail?"

"We found a match for those prints."

• • •

For weeks I'd been trying to figure out who Bishop really was. Not just to help make the case, but because I needed to know, I needed to determine not just his identification, but his identity. Why? What made him different from a dozen other John Does whose murders I had investigated? That question had been darting around the edges of my awareness since the very first night by the river. The fact that he died by fire, as Megan had, was certainly part of the complex equation, but I think I knew even then that there was more to my need. Even as I was about to learn his real name, I still didn't quite grasp the significance of what I'd been doing all along—idealizing him, transforming him into some kind of a mythic figure, denying the truth of who he really was, who he must have been. Again, I asked myself why he was different, or more accurately, why I needed him to be. I still couldn't figure it out.

26

BUNGEE CORDS, FIVE: ASSORTED LENGTHS AND COLORS.

Bishop's real name was William Fischer, DOB 8/26/51. He'd been a resident of Bishop, California, for most of the 1980s. He had a wife, now deceased, and a daughter. He'd never been listed as missing, but he had an arrest record that included three domestic disturbances, two DWIs, a drunk and disorderly, and a misdemeanor charge for battery.

Pam had sent me his record. I looked at the photos from his arrests. It was hard to tell that he was the same man from the photo Henry had given us. I had to look closely at the bone structure, the shape of his nose, the set of his eyes. But the more I studied the face, the more certain I became. It was him.

With the solid ID, I was able to find a half a dozen more arrests spread across California throughout the early '90s. Based on the dates, it appeared he left Bishop sometime in '88 or '89. Then he apparently headed to the coast, where he was picked up for assault in Santa Cruz. The charges were dropped. The first vagrancy hit was in '92 in Salinas. He spent a few days in the city lockup and was released on his own recognizance. He drifted south over the next few years. The most recent arrest had been in Oxnard in '96. No charges were filed in that case either.

I would have expected to get a fingerprint match from at least one of those incidents, but they were relatively minor infractions in small towns like the city of Bishop, so it wasn't too great a surprise that none of his prints had found their way into the federal database.

That was the last record I could find of William Fischer. I'd need to follow up on everything I found in regard to the arrests. But first I'd need to find his daughter, Rose.

With the help of public records and the DMV, I had an address and a phone number for her in less than an hour.

When I told Jen I had Bishop's daughter, she asked, "How are you going to handle it?"

"I'll call."

I did. It went straight to her voice mail.

Her message was short and direct. "This is Rose. Leave a message." Her voice was indistinct—neither particularly high nor low, and there wasn't much affect to it. Nothing that gave me any sense of her personality.

"Hello, Ms. Fischer," I said. "My name is Danny Beckett. I'm a detective with the Long Beach Police Department. I may have some information regarding your father." I left my number and asked her to call me back as soon as she could. "You can call anytime. Thanks for your assistance."

"Thanks for your assistance?" Jen said.

"What's wrong with that?"

"She hasn't assisted you with anything yet."

"I'm thanking her in advance. That way she'll feel compelled to call back."

"You don't think news of her father is a good enough reason?"

We bickered over the inconsequential comment because we didn't want to address anything real. The emotional rush I'd felt when the ID came through was beginning to wane. I knew better, but on some basic level I'd hoped that discovering Bishop's real name would somehow magically fill the emptiness, that it would grant me some sort of grand epiphany that would bring sense and order and closure to the last few weeks of unanswered questions.

Instead, it was only a name.

And a rap sheet.

Now, I realized, I was transferring that burden to a dead man's daughter, hoping she'd somehow be able to fill the gaping hole that was not knowing, hoping she'd finish the story. I was doing what I'd done all my life—trying to understand the people I'd lost. My father, Megan, and every victim whose death I'd ever investigated. Why would I expect to find the answers here?

• • •

It was after nine when I got the return call. I had already added her number to my contacts so I'd know who it was before I answered. That was the thing I liked most about cell phones. Caller ID. Those three or four seconds between the moment the call comes in and the moment I answer have become so necessary to me that I feel disadvantaged when I answer a call from a number I don't recognize or when the display reads "Unknown." But I knew who was calling. I knew what I was going to say and how I was going to say it.

"Detective Danny Beckett," I said in what might have been the softest tone I'd used with that particular combination of words.

"This is Rose Fischer." There was a familiar nervousness in her voice. No one associates messages from detectives with good news. That usually comes across in people's voices when they return our calls. If they return our calls. "I'm sorry to get back to you so late."

"No, please don't worry about that." My voice was warm and friendly, but with a practiced seriousness underlying the pleasantry. It was the voice I'd developed over the years for talking to victims' families. "When I said 'anytime,' I meant it."

"How can I help you?"

"What can you tell me about your father?" I asked.

She said, "He's dead, isn't he?"

"I don't know," I said. "I've been investigating the murder of a man here in Long Beach. We've been having some difficulty positively identifying him."

A nervous edge slipped into her voice. "Do you need me to look at him or something?" And a tinge of trepidation. "I don't even know if I'd recognize him."

"No, I'm afraid that wouldn't help in this case." I shouldn't have said that. In the silence, I could almost hear her mind running through the various reasons why a body might not be able to be visually identified.

"Why?"

"The victim's body was in a condition that would make that kind of identification difficult." Now I was just sounding like a dick. "What we'd really like to do is a DNA test. Would you be willing to help us with that?"

She thought about it. "Yes, of course. I could do that."

I made arrangements to meet her the following evening after she got home from work. It would have been easier to arrange for the sheriff's department to do the test in La Quinta and forward it to us in Long Beach, but I didn't want to wait. And I didn't want to trust it to anyone else.

I'd be heading out to the desert again.

• • •

"Want to go to La Quinta?"

"What do you mean?" Jen asked. We were eating takeout from Enrique's in her backyard. I thought it was still too hot to eat outside, especially since she had air-conditioning. She didn't agree. "The motel?"

"No," I said. "The city."

"I didn't know there was a city. Where is it?"

"Out by Palm Springs. It's 'The Gem of the Desert.'"

"That why you want to go there?"

"No."

"Then what's in La Quinta?"

"Bishop's daughter."

"When do we leave?"

• • •

We took my Camry. The overtime request had been turned down, so that meant we'd have to make up the time, but Jen was still on board. We cleared our call lists and messages and wrapped up as much paperwork as we could after lunch in order to get on the road by two thirty. Much later and the traffic would have doubled our driving time.

I kept waiting for Jen to ask me why we were doing this. By the time we passed Riverside, I went ahead and answered the unspoken question myself. "I know we could have had the locals do it."

"What?" she asked.

"The DNA swab. We didn't need to make this drive ourselves."

"I know."

"I figured it would be quicker this way. How long would we have to wait for some deputy to make time for a low-priority request?"

"It's okay."

"And then how much longer would it take to get it processed through their office and transported to us?"

"You don't have to explain."

"And you didn't need to come. I could have managed myself. But thank you. I'm glad you did."

"You're welcome."

I was tempted to keep explaining, but I knew better. I think I also knew, on some level at least, that the explanations were as much for me as they were for her. I needed to rationalize my connection to the case. Driving two hours one way to do a simple DNA test wasn't unheard of, but it also wasn't something we'd do for many investigations. We were going out of the way, and not just in the geographic sense. But I needed to do this one myself. I needed to make the connection. And I needed to know. Jen understood.

On the stereo, the *Fresh Air* podcast that had been playing ended with Ken Tucker reviewing Bob Dylan's *Another Self Portrait.* I wondered if I was still interested enough in him to give it a listen. I probably was, but I realized I wasn't really invested in what I was listening to and that within five minutes I'd forget I'd ever heard the review. Bishop and his daughter were the only things I could actually focus on.

My iPhone cycled another installment through the Bluetooth connection.

"Are you kidding?" Jen said. "How much Terry Gross do you have on that thing?"

I stopped it and said, "You pick something."

She took the phone out of the cup holder and began searching through the music. Her choice surprised me—Loudon Wainwright III's *High Wide & Handsome.* I don't know why she chose it, but it didn't take long for his banjo frailing and his buoyant voice on the title track to get me out of my head.

• • •

Rose Fischer lived in a gated community called Solida del Sol. It looked like just about every other gated community we'd passed since Orange County. It was just after five when we got there. The guard had our names on a list and gave us directions to her house. Everything looked the same inside, too, all beige stucco and red-tile roofs, but Jen paid close attention to the signs, so we made our way through narrow and winding streets without any wrong turns.

The guard had called ahead. She was waiting for us outside, surrounded by drought-tolerant plants that looked surprisingly lush. She gave us a small wave as we pulled up to the curb. I opened the door, and it felt like I'd stepped too close to a bonfire.

"Ms. Fischer?" I said as we climbed the two glazed-tile steps up onto her porch.

"Yes, hello. Detective Beckett?"

I nodded. "This is my partner, Jennifer Tanaka."

Jen shook her hand.

She led us inside and closed the stout alder door behind us. Jen had almost chosen one like it for her house, but decided the wrought-iron detailing made it look like it was trying too hard. It wasn't a big house, but it was very comfortably furnished. Everything seemed to be at least a few years old, not worn or shabby, but well used. After the door, I was expecting something that looked a lot more like a Pottery Barn catalogue.

She led us into the living room, and we sat on a plush, rust-colored sofa with a subtle geometric print.

"Can I get you anything?"

"No," I said. "That's all right."

She lowered herself into a matching chair and folded her hands in her lap. From the information I'd found on her, I knew she was thirty-nine, five foot seven, and that the last time she'd renewed her driver's license she weighed 139 pounds. She might have gained a little weight, but she was almost exactly as I thought she would be. I also knew she'd been divorced, hadn't taken her husband's last name, hadn't had any children. She'd lived in this house for nine years, the last five by herself. She worked as an administrator for a retirement community.

"So how do we do this?" she asked.

I smiled as warmly as I could and said, "Can you tell us about your father?"

• • •

In her memories, her father seemed like two different men. The daddy from her early childhood, the doting man who always needed a shave and would take her to the park and up into the hills to play in the snow when the first white fall came in the winter, who would buy her a Thrifty ice cream cone when she skinned her knee, who would lift her so high she screamed with glee every time he came home. But those memories were tinged with the hazy blurs of time, and they faded first into the emptiness of the long absences, of her first- and second-grade classrooms where she never knew what to say when someone asked why she didn't have a dad, and then into much more complicated recollections of the times he'd return to her and her mom, and the way the joy she felt would turn into something dark and fearful almost as soon as he came back into their lives.

"Daddy drinks too much," Mom would say.

"Why doesn't he stop?" Rosie would ask.

"He tries, sweetie, he tries."

The father she remembered most clearly, though, was the one who returned when she was in Mrs. Stephenson's second-grade class. The one who put her mother in the hospital. After that, she never again felt the giddy excitement that she had always associated with his visits. He wasn't *Daddy* anymore.

He was gone a long time after he hurt her mother. Rosie would, once in a great while, hear her mom on the phone, late at night, an exasperated tone in her voice, saying, "No, William, no," and try to remember the last time her mom had called him Bill.

Once, when she was in junior high, he talked her mom into letting him come home again. They'd moved to Palm Desert by then. So it felt different to have him in the home the two of them had built together on their own. He didn't have any history there, and he didn't seem to fit.

But he did try.

Rosie, though, couldn't forget the father he'd been so long ago, and after a few weeks, she began to offer tiny tokens of trust to him. She'd tell him about her day at school and let him help with her math homework. She began to feel that she might be able to forgive him.

It was almost six months until he missed a dinner. Rosie and her mom both knew, but they allowed themselves small measures of hope that gradually faded until the night he came home too late, drunk and smelling of vomit, and shoved her mom across the kitchen and into the refrigerator, shaking it and knocking loose the magnet holding Rose's school citizenship award on the door. She watched the faux-parchment certificate drift to the floor and slide underneath the stove.

"He's gone for good this time," her mom said the next day.

And he almost was.

She was in the winter of her first year of high school the next time he came home. He'd changed. At least her mother said he had. And Rose believed her. He did indeed seem different. She thought she saw the father she remembered from her preschool days, the father who taught her how to make snow angels and why chocolate chip was the best of all the flavors. He stayed through spring and summer and well into the fall, long enough for her to begin to trust him for the first time in ages. She remembered how he'd tell her he loved her and that this time was different and how she began to believe, if not in him exactly, in the possibility of him. Without ever realizing it, she began to allow herself brief flashes of hope for a future in which the three of them really were a family. Gradually, she did come to believe in him again.

She surprised herself one evening at bedtime when he kissed the top of her head and she said, "Goodnight, Daddy."

And he didn't lie, not about it being different. It really was. There were no raised voices, no fights, no nights when her mother would fall asleep long after midnight, still in the living room wondering where he was and when he would be home. There were none of the signs they'd seen so many times before. There were no reasons for either her or her mother to let go of the hope they felt growing inside them.

Nothing was as it had been.

The biggest difference of all, though, was his departure. Rosie remembered vividly the last night she saw him. They watched a baseball game. The Dodgers beating the Padres. He told her he'd take her to the mall on the weekend, and he kissed her goodnight.

"I love you," he said.

She almost said it back to him.

When she woke the next morning and found her mom in the kitchen making her favorite French toast for breakfast, she asked, "Where's Dad?"

Her mother didn't answer.

And that was that.

• • •

"I haven't seen him since," she said. I tried to read the emotion in her voice. The tone seemed more sad than bitter.

"Have you had any kind of contact at all with him?"

"A few cards. Some letters. But nothing in years."

"Would you know how to contact him if you needed to?

"I don't know why I would need to."

"If you wanted to?"

"No." More sadness crept into her voice. "I wouldn't have any idea."

"When was the last time he contacted you?"

"Christmas, nine or ten years ago?"

"That was a card?"

"Yes, with a note."

"Do you happen to remember what he wrote?"

"*Rose, I'm thinking about you like always. I'm sorry and I hope you're happy. I won't insult you by asking for your forgiveness, but I am truly sorry. This probably doesn't matter to you, but I've finally managed to quit. Have my own place and I'm trying to put things right as much as I can. I feel better than I have since you were little. If you want to, you can write back to me here, but I understand it if you don't. Love, your father.*"

I was surprised that she remembered something so long word for word. Judging by her expression, she was too.

"Did he give you a return address?"

"Someplace in Ventura, I think."

"Did you write him back?"

"No," she said. "Not right away, at least. When I finally tried, it had been almost a year. My letter came back with 'Return to sender—not at this address' on it." She looked down at the carpet as if she were trying to decide if it was ready for a shampoo.

"Any chance you still have that?" I asked.

"Yes, I do."

"Good," I said. "That might help." Telling us the story had drained her. I didn't want to push her too hard, so I said, "What we'd like to do is to take a swab from the inside of your cheek and we'll run a DNA comparison against that of our victim. We'll be able to either positively identify him, or rule him out altogether. Is that still all right?" I asked.

"Of course," she said. "Do we just do it right here?"

"Yes," Jen said. She took a pair of latex gloves out of her pocket and pulled them on.

"It's really simple," I said while Jen was peeling away the packaging of the collection kit. "She just needs you to open your mouth, and she'll rub the swab inside your cheek for a sample, and we'll be all set."

Rose nodded and said, "Okay."

Jen unsnapped the plastic tube and removed what looked like a large Q-tip.

"Ready?"

Rose nodded again and opened her mouth. Jen collected the sample, put it back in the plastic tube, and dropped that into an envelope she'd already labeled.

"Could we do one more?" I asked.

Jen looked at me and then said, "Sure."

"I'm sorry, Ms. Fischer. I'd like to get one more just to be safe."

Jen repeated the process, smiled at her, and said, "That's it. We're all set."

Rose Fischer said, "Are you sure I can't get you anything? It's such a long drive."

"No, thank you," Jen said.

"We'll be okay," I said. "We really appreciate your help with this."

She led us back to the door. When we'd stepped out onto the porch and turned to say goodbye, she said, "I hope it's not him."

I looked at her and tried to offer a reassuring smile.

"That last note he sent?" she said. "It meant a lot to me. I wanted to keep hating him, but I couldn't. When I read that, I did forgive him. I convinced myself that he would be all right and that I might be, too."

"I understand. We should have more information for you soon."

"Thank you. Any idea how long we'll have to wait?"

"Probably two or three weeks."

"Oh, I thought it would take longer than that."

"Hopefully not. Thanks again, ma'am."

She closed the door behind us. When we were in the car, Jen said, "So you're going to go to a private lab and pay for the test yourself?"

"Only one of them."

27

LAUNDRY DETERGENT: ULTRA TIDE, SINGLE-USE PACKETS, SEVEN.

By the time we got back to Long Beach, it was nearly eight, and for the first time in weeks it seemed cool when we got out of the car. Even though the sun had set and the last traces of color were fading in the sky, the temperature was still in the eighties. Nothing like a trip to the desert to keep things in perspective. When we had been passing through Tustin, Jen phoned in a takeout order to Enrique's. Because she'd left her car at my place, we decided to eat there. I think it was the first time we'd shared a meal in my living room since she'd moved into her house.

I left Jen in the kitchen with the food and went into the bathroom. As I sat down on the toilet, I looked up into the shower and yelled, "Shit!"

She knocked on the door and said, "You okay?"

"Yeah," I said, pulling my pants back up.

When I opened the door, she said, "What's wrong?"

"Look in the shower."

She squeezed past me and did as I asked.

"What?"

"I forgot to take my old showerhead with me today. They changed it out."

She looked at me like I was a three-year-old who'd just thrown all his food on the floor and was complaining about being hungry. Then she reached into the shower and turned on the faucet.

The water came out in a fine mist that I could barely feel on my hand. I couldn't believe I'd been so careless. "That's horrible," I said.

She watched me for a few seconds, then glanced down at the crescent wrench on the bathroom counter that I'd left out to facilitate the daily removal of the old showerhead. She sighed and went back into the kitchen.

I stayed in the bathroom and spoke loudly so she'd be able to hear me in the other room. "I know you think I'm just being a baby, but I need that water pressure."

She came back into the bathroom with a paring knife in her hand and nudged me out of the way.

"What are you going to do?"

Jen didn't say anything. She just grabbed the wrench and took off the new showerhead. It was dripping, so she shook the excess water off into the bathtub and held it under the light. Then she took the knife and removed the little screened washer and looked down into the opening. She put the tip of the knife back into the hole and wiggled it around a bit. The blade found a bit of purchase, and Jen gave it a twist, then turned the whole showerhead upside down and a small, cylindrical piece of green plastic fell out in her hand. She made a show of holding it up for me to see, and then replaced the washer and screwed the showerhead back into place. She turned the hot water on, dried her hands on the towel hanging on the rack on the sliding bathtub door, and without so much as a glance at me, went back out into the kitchen.

I put my hand in the stream of water. The pressure was amazing. Even better than it had been with the old head. It was already getting hot. I turned the knob all the way up. The water flowed so forcefully it almost stung my hand. *Oh my god*, I thought.

When I went back into the kitchen, she was loading her chicken tacos onto a plate.

"Thank you," I said.

"Really?" She looked at me with disappointment in her eyes.

"What?" I said.

"If you're going to be that sincere," she said, "it's going to take all the fun out of me giving you shit about this."

28

Silva Polaris 177 compass.

The press release showed up on Longbeach.gov the next morning. It read:

> FOR IMMEDIATE RELEASE PRESS RELEASE #2013
> **Subject: MURDER (1000 block Ohio Avenue)**
> **Contact: Media Relations Detail (555) 985-4111**
>
> Yesterday, at approximately 8:45 p.m., Long Beach Police responded to a report of a disturbance in the 1000 block of Ohio Avenue, which resulted in the death of a male teenager.
>
> When the officers arrived, they discovered 15-year-old Jesús Solano, a resident of Long Beach, suffering from multiple stab wounds to the upper torso. He was transported by Long Beach Fire Department paramedics to a local hospital where he was pronounced dead on arrival.

No suspect information is available, and the incident is being investigated as possibly gang related.

Anyone with information is urged to contact LBPD Homicide Detectives Danny Beckett and Jennifer Tanaka at (555) 985-2101. Anonymous tips may be submitted by calling 1-800-777-TIPS, texting TIPLA plus your tip to CRIME (27463), or visiting www.lacrimestoppers.org.

I read it over a few times and went to the *Press-Telegram* website to wait for it to show up there as well. It was surprisingly quick. In less than an hour a single paragraph paraphrasing the release showed up on the Crime page under the heading "Homicide."

• • •

At six thirty, I called Benny War's office line, identified myself to the receptionist, and asked to speak to Mr. Guerra. "He should be expecting my call," I said.

"I'm sorry, Mr. Guerra has gone home for the evening. May I take a message or put you through to his voice mail?"

"Just tell him I called."

"And what shall I tell him it was regarding?"

"He'll know."

• • •

I parked my car illegally in front of Benny's garage door on East Lido Lane. It was really more of a glorified alley. On Naples Island, every extra square foot had been swallowed by wealthy residents remodeling their homes over the years. What had once been a charming neighborhood of small, quaint bungalows had metastasized over the decades into a nearly seamless mass of bloated, multistoried architectural ejaculations that left me feeling claustrophobic and depressed.

I didn't want to ring the bell on the entrance that faced the street, and the buildings were so tightly packed together that, unless I wanted to trespass and cut through one of the narrow spaces between them, I was forced to walk all the way around six of the large houses before I could cut over to the pedestrian walkway they called Vista Del Golfo and walk back past the same six homes to get to the side of Benny's place that faced out toward Alamitos Bay.

When I got there, I stood outside the perimeter of the low stone fence that separated Benny's patio from the concourse. Like most of the residents of the island, he kept the expansive picture windows that ran along the entire first floor of his home unencumbered by shades or curtains. It was like looking into a giant, vainglorious fish tank.

In what I'm sure was described as a "great room" by Benny's real-estate agent when he was creaming his jeans over the sale, Benny sat on a large white-leather sectional with a glass of wine in his hand, watching a basketball game on an immense wall-mounted flat-screen TV. He wasn't alone.

From my vantage point, I was able to see past the living-room furniture and into the kitchen. Gregory, the obsequious assistant who had led Jen and me into Benny's office the first time we went to see him, was doing something at one of the counters. After a few moments, he came out with a pizza box in one hand and a beer in the other and joined Benny. I couldn't make it out clearly, but the logo on the pizza box looked like it belonged to Michael's Pizzeria.

They had a location on Naples Island, too. That one didn't have pepperoni either.

I watched them for a while, wondering what Gregory's job duties included. The only one I was sure of was sycophant. The others could have included anything from hired muscle to personal chef to consigliere. I didn't know, and frankly, I didn't care.

The short wrought-iron gate in front of me was locked, but it was so low I could almost step over it without making any contact. I texted Jen and walked past the teak furniture and the built-in grill and up the three steps leading to the glass-panel door.

I gave it a gentle tap, startling both Benny and Gregory.

They looked at me and then at each other. Benny got up and opened the door.

"Hello, Detective," he said as nonchalantly as if I were a favorite neighbor popping in to borrow a cup of pinot noir.

"Benny," I said.

"We weren't expecting any company, but I think we can spare a slice if you'd like to join us."

I tried to read his expression to determine if he'd heard the news. He knew how to play it cool, but I was betting that his attitude meant that he hadn't yet found out.

"Jesús Solano is dead."

The smirk fell off of his face and his eyes widened so slightly that I would not have noticed if I hadn't been watching for the tell. He held my gaze for a moment and then turned to Gregory, who gave his head a puzzled shake and reached for the iPad on the frosted-glass coffee table.

Benny and I watched him slide and tap and wait and read. He looked at Benny and nodded.

When he looked back at me I thought I saw a twitch of fear in his eyes, but it was probably just wishful thinking.

“We need to talk to you at the station,” I said. “How many of those have you had?” I gestured toward the wine glass Benny had left on the table. “You want to ride with me or have Greg drive you?”

The clenching in his jaw gave me more pleasure than I wanted to admit.

29

USED ALTOIDS TIN SECURED W/ RUBBER BAND, CONTAINING: $8.37 IN COINS.

The timing was crucial. Jen had been waiting for me with a backup unit half a block away from Benny's and listening on a wire in case anything went wrong. While Gregory and Benny were making their way into the garage and loading themselves into the Jag, I texted Jen again and let her know everything was going according to plan. She needed to beat us back downtown.

• • •

The visitors' parking area was nearly empty when we got there. I parked and Gregory took the spot next to me. Seeing my Camry next to Benny's Jaguar gave me a pleasantly smug feeling of superiority. It probably did the same for him.

"Let's go upstairs," I said to Benny. We started walking, and I said, "Actually, Greg, you might be more comfortable out here."

Benny shook his head. "No, he'll be coming upstairs with us."

"You sure?" I said.

"He's my attorney."

Maybe that job description included even more duties than I had imagined.

I led them through the lobby, and we rode the elevator upstairs in silence. Before an interrogation, I often feel a twinge of excited anticipation deep in my gut, and as I watched the ascending floor numbers over the door I felt it deepening. The doors slid open and I moved in next to Benny, forcing Gregory to follow a step behind us.

On the way to the interview room we'd selected for Benny, I escorted the two of them the long way around, through the Homicide squad room and past the lieutenant's office. Benny's head swiveled to the left when he saw who was sitting across the desk from Ruiz. I didn't get a good look at Benny's reaction, though, because I was too focused on the slack-jawed fear that overtook Hector Siguenza as we strode past the glass wall.

We turned the corner and Patrick was waiting at the door of the interview room. "Gentlemen," he said. "Make yourselves comfortable." He gestured inside to the two chairs next to the table pushed back into the corner. "Can I get you anything? Water? Coffee?"

I looked Gregory in the eye. "Sorry," I said. "Our espresso machine's out of order."

• • •

In the men's room, I knocked back a cup of lukewarm coffee, brushed my teeth, and put on the coat and tie I'd stashed earlier at my desk. I checked myself out in the mirror. The face I saw looked a little more tired than I would have liked, but it would have to do. It was game time.

When we'd formulated the plan, I suggested that Patrick interview Siguenza. He had made the most important connections in the investigation, and we wouldn't have been where we were without his analysis of the vast amount of metadata he'd been able to collect. He had earned the interrogation.

But this wasn't a normal situation. The most important lesson I'd been taught about interrogations when I made detective was to never ask a question that you don't already know the answer to. Of course, that's an idealization, a lofty and ambitious goal that we can't always pull off in the real world.

Sometimes, all we have are questions.

Whoever went into the interrogation room with Siguenza wouldn't have many answers to work with. Patrick knew that as well as I did. And he knew that I had spent a lot more time in the box than he had. "You take it," he said. I didn't argue.

I smoothed the front of my shirt, snugged up my tie, and went in.

"Hello, Mr. Siguenza." I closed the door behind me. I sat down and said, "I'm Detective Danny Beckett." I stated the date and time and case number for the recording. "Thank you for coming in."

Ruiz had left him a bottle of water on the table when he'd escorted him inside. Siguenza looked at it.

"Can I get you anything? Are you thirsty?"

He kept staring at the Arrowhead bottle. He was wearing jeans and a sweater. Without a suit he looked like a different man.

"No, thank you. I'm fine."

"Okay, then. Why don't we get started? I just have a few questions. Shouldn't take long at all, then we'll have you on your way."

• • •

You never really know how someone will hold up under interrogation. I thought Siguenza's experience in criminal defense might give him an advantage, that he'd hardline me or try to play me, or just count on his own knowledge of the process to make it impossible for me to get anything useful from him. I thought he might have an ego or a backbone.

Unlike Benny, though, Siguenza had never been on the other side of the fence. He'd grown up solidly middle class, made it into UCLA on his academic merit, and gone straight on to law school at USC. Then it was directly on to defense work. He'd never even committed a crime that we could find, let alone done time.

He didn't have the grit to stand up. And because of that, our play had been a success. He was scared shitless of Benny.

I spent an hour building a rapport with him, asking questions that didn't have anything to do with what we really wanted to know. Who do you root for in the big cross-town football game, Bruins or Trojans? After golfing at the Virginia Country Club, is it lame to play the public course at Recreation Park? Did you look at the Jaguars before you bought your Mercedes?

He'd relaxed as much as he would ever be able to in the situation, so I eased Benny into the conversation so gradually that Siguenza never even noticed the transition from the casual baseline-building questions to those that would eventually incriminate him. You like Benny's car? What's his handicap? Did you know him when he was in law school?

Another hour in and he'd given us the name of the man with the neck tattoo. All it took was showing him the list of cell-phone calls and a few careful lies that led him to believe that we had not only all the metadata but recordings of the actual calls as well.

Rudy Guerra was his name. Benny War had more than one skeleton in the family closet. Rudy was his half brother.

When I pressed him for details about their history, he barely hesitated. A few years ago Benny had asked for a favor, and before he knew it, Hector was involved in a successful side business laundering the income from imports of black-market AK-47s through Long Beach Harbor.

"Hector," I said, "Why did Rudy need to kill Bishop?"

"Who's that?"

"The homeless man."

"Oh. I didn't know his name."

I didn't say anything.

"He saw something he shouldn't have. There was a meeting between Rudy and the suppliers down by the harbor. Omar was a lookout half a block away. Kid saw the old man walk past. Started going on about 'no witnesses' and taking care of loose ends. Rudy didn't even care. Wasn't going to do anything. That old guy wasn't going to talk. Didn't even know what he was seeing."

"What happened?"

"Fucking Omar."

"Tell me about it."

"Rudy hated that little psycho. Didn't want him anywhere near the business."

"Then why was he involved?"

"Omar's father. You know how much juice he has, right? He gave the word, and the kid was in."

I nodded. Hector didn't know that Benny was Omar's real father.

"He had to take it on himself. Thought he was showing some kind of initiative or something. Killing somebody who didn't even need to be killed. And it wasn't good enough for him to just pop the guy. No. He thought if he made some big show of it, that he'd make his bones, impress everybody. Stupid little fuck. This is all his fault."

"Of course it is," I said. Thinking, *Yes, of course it's his fault that you're eyeball-deep in Mexican Mafia gunrunning. It's all on a seventeen-year-old kid.*

"Why'd Rudy keep going after Jesús?"

"Omar said he knew everything. That he was going to spill."

"You think Omar was right?"

"No, Omar was pissed off that Jesús thought he was too good for the rest of them and wouldn't get on board and lick his ass like his brother did. And that was all he needed. Stupid, vindictive little fuck."

Omar was right about one thing. Jesús was too good for him.

• • •

When I came out of the interrogation room, Patrick had already found some basic information on Rudy Guerra. He owned a condo in Brea and supposedly sold Infinitis in Tustin.

"You sure that's the right Rudy Guerra?" I asked.

"Yeah."

"He's a car salesman?"

"Apparently."

"No record?"

"Clean as a whistle," Patrick said. "He must have learned some serious lessons from his brothers."

• • •

We put out a BOLO on Rudy Guerra and sent a dangerous-warrant team to his address. They didn't find him.

In the morning, a press release would be issued, and his photo would be put up online and, with luck, would start popping up on the morning news shows.

• • •

By the time we finished for the night, it was after midnight. But Jen and I needed to make one more stop. We drove north on the 710 and cut back down the 405 to Lakewood Boulevard. At the Residence Inn, we checked in with the uniforms in the parking lot and went upstairs to room 217. We knocked softly on the door. They were probably asleep inside.

"Call," Jen said.

I did. When he answered, I said, "It's Danny. Open the door."

A shadow moved across the peephole, we heard the deadbolt unlock, and the door eased open.

Jesús looked at us and tried to rub the sleep out of his eyes.

"Everything's going to be okay," I said.

He didn't look like he believed me.

30

KNUDSEN LOWFAT COTTAGE CHEESE CONTAINER, WITH SEWING NEEDLES, MISC. BUTTONS, THREAD.

The next day, I took another run at Siguenza. He didn't give us much more than he had in the first interrogation. There were a few more details—he fleshed out some facts, dotted i's and crossed t's. He swore up and down that he didn't have anything on Benny War, that Benny had only made the introduction with Rudy and didn't have any other knowledge about their enterprise. Benny made the same claim. I didn't believe them, of course. There might have been a slim possibility that it was true, that Benny had kept himself in the dark deliberately, but I was betting on one of two things: either Siguenza was a lot more worried about Benny than he was about Rudy, or he was holding onto information in hopes of bargaining with the ADA. At one point, he even asked me about witness protection. I pretended like I thought that was within the realm of possibility and said I'd talk to the prosecutor about it. Either way, he didn't offer up anything on the man we believed was calling the shots, and for the time being, it didn't look like we could make anything stick. Benny War would almost surely walk away from the whole ordeal unscathed.

After we wrapped things up, Jen, Patrick, Marty, Ruiz, and I gathered in the squad room.

"I just got a call from ATF," Ruiz said. "Apparently we cracked a big case for them. They've been chasing those AKs for months. Who wants to liaise with them so they can elbow their way in and claim all the credit?"

After a few seconds of us all sitting there in silence and refusing to make eye contact with him, he said, "Thanks, Patrick. I appreciate it."

"Oh, no, I didn't—" Patrick cut himself off in midsentence.

• • •

That afternoon I tried to come up with leads on Rudy Guerra. Because we had virtually nothing on him prior to the current case—no criminal record, no known associates or affiliations—there was little to work with.

I spent half an hour on the phone with his manager at the car dealership, and the only complaint he had was that Rudy had a way of inconveniently flexing his work schedule, but his shifts were always covered and other than that he'd been a model employee for the eighteen months he'd been there.

And I spoke to his next-door neighbor, an elderly woman who had nothing but nice things to say about him. When her arthritis was acting up, he took her trash out. "Such a nice boy," she said. "I hope he's all right."

The next morning, with a fresh search warrant and backup from the Brea PD, Jen and I tossed his condo and found nothing that would indicate he was anything other than a mild-mannered Orange County Infiniti salesman.

We talked to other people he worked with, and to more of his neighbors, to see if we could turn up anything, but it came to nothing. He'd done such a good job of staying off of the law-enforcement radar for so long that it wasn't surprising he'd never let himself slip up while going through the motions of his upstanding-citizen routine.

We had nothing. We'd keep trying, but it was becoming clear that Rudy had disappeared and that unless he made the kind of mistake he seemed too smart for, like making a withdrawal from an ATM or getting pulled over in a traffic stop or using his burner again, our chances of finding him were diminishing with each passing day.

• • •

That evening I once again waited for Benny in the parking garage beneath his office. When he found me leaning against the door of his Jaguar, he said, "Hello, Detective."

I tried to read his expression but couldn't. When I didn't say anything he added, "I still don't know where Rudy is."

"That's not why I'm here," I said. "Jesús Solano isn't going to testify. He doesn't know anything. He wasn't involved in any of it."

"Are you going to threaten me again?"

"Do I need to?"

As he smiled, the overhead fluorescent light shone on the scar beneath his left eye.

31

Timex Ironman wristwatch: black and gray w/ orange highlights.

By the end of the week, the worst of the heat had passed, and Long Beach was settling into a slow downward slide toward fall. I slept relatively well that Friday night and woke later than I usually do. Two cups of coffee and a shower stretched out and filled more than an hour. I dawdled around the house, checking the news online, trying to play a few bars on the banjo, watching *The Today Show*. Matt and Al and whoever that woman was who replaced Ann Curry were enough to put a sour spin on my enthusiastic aimlessness. So I put on some shorts and a short-sleeved plaid button-up and drove to Palm Beach Park.

I got out and walked along the bike path. The last time I had been there, the relentless heat that beat down onto the concrete and reflected up off of the slow-moving water had made it feel like the height of the summer, but now the cooler temperature and the light breeze blowing inland suggested we were well into autumn. It seemed to me as if Bishop's death had occurred months ago, rather than just a few short weeks.

As I was passing the RV park, a small flock of five or six white birds floated on the water of the biological reserve. I knew they weren't ducks or geese, but that was the closest I could come to identifying them. Some kind of egret, maybe? What did an egret even look like? I really had no idea.

Just when I had started walking again, I heard someone behind me say, "On your left," and a cyclist on a sleek racing bike rolled by. As he rounded the curve that opened up onto the long straightaway north along the concrete river, I heard the chink of his chain upshifting, and he stood on the pedals and accelerated into the distance.

Two miles north, a small park was nestled in alongside the river. I lost track of the time and distance, and before I knew it, I was passing Pacific Coast Highway and wandering along the winding dirt pathway flanked by orange and yellow wildflowers and other indigenous plants. I found a sign that read, "Cressa Park: A Native Habitat." How long had the park been there? I'd never even heard of it. Had Bishop? For some odd reason, I found it easy to imagine him there.

The company, even though it was only in my head, didn't really suit me, so I walked back down the bike path all the way to my car at the river's end.

• • •

"How's the taco?" I asked Jesús. It was his last weekend before going back to school. He'd missed more than two weeks and was worried about returning, so I took him for lunch at Enrique's. Carne asada makes everything better.

"When you said that thing about Jack in the Box," he said, "I didn't think you knew what a taco really was."

"That's why I brought you here. Had to prove I had some street cred."

"It's good."

"I'm glad you like it."

The DA was building the case in such a way as to keep Jesús's involvement to a minimum. It was unlikely he'd need to testify. Once we'd gotten Siguenza in custody, Francisco and Pedro had opened up and given us what we needed. Jesús's knowledge of the plan was so limited in relation to theirs that his testimony would add little to the case. Rudy Guerra seemed to have vanished, and I'd gone out of my way to make it clear to Benny that Jesús knew nothing of any value to the prosecution. Was that enough to keep him safe? I hoped so.

Watching him eat, listening to him worry about his little sister and his mom, about how far behind he was on his schoolwork, and even about his concern for Pedro, I thought maybe he had a chance.

• • •

After I dropped him off at home, I went to see the new Alfonso Cuarón astronaut movie everyone had been raving about. It looked pretty, but ultimately I just got pissed off by its failure to grasp the basic principles of middle-school-level physics and the completely gratuitous underwear shots.

Still, though, I was glad I went. It had been a good day. I felt a kind of unburdened and leisurely ease that I hadn't experienced in a very long time.

I called Harlan. "Got any dinner plans?"

"There's a Marie Callender's chicken pot pie waiting for me in the freezer. Why?"

"How about if I pick up a pizza at Domenico's and swing by?"

"You got yourself a date."

Not only did Domenico's have pepperoni, they had two kinds. Sliced *and* ground. Suck on that, Michael's.

• • •

We'd finished eating and headed out to sit on Harlan's porch with a couple of bottles of Sam Adams and give each other a hard time. He reached into his shirt pocket and pulled out a slip of paper torn off of a real-estate agent's promotional notepad. He handed it to me. There was a phone number written on it but nothing else.

"What's this?"

"Banjo teacher. Call him."

"He have a name?"

"Gary. I told him not to take your call, but he seemed really desperate. His kid needs new shoes or something."

"Thanks, Harlan," I said.

"Don't thank me. Just practice."

32

Bic lighter: purple w/ Los Angeles Lakers logo.

When I dropped Rose's second DNA swab at the private lab, I paid an extra $160 for expedited service.

The results came back in two and half weeks.

"I got the DNA results back on Bishop and his daughter," I said to Jen.

"Let me call you back," she said to whoever was on the other end of her phone call. She swiveled her desk chair around. "And?"

"No surprise. They're a familial match."

"When are we going?"

It was after four, so we wouldn't be able to make the drive before the end of the shift. "Do you mind doing it tonight? I know the Friday traffic will be—"

"Let's go."

"I'll give her a call."

I left my car at Jen's house, and we took her RAV4. She had a Caltrans FasTrak transponder so we'd be able to take the express lanes on the 91. The express lanes had adjustable tolls—the worse the traffic was, the more you paid. I generally refused to use them because I didn't think rich assholes in BMWs should be able to zip past all the poor people who couldn't afford the luxury of paying ten bucks a pop to get home in time to have dinner with their families.

"You sure you don't mind compromising your ethics?" Jen said. Needling me seemed to be the most enjoyable thing she'd done all day.

"Special circumstances." I wanted to enjoy the banter, but I was thinking about having to give Rose the bad news.

"Yeah." Jen laughed. "That's exactly what all the guys in the Caddies and the Corvettes say."

• • •

The guard at Solida del Sol remembered us.

"Ms. Fischer's expecting you guys. You know the way, right?"

Rose had coffee waiting for us in the living room. Two cups, black, with cream, sugar, and Splenda on a lime-green serving tray on the table in front of the comfortable couch.

She was dressed more casually than she had been the last time we were there, in jeans and a brown cable-knit cardigan sweater. There was a sadness and resignation in her posture, and she looked like she might have been crying.

She knew what we were there to tell her.

"How are you doing?" Jen asked.

Rose sighed and said, "I've been dreading this."

Jen looked at me and waited for me to say the words.

"We got the results of the DNA test back," I said.

Rose nodded.

I looked at her steeling herself for the bad news she knew was coming, and something stopped me. I remembered how she'd seemed at peace with the memories of her father, how she'd come to terms with his absence, how she'd been able to believe that his last words to her had signaled some small measure of healing for him. The truth, I thought in that moment, doesn't always set you free.

"They weren't a match," I said. "Our murder victim wasn't your father."

Rose looked up at me, surprised, and uttered a soft "Oh."

I smiled at her. Without even looking, I knew Jen's eyes were drilling into me. I could feel them.

"We thought you might be happy to hear that," I said.

"I am, it's just that I—well, I assumed if you were coming all the way out here it had to be bad."

Rose began to tear up, so Jen pulled a tissue out of the box on the table and handed it to her.

"It's not often we get to deliver good news. It was worth the drive."

• • •

On our way home, Jen was quiet.

"You mad?" I asked her.

"No."

"What is it, then?"

"I've never seen you lie to a victim's family member like that before."

"Yes, you have. We lie with almost every notification we make."

"Not like that."

"What's the difference?" I asked her sincerely, without a trace of irony in my voice. "*He didn't suffer. She never knew what was happening. It was quick.* We lie all the time."

"That's different."

I knew what she was saying, but, in that moment, I couldn't make sense of it. I thought about the truth I knew. The truth I'd seen in the files of Megan's death investigation. Of my father's, too. I thought of the times I'd tried to soften the truth by being less than honest. I thought of all the times someone had questioned me about the death of a loved one and how I'd lied to their faces. "How is it different?"

She just shook her head.

When she didn't speak, I said, "It made her feel better."

After another mile or two of silence, looking straight ahead through the windshield, she said, "You're not worried about it coming back on you?"

"It'll be six or eight weeks before we get the official DNA results back. I'll write it up vague and sloppy so there won't be any actual lies in the paperwork."

"What if Rose finds out?"

"She won't."

"And I'm just going to back you up on it?"

"Yes."

We were still a few minutes away from the freeway. The road ahead of us was dark and empty.

Jen said, "It made you feel better, too."

She was right. It did.

• • •

By the time we'd finished the long, quiet drive home, her attitude had changed. In the silence, I could feel her mood shift gradually and the initial exasperation she'd felt fade away. I knew her well enough to understand that it wasn't so much the lie itself that upset her, but the fact that she hadn't known it was coming, that I hadn't let her in on it. She realized, I believed, that I'd been planning to tell Rose the truth about her father all along, but when the moment came, I just wasn't able to do it. And how could I have let her in on the play when even I didn't know it was coming?

We said goodnight in her driveway, and she looked at me for a few seconds before she turned and walked toward her door. I couldn't quite read her feelings, but I felt a sense of calm resignation in her, and it helped me convince myself that I'd done the right thing.

Ten minutes later, I was getting out of the car in front of my duplex and stifling a yawn as I crossed the lawn.

Something caught my attention.

The lamp in the living room wasn't glowing behind the curtain. On the porch, with my keys in my hand, I tried to remember the last time I had changed the bulb. Could it be burned out?

I stopped and listened.

Did I hear the floor creak inside?

I took out my phone and dialed the number of Rudy Guerra's burner. Three seconds later I heard it ring on the other side of the door.

Something crashed in the living room and I knew he was heading for the back door.

I vaulted over the railing on the porch and ran along the side of the building into the backyard.

Rudy was halfway to the gate.

When he got there, he made the mistake of reaching for the latch, and when he couldn't get it open he readjusted his stance and put his hands on the top edge to pull himself up and over.

It slowed him down.

I charged across the yard and threw my shoulder into the small of his back with all the force I could manage.

The impact ripped the gate off its hinges and I crashed to the ground on top of him. As soon as we hit the pavement I started driving my elbow into the back of his head and bouncing his face off of the concrete.

His disorientation didn't last long, and he bucked up and I went rolling to the ground.

As he tried to stand up, I spun myself a quarter turn and drove my heel into his crotch as hard as I could.

He collapsed back down on all fours, and I scrambled to my feet and threw a kick at his head. I felt it connect with a concussive jolt, and I thought I had him.

I was wrong. He somehow managed to wrap his arm around my leg and rose to his feet, lifting me up into the air and dropping me on my back.

Most of the wind was knocked out of me and I thought I was done.

But the burst of energy that put me down took something out of him, and he rested his hands on his knees and took two deep breaths.

By the time he stood up straight and started toward me, I had my Glock in my hands and I was pulling the trigger.

Five hits. Center mass.

He took two more halting steps, but he slowed enough that I was able to scramble away from him and get up on my feet.

We stood facing each other for a long time, his eyes burning with rage and delirium. I opened the distance between us, watching his chest over the front sight of my pistol and waiting for him to make a move.

The sounds of sirens were rising in the distance when he collapsed down to his knees and slumped over sideways onto the ground.

I closed in on him, drove my knee down into his lower back, and cuffed him.

There was a Smith & Wesson tucked into an inside-the-belt holster. I pulled it, ejected the magazine, cleared the chamber, and threw it onto my back lawn. He had a folding knife in one pocket and his cell phone in another. The same phone that had unlocked the entire case.

Gasping for air, I pulled his head up and held the phone in front of his face. "You're so smart?" I said, the adrenaline pounding in my chest. "You're so smart? Do you even know why they call this a burner?"

He didn't answer.

I was still trying to catch my breath when the red and blue lights flashed across his bloodied face.

33

ONE PACKAGE HANES MEN'S CREW SOCKS, SIX COUNT: SIZE LARGE, UNOPENED.

We were all gathered in the squad room, my hopes of wrapping things up before sunrise vanishing as the first glow of morning light illuminated the window across the room.

The adrenaline surge from my encounter with Rudy Guerra had long since faded, and I was left with the drained emptiness and bone-deep exhaustion that usually follow a violent physical confrontation. The paramedics thought the worst of my injuries were likely bruised ribs, but still they wanted me to go to the ER to have everything checked out. I told them I'd go to the doctor later in the day. The pain in my ribs was minor in comparison to the throbbing burn in my neck and shoulder.

Rudy was in surgery at Long Beach Memorial. They didn't give us a prognosis, and even though none of us acknowledged it out loud, I knew we were all hoping for the worst.

Internal Affairs was responsible for the crime scene. That was standard procedure with all officer-involved shootings. I knew they'd be very thorough and that meant I wouldn't be able get back into my home for two or three days.

"I think we're okay here," Ruiz said. He looked at me. "Where will you be until they release the scene?"

Jen said, "At my place."

I hadn't even thought about where I'd stay until I could go home, and Jen hadn't said anything about it to me.

Marty shook his head and chortled.

"What?" I said.

"Just remembering what Siguenza said about Omar. Called him a 'vindictive little fuck.'"

"That's funny?" I asked.

"It's lucky that it runs in the family."

"I'm not following," Patrick said.

"If it didn't," I said, "we never would have got Rudy."

Marty was the only one of us with enough energy to be amused.

"Make sure he gets some rest," the lieutenant said to Jen. He turned to Patrick and Marty. "You two might as well get to work."

• • •

I woke up in Jen's guest room, my feet dangling off the end of the double bed. The sunlight angling in through the slatted blinds on the window told me it was afternoon. I checked the time on my phone: 1:52. There were also two voice mails. One from Julia Rice and one from Gary the banjo teacher. Sitting up, I cycled through a series of stretches in hopes of relieving some of the deep ache that spread across the entire left side of my body. They didn't help much.

In the kitchen, Jen said, "There's coffee."

"Thanks," I said. In the cupboard over the sink I found a cup with an owl on it and filled it.

"How'd you sleep?"

"Good."

"I'll make you some bacon and eggs."

I took the coffee outside onto her patio and sat at the table. After a few minutes in the crosshatched sunshine under the pergola, I started feeling better.

It was a nice day.

I picked up my phone and began to dial, but I was distracted by the sound of the small Zen waterfall across the yard. I remembered the dream I'd had of Bishop on the river and the sounds of his steps splashing away into the darkness.

I thought of the other man, William Fischer, the drunk who'd beaten his wife and whose daughter, Rose, years later would welcome us into her house. The man who died homeless on the concrete bank of the Los Angeles River.

What was the truth? Which man was he? The two of them were not yet reconciled in my mind, and in that moment I understood that I wanted to keep them that way.

I made a choice. The same choice that, rightly or wrongly, I'd made for Rose.

I would remember the man who played chess with a wounded vet, the man who cleaned a parking lot every week in return for the chance to wash clean his possessions. I would remember the man who, on the Fourth of July, with the aurora of the fireworks flashing in the windows high on the wall behind him, took the hands of an old and frightened woman into his own and swayed with her to the music of a fifty-year-old song for no other reason than that he thought it might provide a moment's relief to another soul burning in pain.

I would remember that Bishop danced.

Acknowledgments

My most sincere thanks to:

Nicole Gharda, Sharon Dilts, Jeff Dilts, and Kim Dilts

Eileen Klink, Bill Mohr, Zachary Locklin, Karl Squitier, and Carlos Dews

Derek Pacifico and Richard Klink

Gary Phillips, Naomi Hirahra, and Tod Goldberg

Alison Dasho, Jacque BenZekry, Tiffany Pokorny, Anh Schluep, Paul Morrissey, Charlotte Herscher, Meredith Jacobson, Andy Bartlett, and the entire crew at Thomas & Mercer.

My gratitude is immeasurable.